CONTROLLING
Charlotte
x x

Charlotte Hains

SilverWood

Published in 2016 by SilverWood Books

SilverWood Books Ltd
14 Small Street, Bristol, BS1 1DE, United Kingdom
www.silverwoodbooks.co.uk

ISBN 978-1-78132-480-6 (paperback)
ISBN 978-1-78132-481-3 (ebook)

British Library Cataloguing in Publication Data
A CIP catalogue record for this book is available from
the British Library

Page design and typesetting by SilverWood Books
Printed on responsibly sourced paper

CHARLOTTE HAINS left the UK for France after deciding she needed a change, taking on the huge project of renovating a house. In the UK her life consisted of getting up, going to work, coming home, going to bed, and just surviving. She now enjoys French life within the community of the village in which she lives, and feels privileged to be part of it. She describes her French neighbours as fantastic, offering her help in every way they can, and says she might have given up long ago if they hadn't been so understanding.

With her house nearly finished she found herself with long nights and lots of thumb twiddling, reading anything she could get on her iPad. In honesty, she admits it was here that *Fifty Shades of Grey* caught her eye. Unbeknownst to her, her sister was reading it as well. Her sister thought that, because Charlotte has such a creative side, maybe she'd be able to write a book too. As a joke, Charlotte emailed her sister her stories, also written on her iPad. She researched blogs and BDSM sites on the internet, and so Charlotte came alive. *Controlling Charlotte* is the second in the series.

Contact Charlotte at misschains@gmail.com or follow her on Twitter (@CharlotteHains), and Facebook.

*To all those striving for control,
enrichment and empowerment*

Chapter One

My eyes close momentarily and every muscle in my body tightens, an impulsive reaction to his hand slamming down on the table. Come on, girl, get with it. I open my eyes, staring at his hand flat next to the contract. Eye contact, keep in control, I think to myself. My head turns and my eyes follow the route of his arm until I reach his neck – not far now. I pause for a moment, taking a deep breath. I continue my journey to his eyes, all the while trying hard not to let him see he has fazed me with his obviously and deliberately exaggerated action of slamming his hand down with such a force. It was to try to make me crumble – well, I'm not going to. Our eyes meet and I suddenly feel confident again, as well as a little more in control.

"Are you feeling brave, Charlotte?" he says as I look straight into his eyes, at the same time remembering that I have to scribble my name on the bottom of the contract. Not really thinking about what he has said, or what I am saying, I reply to his question.

"No, Lloyd!"

Oh shit! Too quick – I must think before I speak. What has he said that for? I wish I could work out his games. No, I am in control; this is my game, not yours. Come on, I can do this if I can get the words out. Come on, mouth, engage with brain, and do not let me say, "What the fuck?" Please.

Anthony shifts forward on the sofa – Oh Hell! Please don't say anything, don't side with Lloyd. I can't handle both of you mentally beating me up, not now. Quick, Charlotte, before they get in first; take control, keep calm.

"I am not feeling brave. I am brave!"

I close the contract and push it towards Anthony. Don't lose eye contact, because if you do he will most certainly take control, changing the game. Keep with it; nearly done.

"That's my choice, Anthony. What Lloyd chooses to do is down to him."

I push myself up from the table. Lloyd's eyes follow me, his expression unchanging, and he's not giving anything away. I move back one step – he stands up straight.

"I am going back to the bedroom now – you obviously have things to talk about with Lloyd, Anthony."

I want to keep eye contact until I am at the hallway. I take another step back; I can feel the sofa on the back of my knees. I start to sidestep, feeling for the edge. God, I never realised it was so big until now. It seems to go on forever.

Finally, I feel the arm of the sofa on my upper legs, and this is a sign that I can start moving in the direction of the hallway. Just a few more steps back and I'll be able to see the back of the sofa as well as Lloyd.

That's it; the hallway is just behind me. I raise an eyebrow, just a little bit of cheek as a sign to him and Anthony, to them both, that this is my game. I have stayed in control and now I have finished. Then, turning, I walk away down the hall towards the bedroom. Neither of them says a word; they just watch me as I leave.

Once inside my bedroom: oh shit! What have I done? Leaning against the door to hold it shut, I feel exhausted, mentally and physically. Have I done the right thing? Oh stop, Charlotte, stop right now. Don't analyse it now. It's done. I am now the property of Lloyd for the next six months. I wonder what they are talking about. Maybe they think I have gone bloody mad. Maybe I was feeling brave – yes, I was, but now I don't know if it's brave or stupid. Well, I am sure Lloyd will tell me soon enough. He will definitely say what an airhead, or smart-arse mouth I am – he's always so quick at telling me this. I go over to the bed and lie down. My legs have turned to jelly all of a sudden, and my heart is pounding. Shit! Not good. These are all the things I have to learn to control. I don't know how Lloyd does it, how he controls himself so well. He is so hard to read. I close my eyes, taking some deep breaths to help me relax. My heart is racing like an express train; I can hear every beat – boom, boom, boom – as it beats faster and faster. I cup my hands over my chest in an attempt to stop it beating so hard; I breathe deeply. I must stop it. I must get myself under control and ready for round two. Think what his next step is going to be. He has to come in here, and I need to recompose myself for when he does.

I wake up with a start. The blanket from the other side of the bed has been pulled over me – heck! I must have fallen asleep. I look at the clock; it's only about an hour since I was out in the lounge. I can hear voices, so I look to the door and it's ajar. The hall light is on and Anthony is still here; they are laughing and talking as normal. Lloyd must have been in, shit! I was asleep, that wasn't supposed to happen. I'm wondering if I should go outside or not. I am thirsty and hungry. I need something to eat and drink at least – all this staying-in-control stuff is such hard work. I get up, and, going to the door, I hesitate for a moment. Yes, go out. Some rules before we go: keep eye contact; don't get fazed.

Only having two rules – is this a good idea? Especially after playing such an intense game with him... I don't know any other rules, do I? I walk into the lounge. Too late now. Keep up with it – just pretend you know what you are doing. He will never know.

"Hi, Charlotte, are you feel rested now that you have had a sleep?"

"Yes, thank you, Lloyd," I say, looking straight at him. I look at Anthony and give him a reassuring, smiling nod before looking back to Lloyd. That's good, I am in control.

Lloyd smiles at me. OK! So why is he being so kind now? Well, he would be pleased, I suppose, he now owns my arse. Careful, kid. He really wouldn't care if Anthony was here or not, so don't let your guard down now.

"Do you want a drink? Coffee or wine?" he asks.

"Err, can I have a fruit juice, please, and maybe something to eat? I don't want wine on an empty tummy."

"Yeah, sure, we put a salad in the fridge. I'll go and get it for you."

He gets up off the sofa as I sit down next to Anthony. "Is he OK?" I ask quietly.

"Yes, why shouldn't he be?"

"He's being nice, and acting as if nothing has happened!"

"Charlotte, he is nice, and as for what has happened, that's all forgotten. He doesn't hold grudges, you know that! He is so proud of you right now."

"Proud? Why proud?"

"I am sure he will tell you later. For now, just enjoy the moment. You do like to enjoy the moment, I hear!" He grins.

Oh God, Lloyd has told Anthony everything, absolutely everything, for fuck's sake! I feel the heat of my red blushing cheeks.

"Here you go, ham salad and an orange juice." Lloyd

places it on the table for me. After I finish eating, we all have a little chat about this and that, Anthony and Lloyd talking mainly about the club, and the next big party.

"Right, I am off now I've sorted you two out again! I will see you when I see you. Kat will be waiting for me." Anthony winks at me. "Enjoy what's left of the afternoon, you two." And he gets up and leaves.

Lloyd looks at me and I him, eye contact all the time.

"Do you want some wine, now you have eaten?" He picks up the bottle of red.

"Yes, please."

He pours me a glass of wine. "How are you feeling?" he asks, passing the glass to me.

"Fine, thank you." I take my wine and sip it.

"Fine, huh? Not panicking over what's in the contract you have signed?"

"No, Lloyd, not at all."

That's it, girl. Eye contact; composure. Keep calm – nothing wrong with me letting him know I am very comfortable with the contract.

"You don't know what's in it."

"Would it make any difference if I did know? You already told me that if I wanted this you were going to own my arse, for the next six months anyway."

"It might have given you clues on what could happen within the next six months. You didn't miss a trick there, did you, Charlotte?"

Crap! Never thought of that. Now he has the upper hand, for fuck's sake! What the hell have you done, you stupid airhead? Wait, the game isn't quite over yet – I can read it now. Anthony wouldn't have a clause saying once you sign you can't look at it.

"I'll read it now then, thanks for the tip."

"You can't read it now."

What? What the fuck has Anthony done to me? Of all the stupid things I could have done. My brain starts rushing. Stop! I tell myself, compose! I calm down before answering him.

"Why would that be?"

"Why would you think?"

"If I knew, I wouldn't have asked, Lloyd!"

He just looks at me. No, no, no! You can't try to psych me out by staring at me, that's not going to do it.

"Lloyd, there would be no way that Anthony would have let me sign anything if it had a 'PS: you can't read this after you have signed it'." I raise my eyebrows.

"You can read it if you want to, but you will need some tape for it first."

"What are you on about?"

Nodding his head in the direction of the bin, he says, "It's in there. As soon as you went I ripped it up and threw it away."

What? What the fuck did he do that for?

"Why?" I take another sip of wine.

"Because I said that we wouldn't have a hard copy, not until you were ready to join the lifestyle Anthony came and spoke with you about today. He told me that you had realised what you had done wrong, how it was all going wrong, what you were doing wrong... He was trying to convince me that he thought you had got it – maybe not all of it, but you were starting to understand, and maybe I should reconsider the contract at this stage. Then when you came out in control for the most part, I saw a completely different, more confident Charlotte. You did everything right, except that you didn't read the contract. But then I can understand that because Anthony is your friend and he would never let you sign anything that he thought would compromise you in any way."

A compliment, a fucking compliment. At long last the Dom knows how to compliment me. I have done something right. I smirk to myself on the inside, being careful that Lloyd didn't see that at this point in time I was feeling very confident with the actions I had taken earlier. Maybe too confident. Lloyd leaned over, picking up the wine and pouring us another glass.

"I have torn up the contract because you really don't need it, and I am glad. I'd much rather do what we have been doing, having fun, and now I think we will have more fun, because you are starting to understand the rules. But if at any time I think you do need a hard copy then you will have one, trust me." His voice hardened on the last part of his statement, making sure I understood that basically anytime he saw fit, a contract would be enforced.

"I don't understand, why would you do that, when you were so adamant that a contract was the only way to go with me?"

"Because I trust you, just the same as you trust Anthony. You trust him implicitly – I hadn't realised that until this afternoon. By signing the contract you indicated that you can trust, and for you to trust me that way I must first trust you, so you will eventually trust me in the same way. It's a two-way street, trust." Glancing down at his watch, he hastily adds, "Hey, listen, I promised Anthony that we would disappear into our room – he has Kat coming up later."

Before I can answer he had picked up the bottle of wine and our glasses and was heading to the bedroom, with me following. Putting the items down on the table, he turned to me, grabbing hold of my hips, pulling me towards him.

"Come here, I want to play now. Shall we start where

we left off downstairs?" he says, pulling me close to him and looking me in the eyes. A slight panic flashes through my head – God, no bullwhips, please, no bullwhips – then I see his eyes looking into mine. Oh my, big, blue, melting eyes – I'm putty. He kisses me, long and hard, pulling my head back by my hair. His other hand goes inside my skirt to my arse, rubbing it slowly; then he stops kissing. Looking into my eyes, he says, "How is your arse feeling, Charlotte?"

Aww, my arse, I had forgotten about that.

"Fine."

"Good, let's have a drink."

He releases me from his hold and gets the wine from the table. What? After that kiss? You have got to be kidding, right? I thought you wanted to play – what the fuck? He hands me a glass and invites me to sit.

"I need to discuss something with you, Charlotte," he says as he sits down. Well, I hope it's discussing – how the hell are you going to fuck me from over there? I think as I sat in the seat opposite him, because I am all discussed out right now. I slouch back in the chair, looking sulkily into my glass of wine.

"We need to discuss your behaviour today."

What? My behaviour? What the hell does he mean? That was normal, do you fucking hear me, normal behaviour. Any fucking normal person would have done the same thing.

"That was just a normal reaction, Lloyd."

"I'm not talking about that – yes, you are right. I am talking about your smart-arse mouth!"

He looks at me. I slump further into my chair, like a sulky kid.

"Charlotte, are you losing control? Are you already forgetting the rules?"

"Rules, Lloyd? What fucking rules? You put them in the fucking bin, not me."

"Oh my smart-arse mouth is back, good! I am so going to enjoy this evening."

With that it's game on: spanking, teasing and turning my head inside out and upside down. He does it so well that I find it so hard to control myself, and the more I drink the harder it becomes. I'm not quite sure if I pass out because of the wine or because I just physically can't take any more of Lloyd teasing me.

Chapter Two

I wake up – shit! It's still dark, I can't see anything; I can't see anything at all. I blink a few times but nothing; they will not adjust to the dark. Oh fuck, I have gone blind! I try to move my arms, and they are above my head. I think. They are numb and they feel so heavy – what the fuck has happened to me? I am paralysed from the shoulders up. My head starts to throb like I have never known it to throb before.

"Good morning, Charlotte, how are you feeling after your night of fun?"

What? Good morning, no, it's not a fucking good morning, is it? I am lying here face down on the bed and I can't fucking move or see anything. I try to move my fingers, but no, not even a twitch from them. Panic starts to set in. I have got some form of paralysis going on, so it's not a fucking good morning from where I am lying.

"Lloyd, I have gone blind, for fuck's sake! My arms will not fucking work, I am paralysed. What the fuck is wrong with me?" I say with some urgency.

He strokes his hand down my back and says, "Charlotte, my little smart-arse mouth, there is nothing at all wrong with you."

His hand reaches my arse and he rubs in circles.

I try to move my head, but somehow my arms are on my

hair, trapping it, and my head is throbbing so much I don't think I really want to move it that much anyway!

"Lloyd, I am being fucking serious, my fucking eyes, I can't fucking see, and I can't move my arms."

Slap.

"Is your arse cold, Charlotte? Is that why you have lost control – you need your arse warming?"

Slap.

"No, Lloyd, my arse is not fucking cold. I am telling you I have gone blind, that's why I have lost control, and I can't move my arms."

Slap.

"I'm going to have such a good day today. Not often I wake up with an arse in the air and a smart-arse mouth to go with it."

Slap.

"Then again, Charlotte, I think this might be quite a regular occurrence with you, what do you think?"

Slap.

"Fuck! Lloyd, please don't!"

Slap.

"Think, Charlotte, think."

Slap.

"How the hell can I think with you slapping when I am blind and so obviously paralysed? What the fuck is there to think about, other than to get a doctor – a proper one – if you don't fucking know what to do?"

Slap.

"Charlotte, now that's a little personal, don't you think?"

Slap, rub. Ah, he's rubbing, well, that's nice.

"Charlotte, do you not remember the last thing we discussed last night, before you passed out?"

"Lloyd, I hardly think this is the time to discuss what

we discussed last fucking night, when I am so obviously ill, so let's talk about your lack of compassion towards me this morning!"

Slap.

"I think it is the perfect time to discuss it."

Slap, rub. Ah, soothing.

"As it was you who took your eye off the game, and it was you who lost control, you who started this game, as usual I am the one who will finish the game. Well, now you are awake again I can finish it. That is if we can get past your smart-arse mouth this morning."

Slap.

"Then again, I do like to play several games at once, it gives a little more edge, an extra bite to the games, don't you think?"

Slap.

"OK, OK, I get it, OK!"

Slap.

"Please, Lloyd, stop slapping my arse now. I will keep my mouth under control."

Slap, rub.

"Shit, that hurt."

I squirm my hips in an attempt to ease the sting from the last slap. Well, they work; my legs too – I noticed them lifting when he was spanking me. My arse isn't paralysed – I felt every spank. So that's good, everything down there is working; if he ever does fuck me I will be able to enjoy it, but to be quite honest I don't know how much longer I can go with him teasing me, not finishing the job. Having hip-twisting, mind-blowing orgasmic moments are fantastic, but there is a little disappointment when things just don't get finished.

"Charlotte, what was the last thing you remember about our last discussion?"

Think, think, quick, think! Oh yes, he said that today he was taking me into the bondage room.

"Bondage room, where you wanted to take me into next."

"Yes, and then what did you do?"

"I got up, saying it was the end of discussions and I was going to bed."

"Are you going to finish, or shall I continue for you?"

Finish what? Oh, what the fuck? What does he want to finish?

"Finish what, Lloyd?"

"What you muttered as you stood up to go to bed."

"You know you want to, Lloyd, I really don't want to spoil the fun you are having. That just wouldn't be right of me, would it?"

My head just isn't giving me any clues, it hurts so much. God, why does it hurt so much?

"You muttered to yourself, words to the effect that you would never leave yourself at such a disadvantage, that I would never get fucking close. Game on, Charlotte, don't you think? And yes, this is just so much fun, so enjoyable. As for mumbling, I really don't think you should."

"Oh shit!"

Slap.

"Yes, my little smart-arse mouth, is it coming back to you now? I also owe you a few – you weren't very pleasant to me last night, when I was taping you up!"

"Oh shit! Double crap! But that doesn't explain why I have gone fucking blind, which by the way, I have fucking noticed you are not fucking worried about, are you, and I have such a fucking headache, I have probably had a fucking stroke over the fucking stress you gave me yesterday."

Slap.

"Charlotte, you are not blind. Your headache is due to the wine you drank last night, your arms are probably stiff from being in the same position for approximately eight hours, and your fingers will not move because I have taped from just above your wrists to your fingertips."

Slap.

"Stop fucking slapping my arse! If I am not blind why the hell can't I see?" I protest.

Slap.

"I am not going to stop until you do, my little smart-arse mouth. You obviously like it. The reason you can't see is because I have blindfolded you."

Slap.

"Crap! Lloyd, what the fuck? Why the hell didn't you tell me before? Why let me panic like that? You could have saved me from thinking I had had a bloody fucking stroke or something!"

Slap.

"Stop fucking slapping my arse with your hand!"

Slap.

"Aww, Charlotte, changing the game so soon. What would you rather I use to slap your arse with this morning, my dear?"

"You arrogant...!"

Slap.

"Stop right there, or you will find you bitten off a little more than you can chew, Charlotte. I have already said that you have been very personal once this morning."

Slap.

"Lloyd, please, I have had enough, honestly I have."

Slap, rub.

"Why do you do that, Lloyd? Slap, slap, slap, rub – it's not even consistent."

"You want consistency? Are you changing the game again, Charlotte? Haven't you worked it out yet?"

Work what out now? What should I be working out now?

"Lloyd, please, I am sorry. I am sorry I lost control, I am sorry I took my eye off the game, but I have really had enough."

"OK, Charlotte."

He lies down beside me and starts softly stroking my back.

"Just for you, as you asked so nicely, I will calm it a little."

"Thank you, Lloyd."

This is nice... My body is starting to tingle from his touch, his fingers gently dancing on my spine... Oh, a kiss wouldn't go amiss right now, what I would do for a kiss; a long, slow, lingering kiss, one of his magic kisses... Even the thought makes my hips squirm. This is heaven; my arse is nicely tingling and glowing warm. I would have this any day of the week, rather than the sight of a farting beer gut walking to the bathroom. I shudder at the thought.

"So how do you feel now, Charlotte, now you know you have not had a stroke?"

"Erm, OK, I do feel fine now you have explained it to me in such a sympathetic way."

"Good, and I am glad you approve of the way I explain things."

"I'm not quite sure I said that, Lloyd," I say, trying to think if I did or not.

"I have noticed that you haven't asked me to release you yet."

Why should I ask him to release me? I am enjoying this part, it's very sensual, but I can't tell him that, can I?

"I just guess that you will release me when you want to."

"Would it be because you like it, would it be because you were wrong last night in what you thought? I think it could be that you are turned on by the restriction."

"How do you do that, Lloyd, how do you read my mind?"

"Charlotte, I am reading your body language, that's all." He chuckles. "Your body is very receptive to everything I do to you. I love playing with you, watching your body, your mind changing. I have already watched your body go from rigid to relaxed this morning. It's different when you *say* you don't like the idea of something to when you *really* don't like something. I know exactly when to act, because of the way your mind and body work now. I am in control of everything, all the time, and you are also gaining control of your body – your control improves with every game we play. You are in fact making everything so much fun, more fun than I thought you would manage, I must admit."

He runs his hand down my arse, to my inner thigh. Bloody hell, God, I want to burst. I moan...

"Keep control, Charlotte," he whispers. "Sex is so much better when you can keep control, I promise you."

Oh God, a promise – you don't get many of those to the dozen paddles. Hold on, hold on, just a sub's brain-picking moment – did he just say sex is so much better? Are we going to have sex? Full-blown sex! My hips move with the anticipation of him fucking me, hard 'n' fast, slow 'n' soft, oh my God.

"Oh yes, oh yes!"

Slap.

"What the fuck—"

Slap.

"Why did you fucking slap me?"

Slap.

"You are so easy to read, my little smart-arse mouth, such good fun."

Slap.

"Lloyd, that was so nice, so why spoil it?"

Slap, rub.

"I know it was – you were carried away in the moment, losing control."

Ah, he's rubbing again, that's nice!

"It's just so fucking heavenly!"

Slap.

"It is just so heavenly watching your arse go red, my smart-arse mouth."

"Lloyd, give a girl a break, please!"

Slap, rub.

"OK, as you asked so nicely."

Rubbing, mmm.

"You still haven't worked it out yet, have you?"

"Worked what out?"

"Oh, nothing. You will, I am sure of that. You look so sexy lying there like that – in fact I would go as far as saying the sexiest I have seen you."

"Why thank you, Lloyd, I assume you look just as sexy as you always do."

"Why do you assume I do?"

"It's a little difficult to see you when I have a blindfold on."

"Are you asking for the game to be changed, Charlotte?"

"I wouldn't dream of asking for the game to be changed."

"Good, because I am enjoying it. You would really have to come up with something spectacular to change this game. However, I can change your position, roll you onto your back if you wish, but be warned, I can flip you over again just as quick if I need to." He taps my arse, meaning he will spank me if he thinks I need it.

"Oh, Lloyd, that is so thoughtful of you, letting me know that you are leaving your options open for all eventualities. Thank you."

"You're very welcome. A word of advice, if I may – just remember that smart-arse mouths come in many forms. Even if you don't say the words 'what the fuck' or such words, your tone and sarcastic manner will say them for you."

He bounces his hand up and down on my arse.

Then with one of his legs over mine, hooking his foot under my other leg, he pulls it across towards him, lifting my shoulders; he flips me over, then sits astride me. Moving my hair out of my face, he lifts the blindfold slightly, and I peek out.

"Good morning, Charlotte," he says, and his face is beaming down at me.

"Good morning, Lloyd, nice to see you."

He gives me a little kiss on my forehead. No, no, no, my lips! Kiss my lips, for God's sake.

"Breakfast?"

Breakfast! That's better, yes, breakfast, I can do breakfast. My hips move as I think about participating in a sexual breakfast.

"Charlotte, does coffee and a bagel turn you on that much?" He raises his eyebrows.

"No, Lloyd, but coffee and a bagel would be fantastic, thank you."

No, coffee and a bagel don't turn me on that fucking much, for fuck's sake! What do you think is turning me on? You are sitting there stark bollock naked on top of me – it would turn any woman on, for fuck's sake.

"Charlotte, I will go and get us some breakfast. I will

leave you with that comment you just made, and when I return I expect you to explain why I could be led to believe it is sarcasm." He pulls the blindfold down over my eyes, and gets off me.

Sarcasm! Why would that be sarcasm? I can't help it if he twists things, can I? He's the one who is twisted, not me. I try to move my arms down from above my head but they feel heavy, my shoulders so stiff I can't bend my elbows. Hold on, he said the tape was from just above my wrists to my fingertips, but he has taped my elbows as well. I'll show him. I grit my teeth and roll over onto my side and swing my legs over the edge of the bed. Right, sit up; on three, I can do this. One…two…three…

"Push." I push myself up and my arms flop forward. "Jesus, that fucking hurts!" My arms feel like they have been pulled out of my shoulder sockets. "Shit! Fuck! What the fuck? Oh my fucking God!" My head falls forward, my hair tumbles down across my face, and I feel it brush on my cheeks on its way past. My arms to one side of me, I feel as if I am disabled in some way. Shit, fucking shit, the pain rushes through to my neck as I try to turn.

"Oh, for fuck's sake! What the fuck? How long have I been tied up for? Eight hours, he said, feels more like eight days to me. I am that stiff it hurts."

I try to move the mask off my eyes by using the side of my arm, but my hair is in the way.

"OK, need to move hair." I try to toss my hair back out of my face, but no! Not going to fucking move is it? "Fucking hair, if you don't move, I will get one of the girls at the salon fucking cutting you off, you won't get in my way again. That's it, see, hair, I will take control of you all right."

I try blowing it, to make it move. "Oh, for fuck's sake! Move out of my way, will you?"

I move my knee up towards my face. "Now, if I can just get my knee under my hair, maybe I can get the eye mask off." As I lean to get my knee up, I fall backwards onto the bed.

"Oh fuck! Great, thank you, God, now look at what you have done to me. I am lying back down. I can do this, for fuck's sake. Come on, Charlotte, you can do this…one… two…three – hup." I push with all my might. Oh, oh no, oh no, oh fucking no— CRASH!

"Ouch, fucking ouch, that must be the floor I have just hit, and a good morning to you, floor. Note to oneself: I must remember to put a big, soft, fluffy rug here, as I doubt it will be the last time I end up here!"

Oh, fucking hell, now! Now I have to stand up. I roll onto my side and manage to get onto my knees in a haphazard way. "Fucking hell, why is life so hard sometimes?" I wave my hands around to find the edge of the bed.

"Found you. Why the fuck did you let me fall off you, bed? That was very fucking rude of you, I think, considering the predicament I am in, and don't you know my head is still fucking hurting? You let floor bump it all over." I crawl on my knees to the bed, and eventually lay my head down on it. "Thank fuck! I'm safe again."

OK, maybe I can get the mask off by rubbing it on the bed; then I will be able to see.

"Why the fuck have I chosen a Dom to be my next partner? They have no consideration for us girlies whatsoever. Tah-dah! Done it, fuc—"

Lloyd is sitting on one of the chairs, watching me. I didn't hear him come in at all, and I look at him with surprise.

"Yes, Charlotte, please continue with your little story. You got to why the fuck have you chosen a Dom to be your next partner – why have you? Since you are the one to bring it up."

26

Shit! How long has he been here? Oh fucking hell! What the fuck have I said out loud? Obviously that. I throw my head down between my arms to hide my embarrassment, not quite knowing what to say or do. I know a way to change the subject that will work.

"I needed a pee! So I tried to get up!" That's good, distract him. I raise my head in hope.

"Yes, I saw you trying to get up, very entertaining it was too. Look, I have finished my coffee while I was watching you."

He holds his mug upside down to show it is was indeed empty. Oh shit! Oh fuck! He has been here for fucking ages, so why the fuck didn't he help me?

"I must say, Charlotte, that little party piece was so funny, even Anthony and Kat had to leave because they couldn't contain their laughter any longer."

What, Kat and Anthony saw me?

"Oh no, oh no, you didn't invite them in, did you?" I feel the redness rush to my cheeks, and as it does it burns deep into the bones of my face.

"No, Charlotte, I had left the door open, I was only going to be a minute. They just saw you and couldn't stop watching until the agony of hiding their laughter got too much. Look, they had a coffee too." He nods at the table, where there are three more coffee mugs.

Why the fuck didn't I hear them come in? Oh shit! Oh fuck, I am naked, for Christ's sake. Oh shit! Oh hell, what the fuck? The comment about Doms, was that out loud or in my head? I have probably pissed Anthony off with that. I bury my head again.

"Charlotte, you are leant over a bed, your hands are straight in front of you, your head down – are you expecting something, or just being very submissive?"

"No, neither," I mutter into the bed.

"Oh! I just thought it was an invitation, with that nice pink arse pointing upwards like that!"

I raise my head in horror – surely not! Surely you wouldn't be that cruel?

"Lloyd, after having me put through such humiliation, don't you think that would be so cruel of you, so damn fu—"

"Charlotte, I could let you finish, but the way it's going so far, I have enough to spank you for the whole of the day if I wish."

I grit my teeth at him. "Toilet, please!" I give him a screwed-up grin.

"Yes, Charlotte, you may use the toilet."

"I wasn't fucking asking your permission to use the fucking loo. It would be nice if you can fucking get up and help me!" Oh shit! Oh shit! Out loud! No, not out loud!

"Charlotte, sarcastic as well as smart-arse mouth, all in one sentence! How much you have learnt, and to think you are expecting me to come over there where your bottom is sticking up, slightly pink now, and help you to the toilet. By any chance would you be thinking I wouldn't be tempted in any way to make that smart-arse mouth of yours shut up?"

"What? Is that a rhetorical question, or do you want me to answer it, because right now, Lloyd, I need the loo."

"Tut, tut, you are giving me all the advantages here, Charlotte."

"I didn't realise you were playing. I thought you and your friends were quite happy watching the show I so unknowingly put on for you all this morning, but now I think I deserve the fucking loo, don't you?"

"The loo is over there, Charlotte. I don't believe that the show is over just yet." He grins at me.

I look at him for a sign of some sort of compassion, but all he does is put his arms on the back of the sofa, crossing his legs as he does so; he has no intention of helping me.

"Oh, for God's sake! If you are not going to help me then, then…" My frustration is starting to show and I screw up my face.

OK then. I can do this, I will show you, I think to myself. I can do this, feet first; I just need to concentrate.

"Then what, Charlotte?"

Aw, he is so cold sometimes.

"Lloyd, it's hard enough concentrating without you mind-gaming me as well."

"Oh sorry, Charlotte, I didn't know you were concentrating." He laughs.

For fuck's sake, what the…? I push my hips up, getting my feet firmly on the floor.

"Erm, Charlotte, great view too – nowhere near the right colour for my liking, though."

"Lloyd, leave my fucking arse alone, will you? I don't need you doing that right now, do I?"

"It would add to the entertainment value of all this, don't you think?"

I grimace as I push as hard as I can on my arms to stand up straight. That's it, good, I've done it. My hair is all over my face again, so I toss my head a little with a smug grin, as if to say, See, I am up! I didn't need your help after all.

"Well done, Charlotte, you are standing up and it's only taken you forty minutes! I will go and get us some fresh coffee while you go to the loo."

I watch him walk out of the room; he leaves the door open, and I can hear fits of laughter. Bastards! Fucking bastards.

I hear Lloyd say, "She still hasn't got to the toilet yet, she has only just managed to get off the bed."

Ha-ha! You are all so funny, I say to myself.

"Now she has to work out how to get in to the toilet – the door is closed."

Again they all laugh. Oh shit! Oh pants! The door, how the hell do I turn the knob with my hands taped up? Why oh why haven't I seen this coming, for fuck's sake? Oh shit. What the hell is going on?

I walk over to the door, looking at it. Shit, I can't open that. I know! This will get him. I will go try one of the other bedrooms; maybe the doors will be open. I turn, and he is standing there. Crap! Crap! I am dancing now. I need a wee, really I do; for fuck's sake, just look at me.

"Oh, Charlotte, I didn't realise you were into lap dancing. Maybe I should get you some lessons, because that dance just isn't doing it for me." He smirks as he sits down with two fresh cups of coffee.

"Please, Lloyd, please put a stop to this. Either untie me or open the door, please."

"Why should I want to put a stop to this when I am having such a good time?"

"Please, I am going to pee my pants."

"Do you want me to put some on for you then?"

"Lloyd, don't, you know what the fuck I mean."

"My smart-arse mouth, I am going to enjoy you so much today – not that I haven't already done so."

"Please, Lloyd, let me go."

"I am not stopping you going anywhere you want to, Charlotte."

"Please! Lloyd, I beg you, open the toilet door for me so I can go to the loo."

"What is it worth to me, Charlotte?"

"Oh, Lloyd, I never thought in a million years that you

would ever stoop that low, to blackmail me over opening the door of the loo."

"Charlotte, have you never heard that there is no such thing as a free pee?" He laughs.

Fuck you, there must be some way that I can open the fucking door, I don't need a fucking man to do that for me. I don't, I will show you. I go to the door and I try to get my hips and my hands to turn the knob, but it will not turn. I stand back and lift a foot. I have seen people do this; I must be able to do this... Oh shit! What? Shit! No, I can't get my foot that high; I will fall over. Crap!

Lloyd sniggers. I turn and look at him. I have a very angry face on now.

"Charlotte, if you wish I can open the door for you, but it will cost you. The price of me opening the door will be that for the rest of the day you do not have a smart-arse mouth!"

"OK! Anything, just open the door, please."

What, what have you done that for? You know now he is going to do everything in his power to make you lose control, don't you? Oh for fuck's sake, you stupid blonde. I watch him walk to the bathroom, opening the door with ease.

"Charlotte, be my guest." He holds his hand out, waving me in. As I walk past him I keep eye contact.

"Very ungainly of you, Lloyd, if you don't mind me saying so."

Slap.

Fuck, my arse.

"Oh, by the way, what a spectacular game you have played so far this morning."

I hop forward, scowling at him.

Chapter Three

After I finish my pee, he invites me to sit and have coffee with him. I sit down and look at the table. Where's the bagel?

"Lloyd, I thought you said we were having breakfast?"

He looks at me, then down towards my hands, then back to my face, pausing for a minute.

"You would like breakfast now?"

"Yes, breakfast would be very nice. I have worked up an appetite. Who would have thought getting out of bed would have been such good exercise? Thank you, Lloyd, I would really enjoy eating a bagel now."

"As you asked so nicely I will go and get you a bagel. I think I might even have one as well. Are you sure there is nothing else I can get you or do for you?"

"No thank you, just the bagel will be fine, but it's so nice of you to ask."

He gets up and leaves the room.

Yes, I should feel pleased with myself. I have negotiated a bagel out of him, plus he didn't even argue with me, no blackmail or anything. I smirk inside at my triumph.

When he comes back in he places one bagel down in front of me. Sitting, he crosses his legs and starts eating his bagel.

Crap! Oh, double crap! I suppose he thinks he is fucking clever. For fuck's sake, how the hell do I get to eat mine, then? You knew! You bloody knew! I toss my head back in frustration.

"Problem, Charlotte?"

"Problem...me? No, I don't think so, what makes you think I have a problem?" I'm trying to look casual, but somehow I don't think I do.

"Are you not wanting the bagel I so kindly went and got for you?"

"Yes, I do want my bagel, in fact I am looking forward to eating it."

Shit! How the hell do I get out of this one?

"Is there something you would like me to do for you?"

Yes, there bloody well is and you fucking know it.

"For fuck's sake, cut me loose." Oh crap! Oh fucking crap! Out loud.

"Charlotte, have you just broken a promise there?"

Think, quick, think.

"Lloyd, I don't know what you mean."

"Oh, must be my mistake! Thought I heard a smart-arse mouth!"

"No, not at all, you are just so good at reading me, and keeping one step ahead, you must have imagined that I said something. You really can't hold me responsible for your imagination, Lloyd."

"Oh well, in that case, eat up your bagel. I did think for one moment there that you had asked me to release your hands. You obviously haven't finished entertaining me this morning, as all these games are yours – I truly don't want to spoil the moment for you. It's the first time you have really played, and you have been so inventive it would be such a shame, don't you think?"

I look at him in absolute amazement. Shit! How does he do it? How does he turn everything to his advantage? I really can't ask him to cut me loose now, can I? I look at my bagel, wondering how I can eat it. Only one thing for it: I will have to bite it on the plate. I lower my head to bite into it, and Lloyd sniggers as I do battle with a bagel from hell, darting around the plate. Oh, for fuck's sake! How have I got here?

Thirty minutes later, I look up and see Lloyd wiping away the tears from his eyes.

"Thanks, Lloyd, the best bagel I have ever eaten."

It takes him a minute or two to compose himself.

"Lloyd, you haven't lost control, have you?"

"No, Charlotte, never! That's to say, not enough for you to get the advantage, but you are the funniest sub-to-be I have ever known." He collapses into laughter as he walks out of the door.

OK, the biggest mistake I have made so far: I was quick to point out that he said it was breakfast we were having – too fucking quick. In fact, note to oneself: do not point out facts like that to a Dom when you are still taped up, for when they do agree you are right, it's usually because they can get some more fucking sport out of you. When you think you are holding all the cards, beware, because from where I am sitting Doms have poker faces and most of them have been playing these games for a very long time. I'm starting to see that now.

There's a knock on the door. Anthony pops his head around the corner.

"Hi, can I come in?"

"Oh, I get a choice now, do I? I didn't see you asking me when you all thought I was being entertaining, as Lloyd puts it."

"I am so sorry, you were just so funny."

He enters the room. Grabbing the duvet, he wraps it round my shoulders.

"Thank you, at least there is one Dom that still knows how to behave sometimes." I give him a sideways glance of approval.

"Oh, now, Charlotte, that's unfair of you. By all accounts Lloyd has given you loads of chances to have him help you, which most of the time you have refused. Your stubborn head seems to be controlling you right now. But hey, that's OK – it's all part of being you, and it's important that you don't lose sight of being you, but I think you have a long way to go before you truly find yourself again. But you will. To be honest, Lloyd wouldn't have you any other way." He gives me a little wink.

"Oh yes, like loads! I don't think so, unless he wants me to beg, and I will never beg him – why should I?"

"By all accounts, you begged him to open the toilet door."

"Oh come on, that's fucking different, Anthony, and you know it! What the fuck? How the hell can I get my head around these games he plays, if you are going to play them with me too? I was scared this morning when I thought I was paralysed, and he did nothing to reassure me!"

"Do you think for one moment that Lloyd would leave you struggling if he thought that you were truly ill? Think, Charlotte – trust him, read him. You went into a panic this morning in your hung-over state of mind – your mind was the one playing tricks on you, not Lloyd. If you had thought for one moment that Lloyd was playing then you would have realised that you weren't paralysed and that you hadn't had a stroke. You need to trust that Lloyd will not put you in danger, that he will make sure you are safe at all times.

The two key words here are 'trust' and 'control'."

I listen to everything that Anthony is telling me. God, it's just so much to think about, I really can't take it all in this morning, and my head is still throbbing.

"Charlotte, I love you so much, I am glad you are in all our lives, you bring so much to us all, but on a serious note, I want to ensure you are OK with everything this morning. No regrets?"

I beam at him. "No, Anthony, no regrets."

"Even after everything you have been through this morning?"

Hold on! Is he here to test the water for Lloyd to see if it's fucking safe for him to release me?

"Anthony, as you are being so kind to me, can you please release my hands?"

"Oh, Charlotte, I would love to, but unfortunately it is against the code of Doms to do such a thing." He winks.

Knew it – he is on the Dom from hell's side, for fuck's sake! I can't even trust Anthony to help me when Lloyd is playing, that's for sure.

"OK, got it. In that case then, Anthony, would you mind telling the Dom from hell that his new plaything has had enough of his fucking games this morning? She wishes to have her fucking freedom now, if he has fucking finished this morning."

"What? You want me to tell him exactly what you have just said?"

"Anthony, you really think it's going to make any difference what I say? He will only do what he wants, twisting every little thing around so he can have his entertainment at my expense."

"I see you are starting to see what's happening. All you need to do now is learn how to stop it from happening, then

36

you will be halfway there. So you are quite happy, then, playing the games?"

"Yes, game on." I wink.

Lloyd enters the room, still trying to contain his sniggers.

"Charlotte, I will run you a shower. When I return I will cut off the tape."

Before I can answer and tell him, Oh yes, buster, you are going to cut me free and when you have done I will show you which one of us has itchy palms, Anthony jumps in and answers for me.

"I think that's an excellent idea, Lloyd. You don't want to be late for this morning's activities that you have planned, do you?"

"No, I don't, Anthony, you are right. Oh, on the other hand I have had such a good morning so far that I am in two minds," he says, disappearing into the bathroom.

"I have to go back to Kat now, so will see you both later."

"Bye, then. Thanks, Anthony, for the chat, it's nice to know there is a gentleman here!" I say.

Lloyd, returning from the bathroom, sits on the sofa and looks at me.

"Tape off, or do you wish to carry on? Please take care in what you say next, Charlotte!"

Take care; I always take care in what I say, for fuck's sake. I will clarify what game we are playing before I answer anything today. I will get him.

"Is this a 'yes, Lloyd' or a 'no, Lloyd' answer?"

"Charlotte!" He looks deeply into my eyes. Getting up, he walks towards me, grabs my hair, tips my head back – yes! Oh yes, a drop-dead, stop-breathing, hip-twisting delicious kiss.

Lifting me up, he carries me to the shower. Standing me

on the floor, looking into my eyes, he then takes off the tape, so much tape.

OK, so is that kiss his way of distracting me from the fact that I want to spank him, judging by my itchy palms? Oh God, oh God! There it is again – another kiss. He wraps me in his arms, kissing with passion, long and hard, pushing me towards the shower. He grabs the shower gel and squeezes it into my hair and starts to massage it, lathering it up. I feel the hot water and bubbles running down my back.

I run my hands over his head, following the water down his T-shirt, sliding my hands up inside to feel his skin. I lift his T-shirt up over his head, dropping it to the ground. Feeling around the waistband of his jeans, I undo the buttons and spin him round, gently pushing him back to the wall. I start to massage his chest with shower gel, then I kiss him down his chest, his beautifully toned chest, water and bubbles cascading down his body; such a hot body.

His hands in my hair, controlling my head, bending to my knees as I go. I start to kiss around his groin, my hands caressing his arse, and I slip my fingers into his jeans, pulling them down. He gives out a moan as I start kissing lower. I look up; his head is leaning backwards against the wall and he looks so deliciously hot with the water running, rippling down his body, his perfectly sculpted body. He looks down at me with a look of want in his eyes, and grabbing my hair, he pushes my head back down. There it is, his manhood. How I have longed for this perfect moment of him inside me. I kiss, teasing him with my tongue, and I hear him moan as his hands get tighter in my hair. I feel him swell, growing bigger as he twists his hips in time with me, thrusting, the water rushing over my face. He moans again.

"Oh God, Charlotte, this is so perfect, you are so hot." Pulling upwards by my hair, he raises me from the floor.

Putting his arms around me, he lifts me; I wrap my legs around him. Kissing my nipples, teasing them with his tongue, he carries me into the bedroom, laying me down on the bed and kissing me hard, still wet from the shower. His body feels so smooth against mine that we seem to slide with ease as our bodies twist and turn together. Then tender kisses as he looks at my face, looking deep in my eyes.

"Charlotte, I want you so much my body aches." He kisses me again softly on the lips, and as his hands clench onto my wrists, holding them above my head, he kisses slowly down my neck. I moan when he reaches my breasts.

"I need you, oh please, I need you inside me!"

His hips twist on top of me.

"Lloyd, please," I beg as I feel his manhood on me.

He kisses back up to my face, grabbing my hair, whispering, "Charlotte, nothing would give me greater pleasure, but not right now."

He stops twisting his hips, plants a kiss on my forehead.

"This is perfect, you are so perfect, but the time isn't."

Oh no, that's not right – come on, for fuck's sake! He must be fucking gay if he can go through all of that, not wanting to carry on. How the hell can a man do that? I have never known a man do this before in my life.

"I don't understand, please tell me this isn't one of your games, please, for—"

He puts his hand over my mouth to stop me from continuing the sentence.

"No, it's not one of my games, I just… I respect you too much. I want so much more than this."

Yes, so do I or haven't you noticed? I want so much more than a steamy shower in every sense of the word without going all the way. I look into his eyes and realise he is very serious.

"OK, I get it, although I don't understand it. Moment gone, then, you are calling time out."

"Yes, I am, if that's the way you want to put it. I also am asking for you to trust me."

Why would he call time out? After all, he has done things to me that are not very nice. I have only called time out once, because it bloody hurt my arse. Have I hurt him? No! I haven't, so why time out on such a perfect, heavenly moment? OK, I can be grown-up about this.

"Time out it is. After all, when I said time out you stopped the instant I said it." I place my arms around him and cuddle him. It's better than nothing at all, and truth be known I need a cuddle just as much as sex. I'm starting to realise that cuddling is so, so nice.

"Thank you, Charlotte."

Oh God, what does he want from me? Another moment gone, just like that. What does he want me to prove? I am playing his games, I've given him good foreplay in the shower, and still no fuck, not even an orgasmic moment, and all he can say is thank you, Charlotte.

We cuddle on the bed for a while, stroking each other's bodies, planting the odd kiss, looking into each other's eyes. At some point the lust I've been feeling has turned to something else, deep inside of me; the feeling of security, something I have never felt with any other man. It isn't the security that you get from a cuddle when you are feeling sad, more a feeling of freedom; freedom from danger. Strange, huh, when the lifestyle I have found myself in is one that can be dangerous in so many ways. I have never had that since I have had adult relationships, and it's like the biggest orgasmic experience I could ever have. I look at him, softly kissing him on the lips.

"Why thank me when it is so obvious that I should be thanking you? You have given me so much, shown me so much." A little grimace appears on my face – did I just say that?

"What, no sarcastic remark? Or a smart-arse mouth? I think this has to be put down for posterity. Never before have you strung a whole sentence together without one or the other. That is twice, Charlotte, within half an hour that you have surprised me. Is this something I should be getting used to, or will it wear off? Mind you, I quite like this cuddly Charlotte. I do hope I see more of her as well."

"As well as what?" I asked inquisitively.

"As well as the fun, funny, smart-arse mouth sarcastic Charlotte. It does make life more interesting, don't you think?"

"Oh, in that case why the f—"

Before I can complete my sentence, he cups his hand over my mouth.

"Charlotte, as much as I would love to flip you over, we are late. We should be downstairs right now, besides which, you have made a promise, one that I would like you not to break again today. Now get up, sort out your hair and I will get you some clothes out." With that he is up, sorting clothes for us to wear. Oh wow, I am honoured today; I get to wear panties and a very tight pair of jeans, two things Lloyd isn't that keen on. I wonder why he has got them out for me.

At the lift I wiggle my arse from side to side. Wow! That's sensitive. I smooth the palms of my hands down the outside of my jeans in an attempt to ease my aroused state.

"Problem, Charlotte?"

There, on his head I see devil horns pushing up. Why is he asking me if I have a problem? OK, what has he done? Why should I have a problem? I fidget again. God, this is... My eyes close slightly. No, snap out of it – it's obviously something he has done to me, and he knows it. Take control.

"No, Lloyd, no problem."

We enter the lift. Oh God, what is this? Whenever I walk my clit is rubbing on my panties, I feel so sensitive down there. I fidget again. This is him; he's done this to me, it must be where he was turning me on and fucking off all the time; now my clit doesn't know if it's supposed to be on or off. For the sake of a sub's arse!

"Charlotte, what is wrong?"

There it is, that glint in his eye, the one that says, I know exactly what's wrong and I revel in your agony – I am not giving the finger-rubbing satisfaction you are looking for.

I am not even going to answer that question.

We arrive at the door of the bondage room. Placing his hand on the handle, he turns.

"Ready for this?"

"Yes!" And we enter.

Jeez, this is so hard. I can feel myself getting wet with every step I take. He must have put something in my under-wear, maybe a powder to arouse the clit – I wouldn't put it past him. That's why they were out for me to wear, obvi-ously, and the tight jeans just to keep everything in place. How cunning of him, and after I was so understanding of the fact that he didn't want to fuck me. Oh, I get it – he thinks this will make me use my smart-arse fucking mouth. Well, how the hell does he think that I am going to concen-trate with this going on down there, all bloody day?

I look around the room. There are so many things in here, and some are scary-looking. I just don't know if I can be tied up! Not being able to protect myself...a feeling of vulnerability sweeps over me.

Earth to Planet Charlotte, come in, Planet Charlotte.

God, I am comatose. I don't know if I want to shout at

him to get me out of here or have an orgasmic experience. I don't want to tell him that the little concoction he has so obviously put into my panties is working, but the feeling of vulnerability is taking over slightly.

"Aww, what nice collars!"

What? Where the hell did that come from? Oh, I am not going to be able to play his games when I am saying things like that. Now he has another advantage over me. He will think I really like them, and the truth is they scare me – everything in this room scares me!

"Sit down, Charlotte, your brain isn't in the right place for this at the moment."

We sit on the sofa and he holds my hand.

"That remark was not what you wanted to say, was it? Are you losing control? You must learn to talk with me."

"For the sake of a sub's arse, you are so cruel to me. How do you expect me to concentrate on the art of control when you are playing such nasty tricks on me, for paddling's sake?"

"I don't know what you mean. Good choice of words!" He raises an eyebrow as if to say, You still haven't quite got it. Well, that's tough luck, buster; you can't do this to me and not expect some kind of verbal disapproval.

"You know exactly what I mean. I don't think you are subbing funny, not at all, Lloyd. And…and I don't like this subbing room, to top it all off."

"Charlotte, you are talking in riddles. I really haven't played any tricks on you – would you care to elaborate for me? In a language that we both speak and understand would be helpful, and then we will talk about the room, as I assume you have another problem, other than the room we are in!"

Well, if it's not him, what the subs have the maids washed

my panties in? No, no, it's you. Oh yes, I can elaborate for you; that will be so subbing easy.

"What have you put into my panties?"

"Nope, Charlotte, you are still trapped on another planet."

"You know what you have done, you have put something in my panties."

"I haven't put anything in your panties, what gives you that idea?"

"Oh yes you have. Man up to it, Lloyd, I have caught you out. You have used some sort of arousing powder and now my clit is all over the place."

He laughs. He is extremely amused. I'm so glad that I am still entertaining him, I think not!

"I haven't done that, I don't even know if there is such a thing. Thanks for the tip – I will have to look out for some. You can, however, get pleasure gel that will give you a slight pleasurable tingle, but that's about it, nothing that makes you this frustrated."

"OK, it's you, it's where you keep turning me on 'n' off like a…like a… You have confused my clit. It doesn't know when it should be turned on or off, does it?" I plant my head into my hands over the frustration of my lady button; trying to have a conversation about it is just too subbing much.

"Are you talking about the wax?"

"No, Lloyd, I am not talking about the subbing ripping wax. That was painful, having my pubes plucked out one by one. This is… Well, you know what this is – you are the one that has done it to me, confused it so subbing much that… Stop subbing laughing at me! This is agony, trying to control it."

"Oh, my dear, confused Charlotte, what you are experiencing is the sensation from not having pubes. It is normal. I haven't confused your clit at all, and although you're giving me credit for such an act, I cannot take it. I might even make it my life's ambition from now on, to see if I can really confuse your clit. And I love this new word. Your attempt to talk dirty, maybe!"

"Oh shit, oh double crap, how the hell do I find myself… How do you do it, twist everything, my mind, my brain, making me say such stupid things? And no, I am not talking dirty. I am frustrated!"

"I don't have to twist anything, you're very good at doing it for yourself. I just sit back and let you as you are such a funny smart-arse mouth."

"Oh, Lloyd, no, Lloyd, I am sorry, I am trying so hard."

"Yes, you are very trying. However, you have been so entertaining this morning. I will pretend I didn't hear your smart-arse mouth this time, but please control yourself for the rest of the day, Charlotte."

"You knew what was wrong with me as soon as we got to the lift, you subbing knew."

"Yes, I did."

"Why didn't you say?"

"Charlotte, I asked you what was wrong. Your reply was nothing, so what do you want – me to contradict you?"

"No, yes, no – oh. I don't know, you could have subbing said, that's all I am saying."

"What? Spoil the fun? I don't think so, do you?"

He rubs the palm of his hand with his thumb; I have never seen him do that before.

"It might be fun for you, but let me tell you, I am not subbing happy. You could have said something, I am sure."

He's looking down at his hands now. What, he isn't paying any subbing attention to me? What the stroke of a paddle is he doing? Not like him not to keep looking at me when he is talking.

"Charlotte, I tell you many things, but they just don't stay in the right place in your brain. Is it my problem that you don't know how to keep your drawers tidied up in that empty cavern you call a brain?"

"Oh come now, Lloyd, who is it being personal now?"

He looks back up at me. "Sorry, Charlotte, yes, you are right, that is a little personal. Now let's have a little cuddle before we carry on, then we can start again."

He cuddles me up to him and kisses my head. This is so nice, this is so cool – I have cuddles on demand if I want them, and the best thing is that I don't feel so vulnerable now either; his cuddles have such a calming effect on me.

"On with the show. I have a lot to explain to you in here, and it will not be long until the others come for the demonstration and question time. Let's see how much you can retain, shall we?"

He gets up and takes my hand, and we go to a table where there is a selection of chains, ropes, collars and other things. I am amazed that there are so many different types of restraints.

"Charlotte, please try to stay with this. You will find so many things that you will be able to apply in any walk of life – just try and remember as much as you can. You will, however, pick up more about this room as we play. Bondage is the art of restricting someone – it takes one hundred per cent of the Dom's control. Usually there are three people in here when bondage is being used, for safety – never let anyone you don't know bring you in here, and never come in here with anyone you do not trust completely, because this is one hundred per cent trust. Firstly, rope."

He picks up a piece of rope in his hand before continuing. "When tied with rope, the sub must stay still. Some ropes, depending on the way they are tied, will tighten if the sub struggles or moves – it can cause extreme pain, as they will cut into your flesh. A good Dom will always check that this is not happening, and will stop at the first sign of stress.

"Straps – these are leather ones, just like the straps that used to be used in hospitals and poor houses. A little gentler on the skin, but as you have found out, Charlotte, very effective."

"Do you do ropes?"

"Yes, I do. Cuffs – always know there is a key for them, and don't let anyone put them on too tight, as they are harsh on the skin. Collars – ah yes, you think they are nice! They go around the sub's neck. The collar symbolises ownership. Never let anyone put a collar on if you are not sure, and always make sure you can get fingers between the collar and your neck. If you are involved in any confrontation anywhere, always, where possible, take off anything that can be grabbed hold of that is around your neck. Chains – always check for yourself that the chains are OK. No rust or snags on them, that they aren't broken in any way. Bars – these are used to spread limbs further.

"Make no mistakes, Charlotte, this isn't the room you want to be in with anyone you don't know you can trust, and by that I also mean that even if there are three of you, don't for one moment think that a Dom with his sub is safe. If anything is wrong don't assume the sub will help you – if they are into much stronger submission, the sub will only do what the Dom wants, and you might find yourself in deeper than you wish to be."

"If this room is so harsh, why have it?"

"Charlotte, trust me, this room here is soft, the limits are set low. This is more of a training bondage room, for practice, for us to explain to little confused subs like yourself, for Doms, or Rope Masters as some like to be called, to practise or demonstrate their art, with a little teasing play along the way. I don't want you to think that as it is play it is not dangerous – never take your eye off the game."

"How do you keep an eye on what's going on if you are being tied up?"

"I was expecting that question from you. It is all to do with trusting your Dom, talking with him, telling him how you feel inside and out, answering him truthfully when he asks you if there is anything wrong. Remember, the lifestyle is trust, control and communication, and Charlotte, you don't have to say anything to communicate with people."

Oh, there you go – a little poke right in my subbing eye. You just couldn't resist that, could you, after this morning?

"You have said that the Dom reads body language, so why does he need the sub to talk? You have said loads of times that you prefer me subbing quiet." Stick that in your little subbie collar. Why does he keep doing that today, rubbing his palm? It's quite off-putting.

"That's an interesting choice of words you have just used, and so I want to answer it correctly. Come over to the sofa, please."

"Sure."

He grabs my hand to lead me. Sitting down, he flips me over his knees.

"Lloyd, what the subbing hell do you think you are doing?"

"Explaining."

"Explaining what?"

"Explaining why your comment was so disrespectful. What else would I be explaining?"

"I don't know, Lloyd."

"You are just about to find out."

Slap.

Aww, not so bad, jeans are protecting me – ha-ha, Mr Not-So-Smart Dom.

"Doms will know there is something wrong through body language – they will not always know what."

Slap.

"Charlotte, how do you expect a Dom or anyone to know what is wrong with you?"

Slap.

Aww, ouch.

"You need to tell the Dom the truth always."

Slap.

"When asking your Dom questions, try limiting your sarcasm!"

Slap.

"Charlotte, you are being very quiet!"

"You haven't given me a chance to answer, you just slap, slap away with that hand of yours."

He flips me up; looks me in the eye. "Charlotte, when anyone asks you what is wrong, tell them straight away. There are too many things that can really hurt you."

"I'm sorry, Lloyd."

"So do you understand everything in here, including saying when something is wrong?"

"Yes, I do, Lloyd, but..."

"But what?"

"Are you going to tie me up? I am worried that you will."

"No, Charlotte, I am not going to tie you up." He grabs me by my waist and pulls me to sit on his knees, cuddling me.

"Lloyd, you are a very tactile person – not what I expected

from you when you said you were a Dom. I never expected so many cuddles!"

"Cuddles? I love them, they have always been a very important part of any relationship. However, in a Dom–sub relationship it's more important to give cuddles, love and affection after play. It's important to cuddle, and yes, talk, after play. I will finish this conversation later. The guys are here."

The door opens and in walk Anthony and Kat.

"Rope Master Anthony and sub Kat at your service." Anthony gives a small wave to me, making me smile.

"Right, Charlotte, I assume that Lloyd has given you the dos and don'ts in the room, so we shall begin with some simple wrist-tying, I think. Ready, Kat?"

"Ready."

Picking up a smallish piece of rope, he starts winding it around Kat's wrists. When he is finished I look closely at her. Even with two neatly placed loops around each wrist, the first thing I notice is that Kat has movement in her hands and fingers. She's still able to pick up a glass of water to drink from it.

"See, Lloyd, even Anthony has left Kat with her fingers and movement in her hands," I say, pointing to Kat's hands.

Mmm, that's nice, Lloyd is rubbing my arse in circles.

"Not like you, you left me with no movement and no fingers this morning," I chirp at him.

Lloyd moves his head to mine, and whispering in my ear, he says, "Are you now telling me that I don't know how to tape you up?"

"No, Lloyd, not me!"

He removes his hand sharply and I clench my bottom muscles, ready for the slap. At the same time Anthony and Kat both look away, pretending they are looking at ropes. How do they do that? Secret semaphore of Doms or something?

Tilting his head back towards my ear, Lloyd's hand makes contact with my arse, and softly squeezing, he whispers, "As much as I would love to spank you right now, I will not do so in front of Kat and Anthony. I really don't want to humiliate you any more today. I do hope we have a deal, Charlotte!" Then he kisses me on the cheek.

I watch for the rest of the day, Anthony and Kat demonstrating the art of bondage to me. Kat loves it; I watch her body language, how she holds her hands and feet, different ways for different restraints, not all the same. She explains how she can move her body if Anthony is doing something wrong and he will change what he is doing. There just seem to be so many factors in the way that bondage is carried out correctly and safely, I don't think I will ever get it. How can restriction to that degree be a turn-on? Somehow I think that maybe one day Lloyd will demonstrate it on me – that's if I ever get the art of control – and yes, for the rest of the time in the bondage room I am able to keep my mouth shut. Well, almost, anyway, but it was nice having my arse squeezed every time I said something that Lloyd didn't quite approve of.

Chapter Four

Monday morning, just Lloyd and me here; it's quite calm compared to the last week. Yes, a whole week since I found out that my friends have an alternative lifestyle and enjoy every aspect of what they do, making them who they are. Lloyd is in the shower, I am still in bed, not quite come round yet, drifting in and out of my hazy, dreamy sleep, wondering what Lloyd has got planned for us, or should I say me. Lloyd bounces on the bed next to me.

"Hey, you OK?"

"Yes, I am, thank you, Lloyd."

"Good. Today I have arranged for you to be with Sophie. She is giving dance lessons, and I thought also you could do with time away from me for a while."

"Oh, but isn't today our last day together? You know, back to normality, work tomorrow for me..."

"We will see if you go back tomorrow or not. Let's see what happens today."

"Why, what might happen, Lloyd?"

"Nothing, but you might be too exhausted to go, or you might just give me reason to keep you in bed all day tomorrow."

Oh no you don't, you are not going to give me the impression that you might go all the way, that's bloody subbing mean. "Lloyd, if I want to return to work I will and nothing you can do is going to keep me away."

"Charlotte, are you challenging me? Because I am so sure that if I phone Nats, telling her you will not be in as you challenged me on this, she will understand. It wouldn't be a problem to her, that's for sure."

"Lloyd, for sub's sake, what are you trying to do, control every aspect of my life?" What is he doing looking at his hand again, rubbing it? Maybe he has a splinter or something. It's so off-putting, though.

"No, Charlotte, I am not. Just the things that you find hard to control, that's all."

"I am glad to subbing hear it, or I would have to phone Anthony for a contract, don't you think?"

Duvet gone – where has the duvet gone? Flip – oh shit.

"Lloyd—"

"No jeans to protect your little arse this time, Charlotte!"

"Lloyd, why, please?"

"I am not going to have you being sarcastic." And with that, in quick succession he gives five slaps to my arse.

"Ouch! Bloody ouch!" I could still feel the sting from his hand burning into my arse, as he didn't once rub.

Sitting astride me, face down on the bed, he whispers, "Charlotte, please never change."

"But isn't that the whole point of this little exercise you have come up with?"

"You know full well it isn't. I love you for you." And he kisses my neck.

"Lloyd, what are you doing?"

"Just checking my assets for any damage."

"Like what damage might there be?"

"Yesterday was hard – so many good situations. I just want to ensure that everything is working right, that nothing is left confused this morning. I know how to read you, I don't want Sophie to think I have dumped someone with sub space on her."

"Don't think you are subbing funny, and what the paddle is sub space?"

"Don't you know? I thought you did, as you are always going in and out of sub space."

"Are you going to tell me, or is this one of those things you put on a postcard, or text the answer to? Mmm, that's nice..." Lloyd has started to kiss my neck, and is nibbling my ear.

"Sub space is when things get so intense your body lets go, sending you into a comatose state, like you were yesterday in the bondage room, remember? Earth to Planet Charlotte, but then again, Charlotte, it is very hard to tell as you are always away with the fairies just lately."

"You are so funny. I was perplexed yesterday, that's all."

"What about now, Charlotte, are you perplexed now?"

"No."

"I will have to see if I can change that, then." He holds my hair tightly, biting my neck.

"You said I was going dancing, so do you think it might be a good idea if you release my hands from the bed now?"

"Charlotte, you know I am enjoying this."

"Far be it from me to spoil your little game, but don't you think that Sophie will be cross if I am late?"

"This is your little game, if I recall rightly. Shall I begin? The four of us were eating cream cakes and you decided that your cream cake would look better in my face when I accidentally mentioned your confusing problem to Anthony and Kat."

"Lloyd, I know what I did, I was there, remember? I pushed the cake in your face, saying to hell with your fucking rules. If I remember rightly, Anthony and Kat thought it was funnier than my confusion. Don't you think that tying me to the bed is just a little bit excessive?"

"No, I don't, because it's where I love my sub to be, sometimes for days, just playing and teasing like I did last night and every night since you agreed to this. Don't forget I like everything I do to be intense, hopefully you will find out just how intense when the time is right."

"Oh, here you go with the 'time isn't right' thing. Can I ask you a question?"

"You don't even have to ask that question. Do you?"

"Good. When the hell is the time going to be subbing right?"

"Now that is an answer on a postcard job."

"Grrrrr!"

"Charlotte, don't lose control. Come, I will untie you now and you can get ready for dancing. I can always put you back here later if I wish."

Chapter Five

I get ready. Today's clothes are little black shorts, a T-shirt and a pair of soft black leather flats. Downstairs, outside the punishment room, Lloyd holds my face up with both his hands.

"You OK? I have to go out for a while but I will be back later. If there is anything wrong you must tell Sophie, promise me. She is in there waiting for you."

"Nothing's wrong, and I promise."

He gives me a kiss on the forehead and I watch him walk down the stairs. Oh, this is strange, very strange – I haven't been without him for a week and I feel a little insecure for some reason. I knock on the door but no answer, nothing; I open it slightly, peeping round.

Sophie is sitting on a chair – she is *tied* to the chair – and she has a gag over her mouth. I walk in.

"Hi, Sophie, are you still playing with your Dom?" I say. As I enter I notice that some of the furniture has been moved in the room, and there is a sofa quite close to the door. I walk towards her and notice her eyes widen.

"I will take your gag off, although I bet I will probably upset your Dom or something. Stupid bloody rules they have, I can't be expected to remember them all. Anyway, he has broken the rules because he has left you tied up on your own in a room, so that would be a good argument, wouldn't it? I can always throw some of these rules back in their big fat Dom faces."

I hear the door close. Sophie rolls her eyes upwards.

"Oh shit! Is that him? Did he hear me?" I whisper to her. Turning, there is a man leaning on the closed door; he walks over to the sofa, then pushes it against the door.

"Hey, what are you doing?" I snap.

"You might get away with talking to your Dom like that, but let me tell you this: I am far superior to any of them here. You are not going to talk to me like that. You are going to learn what this is really about."

"Sophie, I really think it's time you got a new Dom, I don't like this one."

I look at her and she shakes her head in a 'no' motion. Oh crap.

"This guy isn't your Dom, is he?" I say as I continue trying to get Sophie free.

"What are you doing?" he snaps.

"I am untying Sophie. This isn't right, it's not in the rules, is it? You left her tied up on her own and anything could have happened, for sub's sake."

Calm, keep calm. My fingers are all over the place; I can't really see what I am doing.

"You were never a boy scout, were you?" That's it – distract him and buy time.

He shakes his head, not quite believing what I have just said to him.

"What has that got to do with anything?" He looks a little confused now, I think. All I have to do is keep calm and I'll have him tied up in verbal knots.

"You don't know how to tie knots, do you, and I am sure that there must be a rule about tying granny knots.

Surely it's illegal, for fuck's sake!"

"Is she for real, Sophie? Or is she just thick?"

Thick! He is calling me thick, what the fuck?

"I don't think I am the stupid one, do you? After all, how the fuck do you think you are going to get away with this – how are you going to get out? You have broken all the rules."

For fuck's sake, what the fuck is happening here? He takes a step towards Sophie, and Sophie's body goes stiff. Hold on, she never goes stiff; she always stays relaxed. She is trying to tell me something. What the fuck is she trying to say? Come on, brain, think. OK, Sophie, I've got it – I have to move as well. Keep eye contact, watch everything, try to take as much in as I can when I am moving around the room.

I start moving to the side of the chair. The only things that have moved in the room are the sofa that he moved against the door, and the chair that he has Sophie on. Moving step for step, I try and keep the same distance between us.

"I am going to teach you a new set of rules. My rules. I love a fresh sub, and you are as fresh as they come. Nothing like seeing your slave trembling in front of you on their knees."

I look at Sophie.

This isn't going well at all. Lloyd said to tell *her* if there was anything wrong. For sub's sake, I bloody need her now – how more wrong can things get? My knees are like jelly. Sophie, help me, please, what do I do, what the fuck do I do?

"Look, I don't know who you are but don't you think this is a little stupid? You know, if you are finding it hard to get a girlfriend I have a phone chat line number you can have!"

Oh shit, I have just called him stupid. He really isn't going to like that, is he? And implying he can't get a girlfriend – where the fuck did that come from? Everything in my head is just getting scrambled. For fuck's sake, compose, control.

"Charlotte – it is Charlotte, isn't it? Yes, I thought so. Do you think it is wise to insult me when I am holding all the cards?" Oh, he answered for me, how rude of him, I think to myself.

How the fuck does he know my name? What the hell is this? My brain starts racing round and round. What else does this nutter know about me? And why is he holding all the cards? What does he want, a game of poker or something? Get control, I need to get control; I need to work out what is going on.

"Who told you my name, for fuck's sake? What the fuck is going on? I don't like your little game, and if this is anything to do with Lloyd I am fucking calling time fucking out. I don't like this. Lloyd?" I shout. That was hardly keeping control – you would have been over Lloyd's knee for that lot, no messing. Shit, and this guy is different to Lloyd because...oh, for the sake of a sub's arse, what the fuck am I doing?

"Soundproofing. The door is locked and no one is going to come and help you. I have taken the mic out as well, so best you get on your knees, little slave."

Oh God, do I do as he demands of me? I shoot a quick glance at Sophie for inspiration. Sophie moves her eyes from left to right. OK, got it. You don't have to talk to communicate. I just hope that eyes will help me now as that's all that I got, and not being fluent in eye language I will assume that's a no then, Sophie.

Looking straight at him I say, "Aww, don't call me a fucking slave, I am no one's slave. I am no one's fucking sub either, get that fucking right, buster." I throw my arms around in frustration at being labelled by this nutter. Lloyd, where are you? I thought while I was frantically searching my brain for what he would say for me to do – typical, he hasn't given me training on how to deal with a nutter, has he? Oh no, he hasn't spelt that out to me!

The man is now standing in front of Sophie, about three feet from her. Good, I think, that's good, I can see them both. I can see her trying to get free; I just hope I managed to loosen the ropes enough.

"Now, is that the way you think you should talk to a potential new Master?"

Oh for fuck's sake, now we are on *Dr Who*. What the fuck is he on about? Hold on, Masters... Anthony called himself a Rope Master yesterday, and Lloyd has mentioned them a few times but somehow I don't think this is the same thing. The guy starts walking back round to the door – no, no, don't do that, I don't want you to move yet. Think, think – yes, the panic button. Walk backwards, keep a little distance but stay over this side of the room; got it, keep eye contact. And potential? I am not anyone's potential. What the fuck, is he for real? Does he really think I would be caught dead with him – his beer gut's hanging over his jeans, for fuck's sake. Look at him: unshaven, greasy, shoulder-length hair – I think it's brown but it could be blonde if he washed it, which I suspect he doesn't – dirty clothes...he looks like a down-and-out. My brain is just racing around with random thoughts now.

"I am not a potential anything for you, you fucking freak." No, Charlotte, what the fuck?! That last bit wasn't supposed to come out.

"I can see that you are going to need some strict discipline. I am a great believer in starting the way you mean to finish."

What the hell does that mean? Oh for fuck's sake, why has everything got to be in riddles?

"I don't know what game this is we are playing but I have really had enough. Don't you fucking understand time out? Open the bloody door now!" I demand. Not good, don't demand; you can't demand with someone like this. For paddles' sake what have I done?

"I am not playing." He reaches over to the table, lifting something off it. Oh shit, oh no, it's a fucking bullwhip, for fuck's sake – where the fuck has that come from? I freeze to the spot. Remember everything. Shit, I can't do this. I look at Sophie but she is too close, she isn't far enough back; if he cracks that whip he will get her. I have to move. Compose yourself, come on. I can do it. Panic alarm on the side of the fireplace – I need to press it. Shit. He flips the whip out. My legs start to wobble and my knees feel like they want to escape from my legs as they start knocking together. Oh no, not now, please don't crumble. Oh for the love of a sub's arse, stay with it, don't let me down now. I feel very insecure. Where are you, Lloyd? I cry inside. Eye contact – don't take my eyes off him, don't lose sight of the game; it's only a game, yes, that's it, it's only a game.

"I understand that you don't like this – something you will have to get used to now that I have claimed you as mine."

How the hell does he know so much about me? How has he got all the advantages? I need to get an advantage. Shit, what the fuck – he turns and looks at Sophie, flipping the whip as he does so. Say something quick; distract him from Sophie.

"Oh, it's OK, I have got to grips with it now Lloyd has given me some lessons." What? What the hell, why have I said that? Sophie's eyes roll up as if to say, What are you doing?

Crack!

The whip whistles past Sophie. Fuck! I stand stock-still. My eyes widen. Fuck, my hair stands on end. When the whip is still I lift my hand and I push the button, quickly placing my hand back down to my side. He turns, facing me, twitching the whip as he does so.

Stepping slowly around he turns, following me. I take one step back.

"Oh, this is going to be fun."

Oh shit, oh hell, what the... I can't do this.

Crack!

The whip whistles past my ear. Shit, fuck, I want to curl up into a ball; I want to shut my eyes. I don't like this. Fuck, my hair – the whip is caught in my fucking hair. Oh shit, my hair!

"Fuck you! You have ripped out my hair, look! What the fuck have you done to my hair? Nats is going to bloody kill you when she gets hold of you, and she will, you know. She doesn't have any shit from anyone, she will whip you without care when she sees what you have done to my hair."

"Charlotte," Sophie calls.

She has managed to work loose and has removed the gag which I had started to undo for her. I want to ask her what's next, what's fucking next? The man walks over to Sophie and hits her around the face.

"For fuck's sake, that isn't very sporting of you, is it?" Trying to distract him again from Sophie.

"I have told you, I am a Master – my rules are different."

"No, you never hit a sub in the fucking face – rule one, I believe."

He flips the whip.

I have to put some distance between him and Sophie.

Keeping an eye on the whip, I have noticed that he habitually does two flicks, then cracks it.

"You have just punished Sophie, you didn't tell her why, and where is her cuddle? I think that's a few more rules you have broken, and didn't you read your guide on how to be a proper Dom?"

"I do like it when a slave fights back a bit."

"Charlotte, move – the whip is longer than ours," Sophie calls.

Fuck, oh shit, can today get any worse? What the fuck – they make them in different lengths? No one told me that. Sofa, get behind the sofa. I sidestep towards the sofa.

Flick, flick.

It's now or never. Two flicks – go!

Crack!

I dive. "Shit!" Didn't judge that fucking right. I hit the back of the sofa. "Fuck!"

I bounce down behind it. Fuck, the floor – I didn't think about how hard I would hit the fucking floor. Shit, that bloody hurts my shoulder. I scramble to the wall and sit with my back leaning against it. I will be able to see him coming from here, but I can't see Sophie, I can't see anything in the room; the sofa is in the way. It's been fucking hours since I pushed that button, where the hell is everyone? I'm not quite convinced their system works right.

"Hi, Sophie, having fun are we?" Lloyd – it's Lloyd! "Hey, are you a member here? I don't recall ever seeing you here before!"

How the fuck did he get in here? The door has a sofa in front and it's locked, for fuck's sake – what the fuck is going on, I think to myself.

"No, I have come to get myself a new slave," said the freak.

"Well, there aren't any slaves here."

How does he keep so calm? Lloyd is just having a casual chat with the freak!

I hear the bolt being taken off the door and the sofa move. Shit, what the fuck is happening?

"Well, I think you have had enough for today, don't you? Why don't us Masters go and find some real slaves – I have just the place here you can find one. Sophie is no good to you."

"It's so good when you meet a fellow Master with the same thinking as you," the freak says to Lloyd.

I hear movement and then silence. Then I hear someone come back into the room.

"Sophie, you OK?"

"Yes, a little shaken, but I am fine, Lloyd."

"How the hell did he get in? How did he tie you up?"

"I don't know. I was getting ready for dancing, and one minute I was talking with him and the next here I was. I don't remember."

"There – better now you are untied properly?"

"Yes, thanks."

"How did you push the alarm from here?"

"I didn't, Charlotte did. Oh God, Charlotte – she dived out of the way of the whip, I hope, and he didn't half crack it. I haven't heard her since, except for a few fucks and shits when she hit the floor, that is."

Then two faces popped over the top of the sofa.

"Charlotte, are you OK?"

"Am I OK? What the fuck? How the hell should I be? Look, he has pulled half my hair out, for fuck's sake!"

"Thank God for that."

Lloyd smiles down at me. Walking to where I am, he crouches, his eyes darting back and forth across my body.

"Hey, you going to get up?"

"No, Lloyd, I am not going to get up, I have the legs of a scarecrow."

"Charlotte, straight question, please try answering me correctly."

"Lloyd, I can't be held responsible for the way my brain is fucking working right now, and if you had been here you would have known that I called time out fucking ages ago."

"Charlotte, do you hurt anywhere?"

"Yes, I fucking hurt. I have been bouncing around the fucking room, so of course I hurt."

He picks me up off the floor and takes me to the sofa, laying me down gently.

"Sophie, are you OK getting the butler outside the door? Tell him to get George – we need some brandy for you two and we might need my bag."

"Yes, fine." She leaves.

"Charlotte, look at me, let me see your eyes please." His manner has changed. He is being very commanding, but he sounds concerned.

"Lloyd, where were you?"

"Does your head hurt?" He feels all around my neck.

"Yes, it hurts, it's thumping, and the fact he has pulled half my hair out by the roots should tell you it's hurting."

He lifts my hair and looks at the damage to my head.

"It's not too bad, considering."

Sophie returns with George.

"Here you go, Lloyd," George says, putting a doctor's bag on the table. I try to sit up.

"Shit, that fucking hurts – what have I done to my shoulder?"

"Charlotte, straight question: do you want a sedative, or do you want a drink?" Twilight Zone. That's the first question he ever asked me when I was at Anthony's, beaten so black and blue by my ex-boyfriend. What the fuck is happening? The pain shoots through my body.

"Drink – you know I don't take tablets, Lloyd."

Pouring two large brandies, he gives one to me and the other to Sophie.

"Here, you two, have a drink."

I drink it straight down.

"Another?" he says, filling my glass back up.

"Well, Lloyd, I hardly think this is the time for you to try and get me drunk to get inside my panties, do you?"

"Charlotte, you have dislocated your shoulder."

"What the fuck?"

I swig the brandy straight down, then another. Sophie starts telling Lloyd exactly what happened, and all the time she is talking, Lloyd keeps topping my glass up. A little while later he turns to George.

"Ready, George?"

"Yes, OK."

"Charlotte, I am going to put your shoulder back now. How are you feeling?"

"Why, where has it been?" I say, feeling extremely happy from the effects of the brandy, which has gone straight to my head.

Lloyd smiles and places a small kiss on my forehead. Putting his hands on my shoulder and feeling and prodding, he looks at George and nods. George holds me down, bending over the sofa.

"What the fuck? Shit, what? Fucking Jesus, that fucking hurts, fucking stop! I say fucking time out."

George holds me down with some force.

Crack.

"OK, Charlotte, it's in. Are you OK?" Lloyd cuddles

me, stroking what's left of my hair.

"You fucking hurt me, Lloyd, you said you would never hurt me!" I sob in a drunken way.

"This is a little different. I was fixing you and it's all done now, you will be fine."

"Well, why does it still fucking hurt?"

"Here, have another brandy. You will be OK." He passes me another brandy and Sophie helps him put a sling on my arm.

"Lloyd, I don't feel well, I think…maybe… I think…" Then I pass out.

Chapter Six

I wake up. Shit, what's happened? I feel like I have been hit by a steamroller, for fuck's sake. My head feels like I have a steel band playing in it. Lloyd is by my side, cuddling me; shit, why isn't he up? He usually is before me, and he is fully clothed. I try to move out of his grip but I can't. Fuck, what the hell has he done to me now?

He opens his eyes. "Hi."

"Hi."

"How are you feeling?" He is smiling softly. OK, what have I done? Why is he being so nice to me? He isn't usually when I have a hangover. I try to move, but my arm seems to be tied to my body. OK, he has tied me up, I get it.

"Lloyd, I feel fine but do you think that just once I could wake up without finding you have tied me up in the middle of the night?"

"Ah, OK, not quite with it yet then!"

"Not quite with what? Lloyd, please, for some reason I feel like shit this morning and I don't want your mind games, thank you so much."

"What do you remember about yesterday?"

"Please, enough! I can't do this, I have told you my head hurts." I grimace at him.

"Working backwards, you passed out when I put your shoulder back into place."

"Why, what was... Oh shit, that fucking freak. What the hell..."

"OK, you remember now, then."

"Oh, Lloyd, I was so scared, I didn't know what to do or say. Sophie was tied and I just couldn't get the ropes untied. Is she OK?"

"Sophie is fine, just very worried about you, as we all are."

"Oh, Lloyd, what happened? How did that happen? How did such a person get in here?"

"Slow down. I will explain, but first I will help you to sit up and then I think some coffee and maybe something for your head."

Leaving the room after sitting me up, he leaves the door open. I can hear him talking with Anthony, Kat and Sophie in the lounge, telling them that I seem to be OK. He comes back, coffees in hand, and gives me two tablets.

"I don't think I need them, Lloyd. Thank you anyway."

He places them down on the bedside cabinet. "OK, how do you feel now?"

"It's a little strange, like a dream, a little hazy in places but I don't know how I got into that situation at all, and how the hell did you get into the room?"

"OK, all the rooms have walk-in cupboards in them. There are concealed doors but not very many people know about them – it's so we can get in if anything goes wrong, like yesterday. I will add that it's the first time we have had to use any of them."

"But how did he get in?"

"He came in with the guy that tried to grab your arse at the party. He signed him in as a guest in the morning.

Neither of them will ever come here again, that's for sure."

"So why did it take so long for someone to come and help us? It seemed like hours."

"We couldn't hear what was going on. He had taken away the mic, so we didn't know who was in there and we didn't know how many people were in there. We had to make sure that whoever went in would be safe. I decided to try the soft approach to see if I could get the door open. He was so shocked when he saw me standing there. He just froze, so it was easy. I kept control of him by the way I spoke. He is a very sick man."

"Oh, so it was that easy, then? And now – where is he now?"

"He is in custody at the police station – we had him arrested. He is everything that we despise in this establishment, and we don't want the word getting around the scene that we let anything happen here."

"But what about all the cloak-and-dagger stuff, you know, keeping it all secret?"

"Charlotte, it's only kept a secret from narrow-minded people. There are many alternative clubs like this one, if you choose to look for them. The club is exclusive, so it's the people who come to this one that we protect, rather than the club itself."

"So how did he get Sophie tied up?"

"She said he had used chloroform, just enough so he could control getting her on the chair to tie her."

"The whip – he hit her with the bloody whip and he slapped her face. Is she OK?"

"No, he missed her with the whip, thanks to you. He hadn't calculated that you had loosened her ropes, and when he cracked it, she was able to move slightly. Her face is a little bruised but it will mend. It was his ring that did the damage when he backhanded her. Sophie said you were brilliant, considering."

"Oh, Lloyd, I wasn't, I let her down. I should have known there was something wrong when I saw her sitting there. I should never have entered the room when I saw her like that, I should have gone and got George and asked him if it was OK for me to enter in case she was playing with her Dom."

"No, no, you didn't let her down, and it's easy to say what you should have done after the event. You were brave and you tried to be in control all the time. She said you kept changing the subject in order to distract him, you kept your distance and maintained eye contact for as long as you could. There was just one thing she said that she thought was a little out of control."

"What was that?"

"Your smart-arse mouth – apparently I owe you a year's supply."

"Oh, Lloyd, not today, please!"

He laughs, cuddling me. I feel so safe, so secure.

"So what do you want to do today, Charlotte?"

"I don't want to do anything other than what we are doing. I just want to feel safe, I feel like I want to just cry and cry and cry."

"You are safe. Yesterday you proved you could keep yourself safe as well as Sophie."

"Oh, Lloyd, I didn't. I was a blabbering wreck, not knowing what to do or say. My brain was getting in the way, there was nothing about me that was controlled."

"I beg to differ – you managed to keep your distance, stay in control as much as you could, and you kept Sophie safe by bringing the attention back to you. You distracted him long enough to get help, long enough for us to get in, and that's all you could have done. See, you are learning already – you are miles from where you were a week ago, though your brain always gets in the way. That's what I like about you – you are spontaneous, and it makes things exciting."

I think about that. Yes, he is right: I didn't just give in and let the freak do whatever he wanted me to do, like I had so many times with the bastard. OK, I might not have had complete control, but the control I had was good enough for that situation.

"I know you want to do nothing today, but can I suggest you take a shower? I will help you put some clothes on. We need to go and see Nats."

Oh hell, Nats. I need to be in work; she is going to kill me.

"Lloyd, I should be at work, you are right."

"Not quite what I meant, Charlotte. You don't need to be in work – Nats knows why you are not going, but we need to sort your hair out."

I put my hand up to my hair – oh shit, the whip pulled a ruddy great lump out of my head, I had completely forgotten. I get up and look in the mirror. That's why my head hurts so much, and there I was thinking it was a hangover.

"Aww, a man couldn't do anything worse than this – even cutting my panties off wasn't this bad." My eyes fill as I look at my hair, or should I say the lack of hair, just to one side of my head. Shit, how did that happen? "He has scalped me!"

Lloyd comes over; cuddles me into his arms. "It's OK, it will grow back and I am sure Nats will have something she can do so it looks as good as new. It could have been a lot worse. He could have marked your face."

After I shower Lloyd helps me to get dressed, a bit of a mission, as I can't use my arm at all. The pain is unbearable, so much so that Lloyd eventually talks me into taking the tablets he brought in for me earlier. Once dressed I am in need of a rest – I am shattered. Lloyd walks me to the lounge where Anthony, Kat and Sophie are still sitting drinking coffee and relaxing. I look at Sophie's face and tears run down my cheeks: on her left cheek a black and purple bruise goes up to her eye; her cheek is swollen and a small scab has started to form in the middle – I guess that's from the freak's ring.

"Oh, Sophie, I am so sorry, what have I done to you?" Seeing her face for the first time since yesterday when it all happened, and still feeling a little fragile, vulnerable even, I just can't contain the tears.

"Charlotte, you didn't do this to me – trust me, I would probably look a lot worse if you hadn't come in. Thank you, Charlotte, for helping me." With that she gets off the sofa and came towards me, carefully putting her arms around me to cuddle me.

"Coffee, everyone? I don't think we are going out for a bit as Charlotte is feeling a little worn out at the moment."

They all answered yes at the same time, and Lloyd went to the kitchen to get some more mugs of coffee for us all.

"I'm fine, Charlotte, really I am, but how's you? Let me look at you." Standing back a pace Sophie looks me up and down, then says, "Nothing too bad, then. Come dry those pretty eyes of yours." She wipes my cheeks with a tissue as she speaks.

Lloyd returns with the coffees and places them down on the coffee table.

"Here, Charlotte, come and sit down. The tablets will be taking effect soon and I would prefer you sitting when they do."

I sit down between Anthony and Lloyd; Anthony puts his arm around my shoulders.

"You OK, my bestest friend in the whole wide world?"

I lean my head on his shoulder. "Yeah, I think so," I say hesitantly.

"You don't sound so sure. Anything you want to talk about?"

"Well... I'm not sure if I do just yet, and besides which, everyone is here and I don't think it would be fair of me to harp on."

"Charlotte, if there is something you want to say then you must say it, you know that. How can we fix it if we don't know what the problem is?" He holds my hand reassuringly. "Is the problem about yesterday?" he whispers in my ear.

I nod yes.

"See, that wasn't so hard, was it? So come on, tell me."

My eyes start to well up with tears again. I look down so no one can see, and whispering back, I say, "I don't know if I can do this!"

Anthony puts his head close to my ear, quietly saying, "Have you told Lloyd this?"

I shake my head again, as if to say no.

"Well, do you want to tell him?"

I shake no again. The room is deadly silent.

"I think he might know."

"How? Have you told him?"

"No, but he is sitting next to you."

"Oh, it's OK, because he wouldn't listen in to our conversation, would he?"

"Probably not, Charlotte. So why don't you think you can do this?"

"Because I don't feel safe anymore. I thought I was going to be safe, but look – look at Sophie's poor face, she looks like I did. I thought I was away from people being so violent – at least in my so-called vanilla world I could protect myself by curling up in a ball."

"Oh, Charlotte, not only did you protect yourself but you protected Sophie as well, and that man has nothing to do with us or the lifestyle – he is sick and thinks that women are here just to be abused, a little like your ex. They are everywhere, people who are extreme with their behaviour – you can never say for sure that you are safe all the time, and that's what we are trying to teach you: how in different situations you can control them. Your body language, the way you talk, is all part of that."

I look up at Anthony, and he smiles back at me.

"I feel so lost." Tears streak down my cheeks.

"Do you know what I think? I think that yesterday was an extremely hard day for all of us, so you and Sophie must be truly exhausted. I think you need to sleep, get your arm better, get your head clear, and I think the tablets are starting to work as you are looking very sleepy. I also think that now isn't the time for making decisions. In a few days' time when you can get your head around everything again, we will have another talk if you want."

Lloyd moves, and I see his head pop around my shoulder.

"How about you go back to bed for a while, Charlotte, and then see how you are feeling later on this afternoon?"

"I feel so pathetic, Lloyd." My eyes are starting to close.

"No, Charlotte, that's not you, that's the tablets I gave you. You are just feeling very tired. Come on, I will take you to bed." Picking me up, he carries me into the bedroom, placing me down on the bed and making me comfortable before giving me a kiss.

"Get some sleep. I will be right here."

My eyes close. I can hear Lloyd and Anthony talking, but I just can't respond to anything.

"Lloyd, she will be OK, it has scared her, that's all. She isn't thinking, you know that. She is just telling us how she feels."

"Correction, Anthony: she told you how she feels, not me or us, but you – what does that tell you? She still isn't trusting me yet, and now she doesn't think this is for her."

"Lloyd, I am going to say this only once. You are also tired – you sat up all night watching over her. She is fine, and you need rest as well or you are going to drive yourself mad with this. We will sort this out. She will work through this herself, I am sure. Go lie down in one of the other bedrooms. Sophie and Kat are staying here to help you and they will look after Charlotte, you know they will. I have to go to the police station to sort things out now I have a statement from Sophie. I will be back later this afternoon."

"No! I am staying here with Charlotte."

Then I hear Sophie. "Lloyd, please, you are exhausted. I will stay right here and watch her if anything is wrong. I will come and get you, I promise." I feel someone sit on the bed, and Sophie talking to me.

"We will be OK, Charlotte, won't we? Go on, tell him to go to bed and get some rest."

I nod my head yes, well... I think I nod my head. I'm not sure, I know my arm isn't hurting anymore – God, these tablets are good, I feel all warm, soft and squiggly.

Chapter Seven

I wake up some time after. For a moment or two I just lie still; for a split second I don't recognise where I am, and then I heard the soft voice of Sophie.

"You OK, Charlotte?" Sophie was sitting on the bed next to me.

I panic, hastily looking around the bedroom for Lloyd.

"Where is Lloyd?"

"Hey, it's OK, he is asleep in the other bedroom. I eventually persuaded him to take some sleeping tablets and get some sleep. He has been with you here for over twenty hours without sleep. He has been so worried about you, Charlotte."

Kat appears at the doorway with a tray of coffee, some orange juice and bagels.

"I know it's a bit late for breakfast, but it's a shame to waste it." Placing the tray down on the table, she walks over to the bed.

"Come on, Charlotte, up you get – slowly at first, you might have a little wobble in those legs of yours, or they might even be a little confused." She laughs, holding out her hand to help me up.

We sit down at the coffee table and eat our breakfast. It tastes so good, and I am famished. Then Sophie says, "Are you feeling better now?"

"Yes, much, thanks, and you, Sophie? How's your face?"

"Oh, it's fine now. Glad to see you can look at me without crying."

"Oh God, I'm sorry, I don't know what came over me this morning."

"I do," says Kat. "It's emotions and tiredness, that's all – your brain racing away with 'what if's. Well, let me tell you this, Charlotte: there are 'what if's everywhere and it's just one more thing you have to get your head around. You can't live your life looking at 'what if's – now you have to put it to the back of your mind and get on with your life." She is so direct with the way she talks.

"But that's just it, Kat – I don't know what life I want, I don't know if I want this life anymore."

"Exactly, you want a life where you are in control, the same as me and the same as Sophie, and here is the best place for learning how to get control of your life. Yesterday was just unfortunate – it could have happened in an office block, hospital or a shop, the only difference is the way that you handle the situations, and you are starting to get it and yesterday proves that. It's you that keeps yourself safe, not the environment you are in." Kat is so straight-talking sometimes it hurts, but she is usually right and she is right about this.

"OK, so I still have a long way to go with my training?"

"Yes, Charlotte, and Lloyd is the best person for that job, and right now I think you need to go and give him a cuddle, because he was feeling very low before he went to bed. He felt as if it was all his fault, that he shouldn't have left you. He feels that you don't trust him anymore because you talked with Anthony instead of him."

"Oh God, I didn't mean that to happen. I don't know why I spoke to Anthony rather than him – maybe it was because Anthony asked me just at the wrong time, or maybe right time…oh, I don't know, but you're right, I will go to Lloyd now and cuddle up with him. Thanks, you two."

They both smile, and I go to the other bedroom.

I look at Lloyd sleeping on the bed. This is the first time I have ever seen him asleep; he looks so calm and peaceful, I don't want to wake him, and I very carefully get on the bed and lie down next to him so I can look at him. For the first time, he actually looks carefree: no wrinkles on his face from frowning, no stress lines from me driving him mad with the way that I act, no smile – he is never without a smile, that's sad, no smile; I much prefer you with a smile. I wonder what you are dreaming about, or if indeed you do dream. I slowly rest my good arm on his waist so I can cuddle him a little. There's so much I don't know about you, and I do want to get to know so much more about you; in fact I think I want to know everything about you, and one day maybe I will be brave enough to tell you that.

His eyes give a little twitch and open slightly, then close again; he wriggles his body closer to me and gives me a little kiss.

"Hello, you," he says, so softly.

"And hi to you, sleepy head."

"Mmm, this is nice, Charlotte, and why do I deserve you sneaking into this bedroom to give me a cuddle?"

"Well, it's not really a cuddle, is it, but it's the best I can do at the moment, and you deserve a cuddle for looking after me so well, and for just being there when I needed you most. Thank you, Lloyd, so much."

"Do you mean that, Charlotte?"

"Yes, I do." I kiss him on the forehead.

"So does that mean you are happy with everything, and you do want to carry on with the lifestyle?" His face still has no smile, no reaction at all.

"Why wouldn't I want to stay here with you?"

"That's answering a question with a question, Charlotte."

"And your point being, Lloyd?"

"Am I to assume from you not answering correctly, Charlotte, that what you are really saying is game on?"

"Not quite game on."

"Not quite game on, what do you mean by that?" His face crinkles a little.

"Well…and don't get mad, but I have been talking with Sophie and Kat – well, Kat has been talking to me. She pointed out some important facts about yesterday, and I have realised that it isn't the lifestyle that I am scared of, it's nutters like my ex and like the man yesterday, and yes, he scared the shit out of me, and I feel alone and vulnerable, but I want to get that all under control, and Kat told me that you are the right person to teach me."

"And is that the only reason you are here, Charlotte, because you want me to teach you how to take control of your feelings and life?" His face is flat again, no sign of what he might be thinking, and all the time his eyes have stayed closed. Is he playing, or is he dreading my answer?

"No, Lloyd, it's not." I pause, looking at him to see if his expression is going to change, my eyes darting all over his face.

"What's the other reason or reasons, then?" Nothing, not a sign.

"I wanted to give you a cuddle, just in case you had Dom's bottom, or whatever the sub space equivalent is."

"Well, that's a nice thought. Thank you, Charlotte. Anything else you want to talk about while you are here?"

"Lots of things, but only one thing that is really important."

"And what would that be, Charlotte?"

"I really fucking like you, so fucking much that, that…"

And before I can say another word, he springs up with his head leaning on his hand, looking straight into my eyes.

"Thank God for that, I thought you were broken for good. My smart-arse mouth is back, and I was getting worried. I'm sorry, Charlotte, that you got hurt yesterday."

"It was nothing you did, just one of those things."

"Come here, let me cuddle you too."

Lifting my head up, putting his arm underneath me, he cuddles me up close to him and as he does so, I say, "I do trust you very much, Lloyd, but I still have a long way to go, I know that."

"You heard that? We thought you were asleep."

"Not asleep, just more spaced out than usual. Can we stay here for the rest of the day and just cuddle, please?"

"Yes, Charlotte, we can."

He gives me a peck on the forehead and we spend the rest of the day in bed, cuddling and chatting. It's so nice.

Chapter Eight

The next morning we get up and make our way to Nats'. Lloyd has found a baseball cap for me so no one can see that some of my hair is missing.

Nats is waiting for me as usual, hovering at the desk. We go in and she cuddles me.

"You OK?" she whispers into my ear.

"Yes, but my hair!"

"Oh, don't worry about that." Scooping me off, she leads me to the office. Shit, where has Lloyd gone? My eyes dart all over the room, frantic. Christ, what is wrong with me? I feel my heart beating so fast, I start to shake.

"Charlotte, calm down, you are OK," Nats says, as she leads me to the chair to sit down.

All the panic from yesterday has returned, and I feel I can't control myself as the room starts to spin.

"Charlotte, breathe, deep breaths." It's Lloyd. I look at him. "You are OK, just a little panic attack. You will be OK, you are safe."

"Oh, here he goes, Charlotte, putting everything into medical terms. You are having a sub's drop – it's where things get so intense your body throws you on a high, then sooner or later you have to come down. This is it, honey – you have crashed right onto your little arse. The last week coupled with the other day has sent you as low as you can get, but don't worry, you are in safe hands – we haven't lost a sub yet."

"Nats, whatever way you put it the cure is simple – she needs rest and pampering right now."

"When you two have finished analysing what the problem is with me, do you think I can have some water, for the sake of a sub's arse?"

Nats gets me some water and I start to calm back down. God, this is so weird, I think I am starting to become dependent on Lloyd, like I don't want him to leave me – surely that's not right.

"Right, you two, I think you can both go and have a relaxing spa – there is one free, I think," Nats commands in a manner that neither of us can argue with.

In the spa Lloyd cuddles up to me, and it's so relaxing just to be on our own. I am still deep in thought, trying to sort out why I think I am dependent on Lloyd.

"You OK, Charlotte?"

"No."

He sits back and looks me in the eyes.

"Well, there's a first. I am shocked, what's wrong?"

"I don't know if anything is wrong, but I am finding it hard to work something out. It's just going round and around my head and I can't shake it off."

"What is it? Tell me, we can fix it together no matter what."

"I feel as if I am becoming dependent on you, and in such a short time."

"I don't quite understand."

"I feel like I don't want to be apart from you. The other day when I watched you go down the stairs I felt a little insecure – it was the first time I had been without you.

Again in the office when you didn't follow me I felt insecure that you weren't there. It's like I can't function when you are not with me, a feeling that I need you with me all the time – that can't be right, can it?"

"No, it's not right, but you have been in a different world for a week. Some subs get this when they are playing, too, it's all part of the emotional stress, a depression in the emotions. I am sure that Nats would call it sub drop or sub burnout. You will see, a week of pampering will put you right, and you will return to normal. You have to remember, Charlotte, that you have not been in control of your thoughts for such a long time, you are going to have it jumping all over the place. You will see that you will soon start putting everything back into the very untidy drawers you have up there. Also, you wouldn't be having these feelings if it wasn't for the other day – I would have fixed you with cuddles long before if I could have got in. That's why cuddling and pampering is so important. I told you I would finish that conversation, although I wish it was under different circumstances."

"So I am not getting dependent on you?"

He leans me back and cuddles me.

"Trust me, Charlotte, I don't want you dependent on me – that's to say, where you are afraid to do anything without me. I want you to trust me, respect me, and to..." He stops.

"And to what? You haven't finished the sentence."

"Oh now, Charlotte, you know that I have to have something to finish another day." He laughs as he pulls me closer. "Right, I do think we should get out and go see Nats now, see what she can do with your hair, don't you?"

"Yes, OK."

We get out of the spa and Lloyd helps me to get dressed, then we return outside to see Nats busy with another customer. She nods to me to sit down in the chair next to where she is working.

As I sit she says, "I'll be five mins, Charlotte. Lloyd, you get off now, you have things to do, I am sure. I will ring you if there is anything wrong."

"Oh no, please don't go, Lloyd," I protest.

"Charlotte, I still haven't done what I was going to do the other day, I had to come and rescue you instead. I will not be long, and you will be safe here, I am sure. Besides which, I really don't want to listen to Nats' medical diagnoses any more today," he jests, with a little laughter in his voice. Giving me a kiss on the forehead as usual, he leaves.

My heart is racing. Don't race, and stay calm, will you?

"Right, Charlotte, ready now – let's look at what I have to patch up on you." Nats' fingers scamper through my hair, the way that hairdressers' do.

"That's good, the hair for the most part is still fine. It has broken off rather than ripped out from the roots – a little short, but at least I will be able to attach the extensions to it. My biggest worry was that he had pulled it out at the roots. Only a few roots have gone but it's not bleeding or weeping, which is also good. I can attach the extensions without it causing an infection. You stay right there and I will go get you some new hair from the store room."

She leaves me alone – oh no, please come back, don't leave me. Thump, thump goes my heart, and my eyes dart all over the salon. Oh come on, get a grip, this is stupid, you are OK; there is no one here who isn't usually here. I take a deep breath, closing my eyes for a moment.

"Here we go, yup, the right colours too, I'm so good at this." Nats has returned. I open my eyes to see her matching the colours, with strands of hair lying over the top of my head.

"This is going to take some time as I literally have to put in each strand separately, but it will look so much better when I have finished."

When Nats is about halfway through the florist arrives with a big bunch of flowers, sandwiches and cakes. She brings them over and says, "Charlotte, these are for you, but I do think Lloyd is a little cheeky here, making me deliver sandwiches and cakes without buying me one!" She places the flowers on the workstation next to me along with the sandwiches and cakes, then hands me a card.

Nats, in the meantime, has pulled my hair across so that the florist can't see what she is doing, whispering in my ear, "She will never know." Then looking up at her, she says, "Do you want a coffee to go with one of the cakes, Anne? You are very welcome to have some lunch with us if you wish."

I open the small florist card and inside it Lloyd has written:

Hi, I have forgotten to tell you something – I quite like you too.
And tell Anne her cake for delivering everything is in the box –
I know she will have something to say about it. Lloyd xx

"Yes, Anne, please do. Lloyd has put a cake in the box for you."

Anne is in her fifties; a mumsy type of person, the type you could quite happily have a cup of tea with and just chat; a very neat lady, small in stature. With her hair in a pixie cut, perfectly done every day, she reminds me a little of Judi Dench. She agrees, and Nats holds up three fingers to one of the girls on the desk, who then brings over three cups of coffee.

"You and Lloyd make a good couple, but I bet he drives

you mad with all his teasing. No wonder you thumped him."

Me thump him – what is she on about?

Nats laughs. "Anne, is that what he has said? He is such a card."

What are they talking about? Riddles, everyone talks in riddles, even Anne is doing it now!

"Aww, he said she had hurt her wrist when she thumped him."

Me thump him and hurt my wrist – hold on just a minute! As I go to open my mouth Nats jumps in very quickly, handing me a sandwich to distract me from talking.

"No, Anne, that isn't what happened. Charlotte was cleaning Lloyd's place and couldn't reach a cobweb, so she stood on a footstool, lost her balance and tumbled onto a sofa, dislocating her shoulder. Lloyd really should start controlling his stories, they will get him into trouble one of these days. Don't you think, Charlotte, control should be very important to Lloyd?"

"Mmm, yes!" I mumble, not quite knowing what else to say. I wouldn't have put it like that, but I'm still trying to digest everything, including the sandwich.

Then Anne notices the hair extensions on the trolley that Nats has been working from.

"Having hair extensions, Charlotte? I wouldn't have thought you would need them, your hair is so beautiful and thick." Oh God, she has turned into a detective since I have been away. Again, Nats is very quick.

"Oh, the extensions, they are new products I am trying out. You know me, Anne, I never use anything unless I have tried and tested it myself, and as Charlotte cannot do any real work I thought I would make her do modelling for me so I can try it all."

Gosh, I would never have thought of all of that – where

does she get it all from, thinking on the spot like that?

When we finish lunch Anne leaves and Nats returns to my hair. When she is finished it is so perfect you would never know.

"Thanks, Nats, it's fantastic." I look in the mirror – the colour, the cut, all just so perfect.

"My pleasure and our secret. Now go see the girls in the nail bar – they have a surprise for you. By the way, they all think you fell off a footstool as well." She winks at me. As she does so, I notice she is wearing pink contacts. Her eyes are pink to match the delicate pink streaks in her hair.

I walk down to the nail bar to see the girls, and when I walk in they all stop what they are doing and rush over, all talking at once, asking me if I am all right and saying how they have all missed me over the last week or so.

Jane then says, "Here, take off that nasty sling," reaching around my neck and carefully lifting it off before I can protest. Then one of the other girls hands her another, which she promptly puts on for me.

"There you go – it's a bling sling." And they all stand back and laugh.

I look down, and they have attached thousands of shiny jewels and glitz, which they normally use for nails, all over the new sling that Jane has so neatly put on for me.

"We thought that it would cheer you up, having a little sparkle!"

"Thanks, everyone, it's brilliant, truly a work of art."

Then, they all wish me well and get back to their work that they were doing before I entered the room. Feeling like a million dollars, I go back outside where Lloyd and Nats are talking.

"Hi, your hair looks great, and what's this?" he says, pointing to the bling sling and chuckling.

"Stop, the girls in the nail bar made it for me – it's a bling sling."

"And a very nice bling sling it is."

Chapter Nine

The weeks have passed and I'm back at work. Nats' hair extensions still look so good, you would never know there is some of my own missing. Lloyd has spent so much time pampering me, with lots of talking and cuddles, I managed to unscramble my brain a little and he was right: he fixed me with a little TLC. It was like being a normal couple, part of a normal relationship – well, not quite, I should say a vanilla relationship when it first starts! A little bit of play, nothing too heavy, no rooms, just us at his place. I have also moved back to my room at Anthony's. I just don't feel that I want to live over The Room twenty-four-seven. Weekends are enough. Also, the arrangement gives me my space and Lloyd his, although I do see him every day, either for lunch or supper. My life has changed so much for the better: I am confident, I am brave, I walk tall, not afraid of who might notice me, I never turn my head away from anyone, but most of all I am happy, so subbing happy, I feel I am on a cloud. And what has brought about this change? Truthfully, me, I have, with a little help from my friends and the sub training they have put me through, teaching me control and trust; not just trusting them, but most importantly trusting myself. Lloyd still likes his little jokes and has sent me some interesting items to my place of work, with notes as to what he would like to do with them when and where, teasing me, keeping me in that spot, turned on enough so I glow, but not too much that I burst. I am growing more and more fond of these games, and have learnt to play them back, teasing him to hell. Am I happy with the lifestyle they are all in? The truth is I am, but am I ready to cross the line? Now come on, I need to have something to finish later, don't I?

It's Friday and I have the weekend off, the first since I returned to work. I haven't seen Lloyd all week as he has been at a conference and I think somehow he has something big planned for tonight. He has sent me a pressie at work every day. The girls here have been fascinated with what has been in them; I have been intrigued, trying to work out what he is planning. Nats has been watching the game with interest; I am sure she knows what is going on but there is something that is a turn-on about knowing that the end product is a game, one hell of a sexy game, and others not even knowing about it. All the girls think Lloyd is just so lovely, the way he spoils me – little do they know that's all part of the fun. So far this week I have had: bra and panties (black silk and lace), a pair of stockings (black), a little black dress, and yesterday a pair of black stiletto high heels. Today's pressie hasn't yet arrived, and I am getting worried because I only have half an hour to go. There's been no message, nothing all day; in fact everyone has started to worry because they have all asked why he hasn't been in touch. Not only that, but I am not sure where I am supposed to be going after work. There have been no notes, no texts or anything, just the pressies every day, very unlike him.

Suddenly the door bursts open and Lloyd walks in, grabbing my wrist. "OK if I use your office, Nats? I need to talk with Charlotte, it's important." He marches me through the salon.

"You know it is, Lloyd."

What is this? He has never done this before, never – everyone is watching and some of the vanilla girls cheer.

"Oh, look at that, he has missed her so much he can't wait till she gets home."

He opens the door, swings me into the office, following my arse with a slap.

"Don't you think that's a little sexist for such a vanilla establishment, Lloyd?"

"Charlotte, I am in the right mood for a spanking." Oh, breaking canes, what have I done or haven't I done, whichever it is?

He looks at me deeply as he walks towards me. I edge backwards.

"Lloyd, I just thought it was a little brash, that's all, I am just saying."

"Charlotte, shut up for one minute. Come here."

I take another step back.

"Will you keep still?"

He grasps hold of my wrist, pulls me to him, and then grabs my hair, tilts my head back and there it is: a drop-dead, stop-breathing kiss. It's been over a week without one; God, I have missed it. His other hand caresses my body, paying more attention to my arse, lifting my skirt so he can feel my skin.

"I have missed you so much this week," he says when we eventually come up for air. Thank paddles for that, I thought I was in trouble for something.

"I have missed you too. I was getting worried because I hadn't heard anything from you all day."

"I decided I would come straight here, surprise you – I am your package."

"Oh good, can I unwrap you? I will take you back outside, unwrap you there – the girls love to see what I have in the pressies you send me!"

"Charlotte, do you think it is wise to joke with me in such a way when I haven't used my hand for very much other than writing? I'm in need to relieve this writer's cramp somehow, but first I think I need one of these from you." He cuddles me up, holding me tight.

"You smell so good, I could overdose on you right now, and it's been a long week."

There's a knock on the door; Nats pops her head around.

"All right to come in now, Lloyd?" she asks.

Not loosening his grip on me, he says, "Yes, Nats, of course, no secrets from you, you know that."

"Do you two want a coffee?"

"Yes, we will, thanks, Nats."

"I thought you would once you got your hellos over with, Lloyd."

Hey, am I invisible? Can't I answer for myself? For sub's sake! Why do they all do that to me, Anthony included? They all just talk over me.

"It's been a hell of a week, Nats."

"Has it?"

Hello, I'm here, I can talk, you know, I cry inside my head.

"Everything been OK at the club?"

"Yes, fine, no problems, although the relief doctor wasn't any good so we will have to find someone else. You know I like to have someone there just in case, even though it's hardly needed."

"What do you mean, was he called out?"

"Yes, it was only someone who had a little too much to drink and fell down some stairs. He basically said it was of their doing and he didn't get out of bed at two in the morning for something so minor, especially when it was alcohol-induced."

"Oh, he never did?"

"Yes, Lloyd, not good in my book, and that's all he had to do all week so he was paid for sitting around the suite, his meals supplied, to be rude to our customers, so I am sorry but you are going to have to start searching for another."

"OK, not a problem!"

Still here, I am still subbing here.

"Here are your coffees!" She places the coffees on the table and Lloyd releases me a little, looking into my eyes and winking at me. What the hell is that? He has never done that before, never. Holding my hand, he takes me to the sofa and we sit.

"Anything else I should know about, Nats?"

"I don't think so, Lloyd, everything has been handled very well, I think."

OK, they are just talking work, nothing to get upset about; that was such a lovely look he gave me when he released me. That says more than words could ever say. He releases my hand, putting his arm around my shoulders and pulling me close to him, nuzzling my hair.

"So has Anthony sorted out the relief doctor then?"

"Yes, he wasn't pleased with him at all. He had George pack him up and he was out."

"That's good."

"So how was your week then? Any new findings in the world of the brain that we should know about?"

"Oh God, no! Just a load of boring doctors who all have their own theories. This week I am just so glad to be home. You know I am not comfortable when I am not here, I never have been."

"Oh, that bad?"

God, he can't stop touching me, holding me as tight as he can. This is so nice. Nats and Lloyd are sitting chatting and have not once involved me; not once have I said a word, but that's OK as I'm too busy concentrating on Lloyd, looking at him and contemplating what he might have in mind for us both.

"Right, Nats, I am taking Charlotte home now, do you need her for anything else?"

"No, not at all, you two get off and enjoy your weekend."

Chapter Ten

As we get into the lift Lloyd can't wait to get up to the suite. He is kissing my neck and holding me tight, and when the lift stops we tumble out, kissing and caressing as we make our way to the lounge.

"You are not losing control are you, Lloyd?"

"No, not at all, just catching up with some moments that I have missed this week. Are you complaining?"

"No, not at all."

"Good. I hope you are ready for some intense pampering and play tonight, Charlotte?"

He swings me around; I stand with my mouth wide open. I can't believe what I see. Everywhere are roses and other kinds of flowers, and candles flickering; the table is set for two with a trolley full of food next to it, champagne glasses on the coffee table with a bowl of strawberries. I look around at him and he is smiling. I look him in the eye and then kiss him, a drop-dead passionate kiss.

"I have missed you too. All week I have wanted you to come home."

He holds my hand, taking me to the coffee table. I sit down and he passes me a glass of champagne, sitting next to me. I say, "What is the occasion, Lloyd – anything I should know about, like your birthday or something?"

"No, no occasion – does there have to be one? This is just because you are you and I am me, is that not special enough for you?"

"That is perfect, thank you." We clink our glasses.

He leans me back, getting the strawberries, dipping them into my champagne then feeding them to me, telling me how much he has missed me.

"Oh dear, I have dropped some champagne on your shirt. Best remove it, don't you think?" Undoing the buttons one by one, slowly, looking in my eyes and parting my shirt, he looks down at my breasts and caresses them.

"You are perfect, so very perfect." He kisses my breasts softly; I take a deep breath in and raise my breasts to meet his lips. This is heaven.

Oh shit, I have missed this all week, I have been longing for his touch. I am in heaven but I think it's time I changed this game; he is so into touching me but it's my turn, I want to touch him too. I push him away, pulling his shirt over his head and kissing his chest.

"Oh, Charlotte, you are so good at this." He leans back and I move to sit astride him. I look him in the eye and kiss him gently, just a little kiss.

"OK, let's eat." I bounce off him and walk over to the table.

"Charlotte, now that isn't nice, is it?"

"Isn't it, Lloyd? I am hungry."

"Charlotte, come here, I haven't finished yet."

"Lloyd, I am so hungry." I pout at him.

"Aww, Charlotte, don't pout, you know what that does to me."

He gets up and God, he looks so subbing hot, he's toned in all in the right place. He moves towards me and I step backwards.

"Now, Lloyd, you know you don't have to do this, don't you?"

"Yes, I know, but where is the fun in that? What did you just say, Charlotte?"

"I didn't say anything, Lloyd." I look at him quizzically.

"Oh, I believe you did. I believe you have just said game on." And there are his devil horns as he chases me around the lounge.

"No, Lloyd!" I protest.

"Oh, Charlotte, that sounds more like a 'Yes, Lloyd, come and get me if you can, I am sure you can do better than that.'"

"Lloyd, I am out of breath, please, I can't keep up with you."

"I have told you to go to the gym."

"No, Lloyd, I will be even more exhausted."

"Charlotte, I've got you, please come with me."

He leads me to the closest chair, and sitting down, he bends me over his knee. "This is what I have missed, your rosy arse… Oh no, Charlotte, there is something wrong!"

"What's wrong?" I try and twist to see but I can't, he has hold of me too tightly.

"This is what's wrong!"

Slap, rub.

"It's not red enough to please my eye."

"For the sake of a sub's arse, Lloyd, that hurt. Remember you haven't spanked it for over a subbing week."

"Oh, I know I haven't, Charlotte. You know what they say, a cold sub's arse is an unloved arse."

Slap, rub.

"Lloyd, it subbing hurts."

Slap, rub.

"Charlotte, will you please remind me to talk with you

about your vocal expressions at some point?"

Slap, rub.

What the subbing hell does that mean, for paddle's sake?

"Ouch, Lloyd, please take it easy."

Slap, rub.

"Charlotte, have you missed this that much?"

What the subbing…?

"Lloyd, do you want the truth?"

Slap, rub.

"Always, Charlotte, you know that."

Slap, rub.

"Yes, it's subbing fantastic."

Slap, rub.

"Good."

He flips me over, holding my buttocks.

"Charlotte, thank you for giving me a reason so quickly to spank you. Shall we eat?"

He kisses me softly and we go to the table.

"Oysters, what do you say?"

"I have never eaten oysters before."

"Oh good, sit."

I sit down and he brings a chair to be next to me. He picks up an oyster and runs a knife around to loosen the flesh, squeezing the juice of a lemon onto it. Holding it in one hand he grabs the back of my hair; looking deep in my eyes he kisses me, oh yes, a drop-dead subbing kiss, then tilting my head back, he whispers into my ear, "Ready, Charlotte? Swallow down in one."

Oh God, this is so sexy, so sensual, food sex. God, I am in subbie food heaven… Cough, splutter – oh for the sake of a subbing arse, what the subbing paddles is that? – and the oyster shoots out at a hundred miles an hour.

"Charlotte, that is not very romantic, is it?"

"Is it subbing cooked?"

"Charlotte, I really must talk with you about your new vocabulary you have found, but now isn't the right time. You don't cook oysters. Are we going to try again?"

What is he on about? I'm so used to him saying it's not the right time. Nothing is ever the right subbing time. He prepares another oyster, and grabbing my hair he kisses me again, another drop-dead kiss; again he whispers into my ear, "Swallow down in one."

Oh for paddling's sake – gulp, gone. Thank the sub for that.

"That's better, Charlotte, did you enjoy that?"

"Truth?" I say as I look him in the eyes.

"As always, Charlotte."

"It tastes like the sea at Skegness, I can even taste the pollution, t-t-t." I spit into a napkin. God, I thought he missed me, so why is he trying to poison me, for the love of subs? Grabbing my glass of champagne, I down it in one. That's better.

"Charlotte, I can't believe you are finding it so hard to be romantic when I have done all this for you."

"Well, firstly you asked for the truth, that is the truth, and secondly, Lloyd, I think you would behave in the same way if your crazy-arse boyfriend tipped raw, slimy fish down your subbing throat, for sub's sake."

Look, he is rubbing his sodding hand again, why does he keep doing that?

"We have already had the conversation about me having a boyfriend, it's never going to happen. Oysters are supposed to be raw, that's how you eat them. To follow all of that, my dear Charlotte, time is getting very close for one of our little chats."

What chats, oh God, does he want to analyse everything again, for sub's sake?

"Well in that case, may I paddling suggest that when you want to feed me subbing fish again, you take me to Bill's Fish and Chip Bar."

"Oh, my dear Charlotte, I didn't realise just how much I have missed your sarcastic tones. Please come to the bedroom with me." He gets up and kisses me before grabbing my wrist and leading me into the bedroom.

"I didn't realise you wanted an early night."

"What part of that little brain of yours has come up with 'I want an early night'?"

"Well, why else come in here?"

"I don't want an early night. On the contrary, I wish for a late night, a very late night, in fact."

"Oh…" My eyes widen.

He leans his head down to my ear and whispers, "Charlotte, it's not what you are thinking at all. Think some more."

"Why, what is it, then?"

"It's this."

He grabs my waist; kisses me hard, lifting me up. I wrap my legs around him and he walks us to the bed, lays me down and places me in the middle. Lying on top of me he gyrates his hips against mine, taking my arms and placing them above my head. I squirm and he stops kissing me, looks me in the eyes. I feel him place some tape on my wrists.

"Oh now, Lloyd, what are you doing after such a drop-dead kiss like that?"

"You have changed the game and I want your hands out of my way. I have planned tonight to every last detail, even to having the tape to hand for when I got you here – I just didn't think it would be so quick."

He kisses me before I can get another word out. He finishes taping my wrists and my hands to the first knuckle on my fingers; I still have a little movement in them. He sits astride me.

"I have missed you here in my bed like this, you look so hot."

"Lloyd, I don't know what I have done to change the game, and can I have my hands back, please? I am sorry."

"You have done so many things, for which at this moment in time I am so glad. Now shush, I want to enjoy the view." He sits looking at me, his eyes darting around my face. He looks so deep in thought, as if he is contemplating something, but what it could be? I can't think. Then he rolls off, lying next to me, gently turning my face to look at his. What is he doing? He is looking at me again like he did in Nats' office. What is he thinking? God, this is agony...

I twist my hips in an attempt to get some sort of reaction from him – nothing, not even a blink.

"You seem to have an advantage over me."

"Yes, I do, but what is new in that?"

"Why are you just looking at me like that?"

"Why, would you rather I didn't?"

"No, I like you looking at me."

"Good."

I can't work him out at all. I had just started to work him out but now he has changed. For the sake of a sub's arse, what the hell is wrong with him?

"What, no spanking for whatever I might have done in your world, Lloyd?"

"It's not my world. It's *our* world at the moment. Do you know what, Charlotte, I think I just want to cuddle with you at this moment in time."

What, a cuddle, is that all he wants to do? He hasn't seen me in over a week, not even talked with me, and all he wants to do is cuddle me.

"Are you OK, Lloyd, is there something wrong? I don't like this!"

"I am fine." He cuddles me close. This isn't right.

"Lloyd, are you happy with everything?"

"Charlotte, I am very happy."

"What the subbing hell is going on?"

He releases his grip on me, flips me over.

"I was waiting for you."

"For me? What do you mean?"

"I was waiting for you to bring the subject up, the one I asked you to remind me of."

"Lloyd, what are you on about?"

"Your new vocabulary that you have adopted over the weeks, and I knew if I waited long enough you would remind me one way or another, and bang, there it was."

Slap.

"Ouch, Lloyd, your hand seems to have got very hard over the week."

"Charlotte, my hand has always been hard, you have just not noticed, and my hand isn't what we are talking about."

Slap.

"Ouch, oh, for the love of a sub, can you not rub or something?"

Slap.

"Rub or something, how interesting, Charlotte. Let's analyse that, shall we, while I spank?"

"Oh, Lloyd, please not."

Slap.

"Rub! I've thought about that – no."

Slap.

"Paddling subs, that hurt!"

"What was that, Charlotte, you want me to paddle your

subbie arse? How considerate of you, not wanting me to hurt my hand. It just so happens that I have one just here." He reaches to the bedside for his paddle.

Swipe.

"Shit, Lloyd."

"Aww, not all of that smart-arse mouth has been changed then, Charlotte."

Swipe.

"Lloyd, I don't know what you mean, but please rub."

Swipe.

"Please rub, that sounds a little better. You don't want an 'or something' then?"

Swipe.

"For subbing—"

Swipe.

"Oh, Lloyd!"

"Charlotte, are you losing control?"

Swipe, rub.

Ah, a rub, that's so nice, there is a subbing God after all.

"Lloyd, if I am losing control, could it be that I haven't been taught correctly?"

"Now, Charlotte, your new phrases – they are very inventive, however, they are still the same, don't you think? And are you questioning my teaching methods? Do you not like them?"

Don't care, not listening, this rubbing is so very nice. God, I have missed this all week, he handles a paddle so very nicely.

Swipe, rub.

"Are you still here, Charlotte?"

"You subbing know I am, but please can you paddle me with a little more subbing care tonight?"

Swipe.

Swipe.

"What, like this, Charlotte?"

"You are the Dom from subbing hell."

"Oh, Charlotte, what a nice compliment you give me."

Swipe, swipe, swipe.

"Your arse warm yet?" he whispers into my ear, and nibbles while he waits for my answer.

God, this is heaven, there is nothing wrong with him after all – he was just playing, thank the great sub goddess for that.

"Yes, I was getting worried though."

"I know you were, Charlotte. I have a week of teasing and playing to catch up on and it's all going to happen in the next two days, I do so hope you are up for it?" There they are, his devil horns up on his head.

"I sure am. I have missed you so very much, Lloyd."

Swipe.

"Good."

Swipe.

"Now that our hellos are over with, my sweet, with a little fun warming up, shall we go and eat?"

"As long as it's not subbing oysters."

Swipe.

"Ouch, what was that for?"

"Do you really want this conversation again? I am so hungry, and I would like to have some sexy food fun at the same time. Your choice, so choose wisely."

"Oh, OK! Eat it is," I say with a hint of reluctance in my voice.

He leads me into the lounge, still taped by my wrists, and sits me down on the sofa. He looks at his watch.

"I have to phone Anthony to see what his plans are. Here's your glass of champagne."

He wedges the glass between my fingers and sits opposite me, watching me as he takes his phone out of his pocket. I look in the glass – it is empty, the subbing thing is empty. I look at him and he smiles; glancing at the bottle of champagne he says, "I will have one too, thank you."

OK, I see, I will show you, how hard can this be? I sit forward, and leaning towards the table I place the bottom of the glass down. Oh paddles, for the love of a sub, he knows I can't put this down; he has bound me in such a way that now I have the glass in my hands I cannot let go. I look at him and he is smiling, his phone to his ear – you know what you are doing all right.

"Hi – yes, not too bad." He chats with Anthony.

I try to twist and turn, my hands trying to release the glass. That will not work, will it – come on, think. I hate it when he plays these games, strategies, but I am getting better at them. OK, got it – foot, come here; hold the bottom of the glass with my toes. I kick my shoes off and lift one foot to the table. I hear him slump down on the sofa; pants, what is he doing? I look up and he has his head to one side, and he is looking up my skirt. For the sake of a peeping Dom, he is looking straight up my skirt! He glances up at me.

"Nice view… Not to you, Anthony, I was talking to Charlotte… Yes she is… I am sure it is going to get very interesting, yes, Anthony…"

That sounds like coded Dom talk for 'yes, they will both have a bloody good laugh over this one.' For sub's sake! I look back at my foot: OK, foot, I need to get my toes around the base of the glass to hold it down so I can slip my hands off the glass. Got it? I hope so. Paddling stockings, I forgot I had them on. I look at my hands around the glass – well, they aren't going to be much help, are they? Elbows – I will use them to roll the top a little, then I can get them off by standing my other foot on the toe end of the stocking and pulling my foot out. Oh come on, all day long I spend pulling you up and now I want you down you have stuck to my thigh like glue, but it's a good job I have hold-ups on – if I had suspenders on I wouldn't have a chance. Got it! I roll them down as far as I can, then placing my other foot on my toes I rub until it starts to come off; then I stand on the stocking and pull my foot out. Then raising my foot up onto the table, I place my foot on the base of the glass.

"Oh, for paddling's sake!" This isn't easy at all.

I wedge the stem of the glass between my big toe and the next toe. Got it, right, come on, hands, lift up. Paddles – my hands are moist and they are sticking with such a firm grip to the glass they are completely stuck now. I pull harder – oh no, oh shit, that's not what I meant to do; I tumble backwards, foot and hand following. Oh good, this is very subbing ladylike; he probably can see what I had for breakfast now. I lower my leg after getting my foot released from the glass, struggling to sit up. Lloyd is sniggering to himself. Oh yes, you would see that as funny. I take it back. You are not a subbing Dom from hell, you are hell itself. He carries on his conversation, still looking up my skirt. I will spoil your fun – watch this. I cross my legs and he raises his eyebrows. I smirk back, pleased with that little move. He looks at his glass; leaning forward, he picks it up, turns it upside down, placing it back on the table. What the paddles has he done that for? If I do eventually get this glass out how the sub does he think I will be able to fill it up? Oh shit, for sub's sake, just something else to work out how to do now. God, this is going to be a game of chess, I can see it coming now. Well, buster, I will have checkmate, you wait and subbing see. OK, think, what next? Release hand from glass. I turn sideways, replacing my foot on the glass. I look at him –

smug again. He shakes his head; leaning forward, he takes the open bottle of champagne. I look at him, my face agog; my eyes follow him as he gets up and walks to the kitchen.

What is he doing now?

"Anthony, if the champagne has been open for about an hour, do you think we need a fresh bottle…? Yes, I thought so too…" What the sub is he doing now? Returning, he has a fresh, unopened bottle of champagne in his hands. I look at him in shock. What the subbing hell has he got that for? I watch him come back and place it on the table; looking at me smugly, he sits back down.

"Yes, Anthony, I have a fresh bottle here, it's on the table." What, he is still including Anthony in this game? How for sub's sake am I going to open that? OK, concentrate on one thing at a time. Release hand; get my foot in place. I semi-stand – yank! Oh no, oh shit, the glass has shot over the table – free at last, but I have fallen between the table and the sofa now. I have to stand. I look over at Lloyd and he is now laughing, still talking with Anthony. Quiet with the talk, will you? I really don't think that Anthony wants to know what you are doing to me, what agony you are putting me through, and if Anthony was any subbing friend he wouldn't let you do this to me. I get up, shaking my hair. I think to myself, right, you two, this is Charlotte, check-mate coming up. I go to the bottle of champagne. God, this is going to be hard. I lift my foot to steady the bottle, and with my fingers start twiddling the wire to undo the cage. Steady, girl, keep in control; don't lose it now! I keep looking at him: he seems to be impressed at this bit. He glances at his glass and mine on the floor by his feet. I remove the cage and loosen the cork, placing my fingers around the neck of the bottle, and it's not that hard to get hold of because it's smaller than the glass. Then lifting the bottle slowly…

"Charlotte, nooo…"

"You and Anthony think it's so funny."

I shake the bottle with all my might.

Bang – shhhhhhh! The cork shoots out and the champagne follows like a fountain, cascading down Lloyd's body.

"Champagne, Lloyd?"

When the fizz dies down I see Lloyd sitting there perplexed at what I have just done. With the phone slightly away from his ear I can hear Anthony laughing – I think he has guessed what has happened.

"Checkmate to me I think, Lloyd?" With a smirk on my face and trying to place the bottle back down on the table carefully, he shakes his head at me.

Slowly moving forward.

"You really should not have done that, Charlotte, you really didn't want to do that!"

I run, and the bottle tumbles onto the table where I hadn't quite let go of it. He chases after me but I get to the bedroom first and shut the door, leaning all my weight on it in an attempt to keep Lloyd out.

"Charlotte, I am very impressed, please let me in."

"No, I will not let you in."

"Please, that was such a good game."

"I know you are going to beat me hard for that one."

"How can you say I beat you hard? I only ever beat you as hard as you want and no more."

"I know you are going to make me pay somehow."

"Well, can I suggest you get it over with?"

"Don't laugh, Lloyd."

"Charlotte, you haven't thought this through, have you?"

"Not quite, but I am sure if you leave me alone I will be able to think some more."

"Now you know that isn't going to happen, don't you?"

"Please!"

"OK, I will give you five minutes, then when I come back I will expect you to be away from the door, sitting on the bed. How's that?"

"OK, yeah, that's good, I think."

"OK, you have five."

I hear him walk down the hallway. He must be going to get cleaned up in one of the other rooms. Good, I need to think. For the sake of a sub's arse, why did I do that? I hear him walking back to the lounge. He doesn't even stop at the door, but then he always keeps to his word. I have about three minutes, and I still don't have a clue what I am doing, not even a hint of a plan. I hear him walking back down the hallway. What is he doing? Two minutes left, oh shit. I know, I will look all sexy and alluring for him on the bed, a come-and-tease-me look – that will distract him. I get on the bed and I try to look drop-dead sexy, making sure my bound wrists are in view. There is a knock on the door; he opens it...

"I think your five are up, my sweet."

I flutter my eyelashes at him. "Oh, are they? How time flies when you are having fun."

"Yes, quite, my dear." He sits on the bed, looking into my eyes.

"You know I should spank you for that, don't you, but how can I spank you when you are looking so hot?"

Good, it's working, keep fluttering, girl, you have him. He leans towards me and gives me a small kiss. That's it; you have him. He runs his fingers down my nose across my lips, down under my chin; I raise my head slightly and close my eyes. That's it – he is softening.

"What am I going to do with such a hot sub? I just don't

know." He runs his finger back up to my chin, and with his thumb and finger pinching softly on my chin he pulls my head forward slightly, and softly plants a tender kiss on my lips. He slips his hand under my knees and the other round my back; picking me up, he gives me the best of his kisses, a drop-dead, eye-closing, stop-breathing kiss. I am aware of him walking somewhere but I really don't care where he is going because this is the everlasting k— Oh shit, oh fucking hell, that's fucking freezing!

He has taken me into another bathroom and dropped me into a bath of ice-cold water with lumps of ice floating in it.

"Need cooling off, Charlotte?"

"Fucking shit, what the fuck?!" I look up at him, shocked and amazed.

"Another rule, Charlotte: never give anyone thinking time, especially a Dom." He turns, laughing as he walks out.

"And *that* is checkmate, I think, Charlotte."

"How the hell…what the hell? Don't you think that this is a little excessive, Lloyd?"

He returns with a towel.

"Not at all, a little excessive would be to leave you in here."

Lifting me out of the bath, taking the tape off my wrists, removing my wet clothes, he wraps the towel around me.

"You gave me time to think. Giving anyone time to think is not good, I had to show you that. I keep telling you, think things through, what will the reaction be to the action? You didn't think it through all the way."

He carries me back to our room and places me on the bed.

"You having to think about what to do to avoid the reaction just gives the other person more time to think. You don't want to give them an advantage like you have just given me."

"Shit, I messed it up, didn't I?"

"You will always be learning but you have at last taken control. The rest will come – it will soon become a game of nerves between us, very much like chess. Sometimes you will win and sometimes I will win, depending on who gets tired first. Now, back to our game. Where was I?" Taking off his jeans, he lies down on top of me. "I think you need warming up, my sweet."

"You didn't mind the champagne?"

"No, I didn't mind the champagne, it's one of your better plans. I didn't see it coming until it was too late or it would have been you wearing the champagne, not me, and this game would have had a completely different ending. Are you OK, you didn't mind the cold bath?"

"It was a bit of a shock, but yes, I'm OK," I say, shivering.

"Good. Not going too fast for you, I hope?"

"No, not at all, I love it when we are playing a few games at once – keeps you on your toes."

He is gently rubbing his hand over the towel, gyrating his hips slowly... God, if I wasn't so subbing cold, this would be lovely.

The towel is wrapped tight around me, encasing my arms. Lloyd places a leg over mine and pulls me close to him, huddling me up like a sack of washing.

"I can't move, Lloyd."

"Can't you, Charlotte? And why would that be, do you think?"

"Are we still playing? I thought you were explaining."

"Charlotte..." He looks into my eyes, pausing for a moment. "You haven't taken your eye off the ball again, have you?"

Subbing breaking canes, he is still playing; he knows I can't do both very well yet.

"Who me, Lloyd? No, never, just thought I would clarify that you were still up for playing, that's all."

"Relax, Charlotte, I am teasing you, unless..." And he looks me in the eye.

"Unless what, Lloyd?"

"Unless that was sarcasm I heard in your voice then." And he laughs. Then whispered in my ear, "With you, Charlotte, I will always be up for playing."

"Lloyd, can you please let me loose a little?"

"OK, do you want some more to eat?" he asks as he loosens the towel.

"No, not really, I don't, but I do want something."

"What do you want, Charlotte?"

"This." And I place my hands on his face and pull his head towards me and kiss him hard. His body turns and his hands tighten on my back, pulling me closer to him. My hands run down his back and then around to the front of his shoulders. Then pushing him firmly to make him roll onto his back, rolling with him, I sit astride him. Slowly moving my head down to his mouth, I start teasing him with my tongue on his lips, just touching softly; then pulling away when he lifts his head for a kiss. He runs his hands up my back and tries to push my head down to meet his lips. I push back and turn my head; I feel my wet hair tumbling around my shoulders. I kiss down his chin and follow the line to his neck, inching my way down to his chest, arching my back as I do so.

Pushing myself up with my hands on his chest to a sitting position, I start to slowly massage his chest and shoulders. I look at his face: eyes closed, lips slightly apart; he looks so relaxed and into what I am doing. I place my hands back on his extremely toned chest and lean forward, teasing his lips once again, running my tongue softly over them. He moans and raises his head to try and steal a kiss, but I move just out of his reach. Kissing his chest again; going lower down his body. My clit rubs on his erection and he moans some more. He places his hands on my head and tries to push it down further. I lift his hands off my head. Changing direction, I'm moving slowly back up his body, kissing and licking. I sit up, and begin running my nails slowly across his chest, and I see his muscles flex when I find an erogenous zone. I can feel his manhood throbbing beneath me. I lean forward; another soft, gentle tease on the lips, then I kiss his ear, giving it a nibble as he moans. I whisper softly into his ear, "You are not losing control are you, Lloyd?"

He slowly moves his hands onto my hips; kissing my neck, he moves his left leg and somehow he has placed it under my left leg. Oh no, what's happening? All at once he lifts me up, pushing me over to the other side of the bed, face down, slapping my arse and whispering in my ear, "Never, Charlotte!" And with that he gets off the bed, saying, "Come on, let's eat now."

I push myself up onto my arms, mouth open wide with surprise, just in time to see him grab his robe off the back of the door and his lovely toned arse walking out of the doorway.

What? What?! I throw myself back down on the bed, kicking my feet and thumping the mattress with my hands. I scream into the quilt so it will muffle my disappointment and frustration.

Why did I say that? I had him on the ropes; I could have taken that all the way. Stupid, stupid, stupid.

I hear Lloyd call me and I push myself back up on my hands to listen to what he is saying.

"Charlotte! Here, I have something for you!"

Maybe he is teasing me and he still wants to play. I get off the bed and grabbing my robe I run out, eager to see what he has for me, all excited. I stop as I get to the lounge; looking around, I can't see him. Oh, he must be somewhere else, he is playing hide and seek; I bet he must be in one of the other bedrooms. I turn, and there he is, leaning against the wall.

He holds out a bucket with cleaning stuff in it. I look at it for a moment, amazed at what he has got, then as I look up at his grinning face, he says with a broad smile, "Your game! You clean it up."

Stunned, I raise my hand slowly and take the bucket. As I take it, he walks over to the table and sits down. My eyes follow him as he walks. I turn around slowly and watch him pour a glass of champagne and sit on the chair next to the table. He places his feet onto the chair where I was sitting earlier and takes a sip from his glass. Then picking up a strawberry, he dips it into his champagne, lets it drip a little as he lifts it slowly out of his glass and raises it to his mouth, bending his head back slowly. When he gets it to his lips his tongue slowly and sensually meets the last remaining drip from the strawberry, and in a teasing motion he licks the bottom of the strawberry before taking a bite. I tip my head backwards and close my eyes, thinking, that's my lick, my teasing bite, and you had to open your big mouth, for the sake of a sub's arse.

I put my head down and open my eyes, looking at the coffee table and the sofa where I aimed the champagne. What a mess. I will be here all night cleaning this up. Where I tried to place the bottle down carefully it has fallen over onto its side and is now sitting in a pool of champagne, which is escaping and dripping onto the floor. There is champagne also dripping off the back of the sofa which is forming puddles on the floor. I look back at him and there he is, eating strawberries and drinking champagne, smirking at me, then another tease and bite of a strawberry. Oh, you think you are so funny, don't you, Lloyd?

I go to the sofa and start to wipe the champagne from the back of it onto the floor. When I finish that I move to the front of the sofa, and the glass that was in my hands is still on the floor. I bend down, picking it up, as Lloyd says, "Remind me I have to get you a new robe – this one is far too long for when we are here alone."

Still bent over, I look round at him. For the love of a sub, is there nothing that he can't turn into one of his games? He gets another strawberry – nope, not looking, not playing. You know what you are doing, trying to turn me on by eating so seductively… My arse wiggles with that thought. No, arse, don't do it! God, you will let him know he is winning. I try to make out that the arse wiggle was just me moving to stand back up, but I think he guessed: a small snigger slips from his mouth.

"Careful, Lloyd, there are killer strawberries around this year. They might try and choke you!" As if I would be so subbing lucky that a strawberry would get stuck in his throat and I would have to save his life, and then when he was unconscious I could have my wicked way with him. That would never happen, would it?

"I'll be careful, Charlotte, no need to worry. I checked for killer strawberries earlier – none here so I will be fine."

Holding the glass in my hands, I look at it. Strange, it feels strange. It's plastic, the bloody glass is plastic, and I didn't even notice earlier; I was so busy trying to get it out of my hands that I didn't notice. I look back at him.

"Told you I had every little detail worked out. I didn't

want you to cut your hands with a real glass – your safety as well as mine always comes first, no matter what we play." And yet another smirk.

I finish cleaning up the mess after Lloyd and I have sat down to eat together. Food teasing and playing, enjoying each other's company, like so much of our time, is spent with me learning more and more about Lloyd and his likes and dislikes, and more importantly mine. When I am with him, I trust him so much, in everything that he does and every game that we play, I fix another bit of the jigsaw, tidying those drawers in my brain, and so much now makes sense. I still don't know what it is he is into, not really, all he says is the time isn't right whenever I ask him. I also think he must be very frustrated as we still haven't gone all the way.

The truth is, I am glad; it proves his point that a good relationship is more than a fuck – it's about trust and respect. Yes, sure, sometimes I question where is the respect in what he has just done, like when he has me tied up on the bed starfish fashion, and he has been teasing me for hours, gently dancing his fingers over my body, getting me to a point of what I think is no return; then leaving me while he goes and sits enjoying the view, as he calls it, while I twist and turn, almost making myself burst. He loves seeing me in sexual agony, I think; sometimes he will get me all hot and place the Ann Summers rabbit switched on just close enough to cause a sensation, but not close enough for me to do anything about it, and he will watch, saying, "Keep control, Charlotte. No, that's not respecting me is it?" For the sake of a sub's arse, I just want to have satisfaction. After all, he is getting his by watching me twist and turn in agony, isn't he? But on the other hand he never does anything through anger, spite or malice, for which I am grateful. Everything we do is perfectly controlled by Lloyd, so I can and do enjoy every little game we play. After play, well, we just can't get enough of the cuddles, and of course that leads to more sexy play, and last but by no means least, light bondage and spanking which is just heavenly.

Chapter Eleven

It's Saturday evening. Lloyd has spent the day pampering me with nails, hair, make-up, oh yes, and the unspeakable wax. For sub's sake, he sprung it on me again! Yes, there were full-blown expletives and yes, afterwards he did what he threatened to do the first time: he locked the door and spanked me. There was something dead sexy about it, knowing there was a shop full of people outside, not knowing what was going on. Afterwards cuddles, and with teasing he has kept me on edge all day. Even in public the little kiss at the back of my ear, the soft stroke of my arse as I walk in and out of doors, subtle looks of approval and disapproval – they all work so well. The one I like the most is when we are at a table in a restaurant side by side and he slips his hand up inside my skirt just for a light tease, not quite getting right up to my clit but close enough, at the same time eating slowly, suggestively; it just makes me wriggle a little. He hasn't said what he has planned for tonight, all I know is we are going out; a need-to-know basis is what he said.

He has showered me and dressed me in all the clothes he sent me during the week, all fitting perfectly. Well, what would you expect from a control freak of a Dom? I even got to put on the panties, what a surprise! He has said it's because he wants to be able to take them off later. Well, if he undresses me as sensually as he dressed me, kissing everything before he tucked it in, then I think I might enjoy him taking them off even more. The top of the little black number shows just enough cleavage to be classy but not trashy. The shoes just set it all off, an ensemble that would be the envy of any girl.

We have just arrived at the hotel and he helps me out of the taxi and walks me to the door. Just before going in he pulls me to one side into a dark corner – oh, here we go, the talk on how to behave. I am starting to think I have turned into Eliza Doolittle from *My Fair Lady*.

For the sake of a sub's arse – leaning me up against the wall, he looks me in the eye and says, "This is a test of ultimate control, also a little fun too. Now you must listen carefully – at any time if you are not happy you must text me *TO* so I know you want time out."

"Why text?"

Holding his hand to my mouth he says, "Just listen, Charlotte." He removes his hand and kisses my lips softly. "I will continue as this is important. When you go in I want you to walk to the bar, sit on a stool sideways, legs crossed, and look straight at the bar. Do not look around, do not look back. You can order a drink – it goes on room 433. If anyone stands next to you, you may talk with them if they talk to you first, do you understand?"

No! What is happening, does he think I am Pussy Galore or someone? He is talking as if I am going on a mission for James Bond. Oh yes, James Bond wouldn't be too bad – at least he goes all the way with his playmates.

"Lloyd, what is going on? Where will you be?"

"I will be there. Are you happy with what I have said? Do you understand?"

"Yes, I understand but I am not sure that I am happy just sitting at a bar without you!"

"You will be fine." He kisses me long and hard, a drop-dead kiss, then looking at me again he says, "Take off your panties."

"What the sub's arse for?"

"Charlotte, it's nothing I haven't done before, but I am sure I will enjoy spanking your arse al fresco."

I give him a disapproving face, knowing damn well he will spank me somewhere here.

Taking off my panties and handing them to him, he puts them in his pocket. He hitches up my dress, looking me in the eye, kissing with passion, and pressing me hard to the wall. God, this is so nice...hold on, what is that? His hand is on my clit, subbing hell, that's nice, oh for... What is that? He has popped something inside me!

He stops kissing, and pulling down my dress he says, "That is a love egg, you are to keep it in all night." There they are, devil horns, those bloody devil horns are back.

Making sure my dress is straight, he then takes my hand. "Ready for some fun?" He winks.

"Yes, OK."

"Remember, *TO* by text if you need out." He opens the door and slaps my arse.

I do as I have been told, or should I say instructed, and I go to the bar. This thing inside me is driving me mad. I fidget as I walk. God, what if the subbing thing falls out? Oh, for sub's...how embarrassing would that be? I look around for a vacant stool at the bar; as I arrive I place my bag on the bar, put one foot on the stool bar, and I hear my phone beep as I sit on the stool. What the hell, what the subbing hell is that? The stool is vibrating. Clutching hold of the bar for grim death, I try and sit down. No, it's not the stool, it's that subbing egg, it's vibrating! Bloody hell, how the hell am I going to control that?

I look at my phone: it's a message from Lloyd.

Hi, how's the new toy? Exciting, I hope. I have some more instructions for you. You must not talk or acknowledge anyone when it's vibrating. Have fun, stay in control, Charlotte. xxx PS: Sit how I told you, please.

My return text:

This is not funny. I do hope you switch it off so I can at least have a subbing drink. xxx PS: Where are you?

It beeps again.

Sit correctly, please. I am not too far away. xxx PS: Anthony and Kat will be here soon for dinner, so please let's play before they arrive.

Oh for the love of a sub, please help me, this is just... I swing my legs round and cross them, just as he has instructed. Jeez, that's worse, I want to burst! I fidget on the seat. I bet he knows it is. Compose, concentrate, I want to burst, I need to burst – no, think of something else, quick. Hold on – if he knows how this thing works who in sub's heaven has he done a test drive with? You can do this. I feel hot tingles go up my spine. A drink, that's it – a large vodka and Coke, I think.

"Can I help you?" asks the bartender.

"Erm, yes, a large vodka and Coke, please, with loads of ice." That's it, ice; ice will help.

The bartender sets it down.

"Thank you, can you put it on room 433 please?" I say in a squeaky, clear-my-throat voice, and with a very strange look he goes off to serve someone else. Oh paddles, he knows, I can tell he knows. I wonder if he can hear it vibrating inside me. Jeez, this is so hard to control, and there I was worried about it falling out. No chance of it falling out, is there? Nope, I wouldn't be so subbing lucky.

A guy in jeans and T-shirt, quite hot-looking, orders a beer and looks at my legs. I fidget back in the chair. Please don't talk to me, you will think I am some sort of demented woman and you are much too hot to think that of me.

"Hello!" Oh God, he has a lovely husky voice, one that sends shivers up and down my spine. Please stop this vibrating. I fidget on the stool and look down at the bar.

"Are you OK?"

No, please, don't try and look at me. I lower my head and he lowers his.

"It can't be as bad as all that, you know."

Oh little sub bottoms, what would you know? Please, Lloyd, switch it off. Oh shit, if this guy gets any lower he might hear it vibrating. I fidget and lift my head up. Oh shit, oh yes, I would jump your bones, OK, if only…you are well fit. I can feel my stomach muscles clench. No, don't. I start breathing a little heavier. Yes, I would have sex with you here, right now.

His eyes are full of sympathy for me…oh, it's stopped.

"I am sorry, I just don't feel like talking tonight. I have had some bad news."

"I'm sorry, hun, are you sure you don't want to talk about it? A shoulder sometimes helps."

"No, I will be fine, I just want to be alone. Thank you anyway." Oh, I can't believe I am sending an Adonis away, he is a god. No, come back, I shout inside as I watch his arse, his perfectly formed arse in those jeans, out of the corner of my eye, being careful not to look too far back.

Buzz.

Shit, no, don't – oh God, Adonis, come back. I want your shoulder, truly I do… I want it to bite into. This is agony. You know exactly what you are doing, Lloyd, don't turn it off. No, no, that's not right, is it, turn it off. No, don't, turn it off, for God's sake. I know you can read my mind. Shift your arse back, that will help. Why are you doing this, Lloyd? My phone beeps: a message from Lloyd. He is probably changing the rules now.

> Did he have a nice arse? xxx

Reply:

> I don't know, Lloyd, did he? But you obviously do have a nice arse! Is it subbing spankable? And quit with the subbing vibrator.

It beeps again:

> Charlotte, you looked, I saw you. And the vibrator isn't going to stop until I have finished the game. xxx

And again:

> Yes, I do have a very spankable arse. It's attached to you, and yes, I will spank it tonight for that remark. xxx

For sub's sake, please, how long is this going on? I sit fidgeting. Another guy comes over, and standing next to me, he orders a drink. He runs his eyes down my legs, mentally undressing me as he looks up at me. Oh for…bloody hell, the vibrating stops. Oh no, oh no, not him, don't let him talk to me. Shit.

"Hi."

"Hello."

"What's your name?"

"Charlotte."

"Well hello, Charlotte, can I buy you a drink?"

Oh God, it's vibrating. I don't want a drink, thank you. I fidget a little. Please turn it off; this guy thinks I have gone mad. I look straight back at the back of the bar. Please go away.

"Did you hear me? I asked if you wanted a drink."

I look at the bartender, fidgeting, trying to hide my awkwardness. This is hell. The phone beeps.

How you doing? You look so funny. Lloyd xxx

Reply:

I have already told you this is not subbing funny. Charlotte xxx

Ah, it's stopped buzzing.

"Are you always so bloody rude when people are talking to you?"

No, how bloody dare you? You haven't a clue.

"Sorry, I didn't realise you were talking to me!"

"Well, I was going to buy you a drink, maybe show you a good time if you're up for it?"

"I don't think so, I am waiting for friends."

"What, girlfriends? Maybe you can introduce me to them."

Shit, it's vibrating again. For God's sake, I have a sex-mad idiot trying to get inside the panties that I don't have on, then Lloyd turning me on and off as usual. God, I can feel myself getting wet. I look around the bar area, trying to control my thoughts. Right, I need to get rid of this idiot when it stops next.

"Hey, what about your friends, are they a little more friendly than you?"

It's stopped. Right, now this is it, twat.

I lean over and place my hand on his arm.

"I don't think we are your type, we prefer women." That will shut him up. Ingenious comeback, if I do say so myself.

"Cool, can I watch?"

What? He wants to watch me with another woman? Paddle's sake, who does he think he is?

Lloyd, turn it off, for Dom's sake, I want to tell him where to go. I give the guy a smug grin.

"That's my girl. What room you in, then?"

Oh no, I am not your girl. That wasn't a yes grin! Get out of here. Go away, you creep. No way are you going to get anywhere near me. Then for the love of a sub, he places his hand on my leg. I move back in amazement; I look down at his hand, then look at him.

"Remove your hand now," I say curtly.

"Oh come on, all you need is a real man!"

"I said remove your hand now and when I want a real man I will not be calling you, because by the looks of it there is nothing real about you." I look down at his groin and then at my foot that has started to sway back and forth in his direction.

"Nice one, Charlotte!" And two hands embrace me from behind. "Are you bothering my wife?"

"No, no, I am just off. How do you get to be the husband of a lesbian then?" he says as he walks away from the bar. A kiss on the back of the neck, and with the vibrator still switched on, I start to become putty. Lloyd saved me from him. Or should that be he saved him from me?

"You OK?"

"I am now."

"You were in control so well with the way you handled him. I should have left you to sort him out, but I didn't like him touching you. It's not done in the lifestyle, touching without a verbal invitation."

"I am glad you are here. You called me your wife!"

"Best way to get rid of him. You told him you were a lesbian?"

"Backfired on me – he wanted to watch."

"Erm, can I watch instead, then, now he has gone?" And he nibbles some more on my other ear.

"What?"

"That's something we haven't discussed – your sexual preferences."

"Please, Lloyd, could you turn me off or stop kissing my ear, or I will burst!"

He hands me something that looks like a key fob with two buttons on it and I turn the vibrator off.

"Be my guest, job done for now."

"What do you mean?"

"Well, it was to test your reactions in a public place, to see if you would cope or crumble, what limit you would reach."

"We will never know now, will we? You stopped the game."

"Oh, I do know. I think he would have removed his hand, or if he didn't I think he would have been crawling out."

"How do you know that?"

"I saw you move your foot, my dear – that's why I put my arms around you and placed my hands on your knee. See, I was in total control of you and the situation all the time – I was never further than three steps away from you.

Anthony is behind with Kat sitting at a table – I had all bases covered and so did you." He kisses me again on my neck.

"Come on, let's join the others." He grabs my wrist and I turn on the bar stool, collecting my bag from the bar at the same time, and we went to see Anthony and Kat who were sitting just a short way from where I had been sitting. There were three glasses of red wine on the table; one of them must have been Lloyd's. He must have been here too. Lloyd released my wrist and grabbed a chair from another table and placed it for me to sit on.

"Thank you, Lloyd." I sit down, and Lloyd sits next to me.

"Hi, Anthony, I assume you were in on this, and you call yourself a friend?"

"Now, Charlotte, you know I don't stand in the way of anything you and Lloyd do. A little unfair of you, don't you think?"

I smiled sweetly at him.

"Hi, Kat. No use asking you anything, I don't want to get you into trouble! Are you OK?"

"Hi, yes, I am fine." She leans towards me and whispers, "Anthony and I have been trying out this new toy all week – we even tried it out in here to make sure that you would be OK. It has been a very good week for me. It was such fun working everything out, and trying the love egg. I thought it was sensational on all levels, don't you think?"

I can't believe that everyone here has been sorting out this little task and then sniggering at my pain while they all watched me trying not to burst.

I turn to Lloyd.

"Oh, what's next then, a rabbit while shopping in Marks and Spencer?"

"Could be interesting! I will have to think about that one. Thanks for the tip, Charlotte!"

They all laugh. Standing up from my seat, I excuse myself.

"Excuse me but I need the toilet."

Lloyd hastily gets up.

"Here, I will show you where they are." Taking my hand, he walks me in the direction of the door where we came in, then turns right into a corridor.

"I am sure I could have found them by myself."

"I am sure you would have done." He turns and looks at me; moving me to the wall, he leans against me and looks into my eyes. "You look even more beautiful than ever. I love the way you look when you are sexually frustrated." He kisses me long and hard. Oh yes, that's the kiss, the drop-dead kiss from heaven.

When we finish kissing my knees have turned to jelly. He whispers softly, "Don't take it out."

What? What does he mean, don't take it out?

"Why not?"

"Why do you think?"

"Oh no, Lloyd, not in front of Anthony and Kat!"

A grin and devil horns, and a small kiss on the lips.

"Come on, Charlotte, it's a new toy – I haven't finished playing yet!"

"Oh but, but…"

"Now, Charlotte, please don't, I really want to have some fun, although punishment is just as much fun for me."

"But what if it falls out? Anthony and Kat will be able to tell!"

"That's all part of the fun – you will have to make sure they can't tell."

"But what if it falls out?" I persist.

"Well, if it makes you feel safer I will give you your panties back." Putting his hand inside his pocket, he pulls out my panties. I snatch them out of his hands as he dangles them in mid-air, looking around to see if anyone might have seen them.

"I take it as game on as you have taken back your panties so quickly, Charlotte. I will see you at the table." He turns and starts walking away and I turn to walk towards the toilets, which are at the end of the corridor. Huh, not so clever after all, are you, devil Dom – I still have the magic switch in my hand. And I will not give it to you in front of Kat and Anthony – I will face the consequences later. Then I feel hands on my shoulders just as I am opening the door to the toilets.

"Buttons please, Charlotte?" I turn and Lloyd is standing with his hand out.

"What's the matter, Lloyd, having trouble with your shirt buttons?" I say, knowing full well he was asking for the buttons for the love egg.

"Charlotte, shall I assume by that you are saying game on for a spanking tonight? Am I to count your sarcastic remarks, as you already have a few saved up from the texts you sent me earlier this evening?"

Handing him the buttons, he gives me a peck on the lips.

"Good, I will see you back at the table."

How does he do that? I couldn't even find an answer to shoot right back at him. Every time I think I have the upper hand within seconds it's gone, just like that. I don't even have to say anything out loud to remind him of things, I just have to think it and he knows… Why is this? Deliberating the reasons for this I enter the toilet; as the door closes my phone beeps. Yet another message from Lloyd.

> You should have just handed me the buttons and not thought
> you had got one over on me LOL. Lloyd xxx

Double subs' arses, he is just so good at this, and I will never
get it. I enter a cubicle. I know – I will text back and tell him
I was caught up in the moment and I forgot I had it in my
hands.

Reply:

> I was so caught up in the moment that I forgot it was in my little
> hands. Charlotte xxx

Send, that will do it.

Beep.

> Tut tut, you were caught up in the moment. Does that mean
> you have lost control? Lloyd xxx PS: Do not remove ;)

Smiley winking face? No, don't put smiley winking face on
the bottom of your text, I now know that you have devil
horns coming out of the top of your head. That what you
are planning is going to be hell for me.

Reply, quick, reply.

> I just meant that we are playing such good games tonight I am
> caught up with the thought of what is going to happen and
> how enjoyable you are going to make the games for me. That's
> all, Lloyd, I was going to give you back the buttons when I got
> to the table. Charlotte xxx

Send.

I put my panties on and straighten myself out, before
leaving the cubicle. I did wonder about taking the love egg

out, but I am sure that if I did do that whatever Lloyd would have thought up as punishment would be even worse.

Beep.

Charlotte, I do think I know you and that reply is a hasty, panic one. Now hurry up and come out. Stop texting me. We are all hungry LOL. Lloyd xxx

I wash my hands and return to the table. As I walk closer Lloyd stands and moves the chair for me.

"What took you so long?"

"You know, just girl's stuff as usual."

As I sit down – pants! There it is, he has turned the thing on.

"Thank you, Lloyd," I say to try and hide the fact that I have something inside me vibrating. I say quickly, "What and where are we eating?"

"Oh, didn't I say, Charlotte? Sorry, we are eating here tonight, as well as staying here. We want to try it out, see what it is like."

"No, Lloyd, you didn't say, but it's not far from where we live, so why don't we go home afterwards?"

"Well, how can we try everything if we go home? We want to try out the bedrooms, make sure the beds bounce properly too."

"Oh, OK, a little strange though." I fidget back a little and the vibrating stops.

Lloyd puts his arm around my shoulder and leans in, whispering, "All will become clear."

I look at Anthony and Kat to see if they are giving away any clues about what is going on, but no, nothing as usual, I can't even count on them. Hold on, hold on, did he say beds bouncing, that he wants to see how well the beds bounce? Beds bouncing to me only means one thing. Maybe tonight is the right time, right moment; yes, that's it, tonight will be the night – there is a great sub God after all. I feel myself going all dreamy as I think about hot passion with Lloyd and what he will do to me. My mind is racing.

A waiter comes over and Lloyd moves to stand up, waking me from my dreamy state.

"Are you ready to eat now, sir?" the waiter asks.

Lloyd removes his arm from me and getting up, he says, "Yes, thank you, we are all ready."

We follow the waiter to the dining room. There are loads of round tables all dressed with white tablecloths, long ones nearly to the floor, with settings on each table. Our table has four settings, with every knife and fork that you can think of on it. There is a white wine glass, a red wine glass and a glass for water. Very posh.

We sit down and Lloyd holds my chair and tucks it in; at the same time Anthony does the same for Kat. Then they both sit down. Order of seating is Lloyd, Kat, Anthony, then me, on the right side of Lloyd.

"This is nice in here. You wouldn't have thought so from the bar and entrance, you would have thought it was just a bog-standard hotel!" Anthony says.

I look around: there are chandeliers on the ceiling, all sparkling with the lights dancing around, as well as five candles alight on every table, including ours.

"No, you wouldn't. I have ordered for us, I hope you don't mind." Oh, here we go, bloody oysters – he knows I can't put up a fight in here.

"I am sure whatever you have ordered will be fine, Lloyd," Kat says.

I place the napkin over my lap and Lloyd grabs hold of my hand; lifting it, he places both our hands on the table, still holding mine. I look at him and his eyes are sparkling in the candlelight; he winks at me and I feel like melting. The thoughts of long, hot passion come back – at last, tonight's the night.

The waiter comes with some white wine. Lloyd tries it and nods in acceptance to the waiter, who then fills all our glasses and places the bottle of wine in an ice bucket just between Lloyd and Kat.

"So what do you think, Anthony? Perfect for a vanilla night, don't you think?"

"Yes, Lloyd, perfect."

"What do you mean, Lloyd, vanilla night? I don't think this is a vanilla night at all, do you?" I scowl at him.

"Charlotte, you are so funny. I have said we are testing it out. Nats wants a venue for a party, she wants to treat all the girls to a night out with their partners, and I thought about this place, so here we are."

"Well, you could have said, I thought that you and Anthony were turning straight."

And they both say simultaneously, "That will never happen, Charlotte."

"Phew. Thank God for that, I thought for one moment there I was going to have to advertise in the *Dom Times* for a new Dom."

They all look at me and I can feel their eyes burning deep. For the love of a sub, what have I said now? My eyes dart between the three of them, not quite knowing what to say.

"Charlotte, do you mean that you are in full submission to the lifestyle?" Anthony says quietly.

Full submission, what exactly does that mean? Or more to the point, what exactly does Anthony mean by full submission, and what is my interpretation of that statement? Oh paddles, what can of worms have I opened now? They are going to run me around in little circles.

"Well, Anthony, if you mean am I comfortable with everything that it has to offer, then my answer is that I am still exploring my options. If you mean am I happy to be in the lifestyle the answer is yes, I am happy – there are alternatives and I'm very happy to be part of it." I grimace in contemplation of the next question because there are going to be a lot more questions; I know that.

"It's the first time you have even indicated that you are happy with the choice you have made." Anthony raises an eyebrow.

"That's not true – when anyone asks me if I am happy I always say yes."

"Yes, you do, but that's the only time you have mentioned this aspect – up until now, that is." Anthony looks at Lloyd as if to say, Have you got anything to say?

"Charlotte, you have surprised me. I just thought that you were going along with the games. I thought that you were happy with what we were doing. There's a lot more to the lifestyle than just what we do."

"I know that, Lloyd, and I also know that we are just playing at the moment, but the more we play the more that I realise that maybe this is OK…"

The waiter comes and we all stop talking. He places four small bowls just to one side of the place settings, then leaves. In the bowls there is warm water and a slice of lemon floating in the middle. I look at the bowl at the side of me and then at Lloyd. He squeezes my hand and smiles. Devil horns, I see you. I knew it: subbing oysters.

"Just maybe OK?" Lloyd says.

"No, yes, no, not quite – what I meant, what I am saying is that I am more than comfortable with the lifestyle. I can't imagine my life without it now."

"So does that mean I can step up the pace more now?"

Step up the pace? I thought he already had with tonight.

I remove my hand from Lloyd's grip and place it on the top of his leg, just out of sight of the others, and give it a little rub, at the same time saying, "Lloyd, you are always stepping the pace up, but do you mean would I be happy to go back down to the room with you? The answer would be yes." Lloyd hasn't taken me back down there since the nutter attacked Sophie and me; he hasn't even suggested that we should go down.

The waiter arrives with three dishes, and again we all stop our conversation as he places the first down in front of Kat. I see that my instinct was right: paddling oysters. He places the other two down, one for Anthony and the other for Lloyd, and then returns to the kitchen. I look at the dishes with horror on my face, then look at Lloyd. He takes my hand and gives it another squeeze.

"Oysters, my favourite!" Kat says.

"Yes, good choice, Lloyd," Anthony says. They all love them, except me. I will have to try and pretend to like the slimy pollution food from hell.

The waiter returns with another plate and places it down in front of me. To my surprise it isn't oysters, it's asparagus.

Lloyd leans towards me. "I do hope you like asparagus, I didn't think I would make you eat oysters two nights running."

"Yes, thank you, Lloyd."

"What, you don't like oysters?" Anthony is shocked.

"Let's just say that Charlotte loses control with oysters, and I didn't think that I would expose you and Kat to the technique of oyster-eating that Charlotte has adopted. I don't think they will have enough napkins for Charlotte to spit into after every oyster." And they all laugh.

"I am sure you will not be laughing in the morning when you have grown another eye in the middle of your forehead from the pollution you are eating as well as the oyster. I am sure they are radioactive as well," I add.

"See, I said she wouldn't get over the oysters, Anthony! I won that bet!"

"What do you mean, you are betting on me?"

"Oh, Charlotte, I thought you knew. It's just our little bit of fun."

Fun, huh? I'll show him.

I pick up an asparagus tip from my plate and I let the excess oil drip from it. Then moving my head forward, raised slightly, I lift the asparagus so that the tip is in line with my lips, parting them slightly as I do so. My tongue slowly meets the asparagus and I lick the last dripping remains of oil, slowly bending the asparagus into my mouth, holding it firmly with my teeth, biting gently into it, slowly and sensually, and as they all watch I say, "I am quite happy with asparagus. I know it doesn't taste of sea pollution." And I look at Lloyd. He smiles.

"Is that game on, Charlotte? It sounds like that to me." He moves his hand down towards his pocket, and a voice inside my head shouts *nooo* as loud as it can. I forgot, I subbing well forgot about the vibrating egg inside me. I start to vibrate. I turn my head abruptly, looking at him with my eyes opened wide. He picks up an oyster, raising it to his mouth, and shoots it down in one, gently licking his lips.

"Mmm, so lovely." He raises an eyebrow as if to say, My point, I think.

For the rest of the starter I eat the asparagus tips while I vibrate. I so wanted to just drag him up to our room and test those beds for bounciness, right there and then.

"So how was your starter, Charlotte?" Lloyd so kindly

137

asked, but something told me he wasn't asking about the asparagus at all.

"Sensational. Thank you, Lloyd."

"You two, how was your starter?"

"They were very good."

"Yes, quite fresh and sweet-tasting," Kat added after Anthony.

The waiter arrives and takes the plates away.

"And, Charlotte, did it taste as good as you made it look?" Lloyd asks, looking into my eyes.

"Every bit so, Lloyd, if not better." I place my hand on his leg and work upwards to his groin, then rubbing softly, I feel a twitch from within his trousers. He looks at me and I smile sweetly at him. I feel another twitch as he starts to grow. Lloyd grabs my hand and lifts it back to the table. Releasing my hand, he puts his hand inside his pocket and the vibrating stops. That's it, see; play him at his own game.

"Charlotte, getting back to our conversation before our starters arrived. Do you mean to say that you trust Lloyd?"

"Anthony, you know that I have always trusted him, but now that trust has grown into something else. What I feel is strong and confident when I am with him. I know that no matter what I say or do he will never hurt me. I also know that no matter where we are he will never let me get hurt if he can help it. I know that if I have something to say I can say it without fear of repercussions. I know I don't know everything about the lifestyle but..." I hesitate, deep in thought about that last comment about not knowing everything. Do I want to know everything, do I want to go further, or am I just happy with what I have now? I question myself.

"But what, Charlotte?" Lloyd squeezes my hand. I look

at him; I look him in the eyes. He looks a little concerned – why is that? Does he know that I am questioning myself?

"I am not sure what the 'but' is, Lloyd, I still have lots of unanswered questions about myself. All I know is that I am very happy with everything, as I have said. My trust in you has grown over the weeks and I have a great respect for you and your values." I pause again, then I turn and look at Anthony and Kat. Are they quite happy with what they have? They must be well suited, but how do you know? How will I know if Lloyd is or will be that happy with me? I look at Anthony. I really need to talk with you, I think.

"Charlotte, whatever it is, spit it out. What are you thinking?" Anthony says.

"Well, I don't know everything, do I, and I don't know if Lloyd and I will be suited, like you and Kat are. How can I? He hasn't told me everything he likes and what he doesn't like."

Lloyd laughs, then says, "Charlotte, that's why there are limits. We all have them. We haven't found yours yet, because your trust is still growing with me. OK, yes, it's taking a little longer than we thought, but you have been through a lot, and trust-building can take a long time. That's what tonight was about, to see if you trusted me enough for you to be able to go through with the game in public. That's another limit you have reached. I now know we can play in public and you can, as far as the public will let you, keep control. We are always building our limits in everything we do. When you get to a place that you are not comfortable with, like that man this evening, I know and I stop the game – limit set. You don't like people you don't know touching you inappropriately and neither do I. You will find out what I like just the same as I find out about you."

The second course arrives. Fresh salmon, with a wild

mushroom risotto. We wait for the waiter to go and then I start up the conversation again.

"But that's just it, Lloyd, I don't know what your limits are. What if our limits are different, not the same things?"

"Charlotte, we all have different limits, that's the point. One of the things I like I truly like is pushing limits to see how far I can go..."

Before he can get another word out I say brashly, "Well, that's not the point – you are to respect each other's limits, that's the point, I think. I wouldn't like it if you pushed my limits."

"But, Charlotte, that's what we have done tonight. Your limits *were* pushed, I didn't know how you were going to take it and I didn't know if you were going to run off to the ladies' shouting at me, 'You Dom from hell,' or, 'What the sub do you think you are doing to me?' That's why Kat is here to help. If you did she would have come and found you, talked with you, seen that all bases were covered. We did expect you to run off, to be honest, but you didn't, you took it very well. That was me pushing your limits. I know that you will do anything I ask when we are alone, I just wanted to see how far you would go in public. Now I know, and now we can play other games and not confine ourselves to the apartment." And he winks. God, you think winking at me makes everything OK.

"But why didn't you tell me first what we were doing if you were so worried about my reaction?"

"Because if I had told you the element of surprise would be gone and I have found that you enjoy things more when there is a little mystery to the games we have been playing. The element of surprise and the power of suggestion are all things you have underestimated, and that you haven't really got a grasp on yet." There's a hint in all of that, I am sure, but now my head is puddled again and I can't think straight.

"This fish is nice, Lloyd, don't you think?" Phew, Anthony has saved me by changing the subject.

"Yes, I quite like the wine as well," I say, picking up my glass and taking a sip.

Lloyd leans sideways towards me and says quietly, "We will carry on this discussion later if you want, and oh yes, remind me of paddling subs' arses, I need to talk with you about my limits on that one." What does he mean? Paddling subs' arses and his limits...how many subs' arses does he want to paddle?

We eat the rest of the meal just chatting about how good the food is and how many people will be coming for Nats' work do. The dessert eventually arrives: rich chocolate round cake with strawberries and handmade chocolates, and a few crystallised violet petals sprinkled over the top.

"It looks too good to eat!" Kat says.

"I am sure you will enjoy trying to eat it, Kat!" says Anthony.

I pick up one of the chocolates, round and white, and a comfortable size just for popping into my mouth. I place it on my tongue, closing my mouth slowly. It's a perfect fit between the roof of my mouth and my tongue. I slowly move my tongue under the ball of chocolate and I can now taste the creaminess as it melts slowly. I move it between my teeth and bite into it gently but firmly. My mouth fills with a slightly fizzy liquid which dances on my tongue and sets my taste buds dancing with its sparkle. It tastes of champagne with a slight hint of violets. Wow, this is nice, the best part of the meal. After I finish that moment, I look at my plate and decide that a strawberry will get it next. Lifting one up by its very handily placed stalk, I place it between my teeth and bite just below the stalk. It is perfect, just soft, plump and juicy, not too cold and not too warm. The juices fill my mouth and I can taste the sunshine that has ripened the berry on the plant; it is just so succulent in my mouth. Next another chocolate, I think, before I attack the cake; a dark one this time. I eye up the two dark chocolates, trying to decide which one is going to have the pleasure of tantalising my tongue and mouth next. They both look as good as each other but it comes down to the fact that one has a violet on it, the other a tiny sliver of gold leaf. Already having the violet taste dancing on my tongue, I decide the gold leaf will have to be the one. Carefully picking it up with my thumb and forefinger as I did with the other, I place it slowly into my mouth; I don't want to lose any of the sensations. Again, a perfect fit. I roll my tongue back and forth to help it melt, the rich smoothness of the chocolate bursting into a deep flavour of heaven. It's so mind-blowingly delicious. I bite into it slowly to release the liquid. My mouth fills with the flavour of pears and the liqueur is soft; my taste buds burst as it blends with the dark chocolate beautifully.

Looking at my plate, I think another strawberry to clean my palate a little, then it's you, cake, yes, your turn, and I am sure that you will be every bit as good as everything else on my plate. Same again with the strawberry: slowly biting, I can still taste everything I tasted before. I never knew there was a chocolate pudding sub god but there must be, as I have never tasted a dessert so good. Picking up my spoon I think to myself, this is it, little cake, your turn. And don't disappoint me, please don't; if I can't have a good fuck this is the closest I will get.

I place the spoon on the cake and then slowly scoop a small amount for the first try. I raise the spoon and place it into my mouth, slowly closing my lips around it, trapping that little bit of chocolate goodness inside my warm, very sensual mouth. Slipping my spoon slowly out of my mouth so that none of the goodness will escape, I keep my lips tight. Oh wow, oh gosh, as soon as it hits my mouth my taste buds are having a heavenly food orgasm. My eyes close slightly and my head tips back. Mmm, this is just divine. I need another spoonful, this time bigger, just slightly, and with some violets. I lower my spoon and scoop up another, placing it into my mouth. Both eyes closed, I feel the creaminess of the mousse as it starts to melt, then the brandy liqueur and slow but slight hint of violets, which starts to fill my mouth. Anticipating the chocolate taste next, I slowly lick my lips. Food heaven here, I— What? What...oh, for sub's sake. I gulp, vibrating. Oh no, Lloyd, not now, for the love of a Dom's cane, not now. I open my eyes wide and swing around, and before I know it my mouth is open and words are just coming out.

"It's not that subbing obvious, Lloyd!"

I watch him raise an eyebrow.

"Caught up in the moment, Charlotte, or have you lost total control?"

I hear Kat snigger and I look up at her. Oh shit, she knows. She was trying to pretend she wasn't paying attention but I know subs always pay attention to everything – except for me, that is. I look at Anthony, who has finished his dessert and is sitting with his elbows on the table, casually sipping his wine. And he knows? Oh for the love of a sub...

"Waiting for an answer, Charlotte," Lloyd whispers. I turn my head and look back at him, and just stare blankly into his eyes for a moment or two, then think, well, how can I answer that, Lloyd? The moment is gone and I am sure you really don't want me to tell you that you really are the Dom from hell, do you? On my planet you just don't spoil such a good subbing moment as good chocolate, not unless you want to know what a woman really thinks about you. Oh no you don't, and when I get you upstairs I will subbing tell you so.

"I think Charlotte and I will go upstairs now, we need a little chat." He starts rubbing his palm. What, a chat? I haven't finished my dessert yet, have I? The vibration deep within, along with the food orgasm I was having, is sending shivers up and down my spine. I just can't answer him. Yes, get up and go – no, don't get up and go, what if your knees go all weak like they do sometimes? Oh, help me please!

Lloyd stands up and my eyes stay stuck to his like glue, my mouth slightly open. I close it and take a gulp. Yup, he is going to make me stand up. He holds his hand out to me, saying, "Are you not going to say goodnight, Charlotte?"

By this stage I am almost bent over double in the chair, trying to make the vibrations stop. I am clenching every muscle I can in my stomach. I slowly place my hand on his and he gives me a little pull.

"Err, yeah, night, you two." A little wobbly squeak comes out of my mouth, followed by sniggers from Anthony and Kat. I turn and look at them again; they look as if they haven't noticed, but I know they have. Lloyd turns and starts to walk away from the table.

"Night, Anthony, Kat. Have fun, I am sure I am going to."

He gives my hand a squeeze and I started to automatically follow him to the lift.

Swinging me into the lift, pushing the button for our floor, he pushes me to the wall with both hands held downwards behind my back. He leans against me, pushing hard on my pelvis.

"How clever of you, Charlotte, to give me such a perfect

excuse to leave. How did you know I wanted to go?" He gyrates his hips on mine.

"Err, err, err." I can't think of anything to say.

"Come, Charlotte, don't be modest now, after all, you have just entertained everyone with your chocolate dessert."

What, everyone? That was in my head! Please say it wasn't out loud, please. I slump my head backwards in disbelief that I did such a thing.

"And yes, it was that obvious, as you asked so politely."

My face cringes. No, surely not, surely I didn't. I couldn't have done. And if I did then it's him, he has done it to me with switching the vibrator on and off all night. He knows it was him – what in subbing hell does he think is going to happen? You give a girl love eggs that are remote controlled, then feed her food that is just so perfect followed by chocolate heaven.

He kisses me on the neck and says, "I am really going to enjoy you tonight."

The lift door opens and as he steps out, I watch him. The vibrations from the love eggs seem to be getting stronger. Lloyd turns.

"Are you coming then?"

"Oh, great choice of words, Lloyd, you never use the word 'come' like that, do you..." Shit, out loud? Nooo, please no, don't!

"Problem, Charlotte? Are you trying to say something?" He holds his hand out, and again I automatically place mine in it, shaking my head. No.

"Good, I didn't think you would be so stupid as to add to your growing-larger-by-the-minute list." He pulls me softly out of the lift into his arms.

"I could feel the love egg vibrating inside you when I was leaning on you in the lift. Feels good."

Feels good? Not where I am, I just want to burst now. I am almost there, buster, best get a move on to the room or I will explode right here and now.

He plants a kiss on my neck that sends shivers down my spine, then turns; still holding my hand tight he walks down the hallway past lots of doors right to the very last door. Unlocking the door, he turns around, sweeping me off my feet, and then carries me in, kissing my neck as he does so, kicking the door closed with the heel of his foot.

"Got you here alone at last. It's been a long evening, I think. What about you, Charlotte, has it been a long evening for you?"

"Yes, and something tells me, Lloyd, that it hasn't finished yet!"

"I don't know what makes you think that, Charlotte." He lowers me to the floor.

"Because you still have the buttons and I am fed up with feeling like a Duracell bunny, always on the go."

Lloyd laughs as he walks over to the bed and lies down.

"Charlotte, here." He holds up his hand, and dangling from his fingers is the control.

"Come and get if...if you want to turn it off."

I run over to the bed and fling myself on the other half, clutching for the buttons. Buttons in hand, I switch the love egg off and sigh with relief.

"Better?"

"Yes, much, thank you, Lloyd." Calmness starts to come back, deep within.

"Now, Charlotte, we do have to talk for a while if you think you can, but first this."

A kiss, a drop-dead, gorgeous kiss. I wrap my arms around him and place a leg over his. He pulls me closer and strokes his fingers gently all down my spine; at the same time he lifts his knee to my clit and there it is – I'm bursting and he's kissing me so hard I can't make a noise. I squirm beside him, longing for him to go all the way, but tonight it only takes a kiss and a gentle stroke and I'm gone, clasping his shirt tightly in my hands and kissing him harder as the orgasm intensifies. I feel his hand reach down and Lloyd hitches up my dress just past my buttocks; he rolls me onto my back, rolling with me until he is on top, still kissing and teasing my mouth. I wrap my legs around his waist and he pushes down on me. My hips raise to meet his, oh yes, oh please, God, please, let this be the night, so perfect, so subbing lovely. I untuck his shirt, pulling at it hastily; I put my hand up inside to feel his back. Perfect, he feels perfect; this moment is just as good as the chocolate moment downstairs. I moan a little as he pushes down on me again; he grabs my arms and places them above my head and pushes himself up on his hands, still holding my wrists, and looks at me deep in my eyes.

"I have never seen you looking this hot, or this horny. All night you have been looking so incredibly horny." He comes down for another kiss; I open my lips in anticipation.

Knock, knock!

He stops, looks at me. Nooo, please, not now, it can't be anyone important; you are not on duty tonight, surely, so it can't be George. No – breaking canes of Doms!

Knock, knock.

"No, Lloyd, let's pretend we are not in," I whisper quietly.

"You know I can't do that, Charlotte." He winks and gets off me. I raise my head and watch him go to the door, shirt untucked and looking very ravishing indeed. I throw my head back and look at the ceiling; that's it, moment gone by the time he gets back. This is a subbing rubbish establishment that they come knocking on your door – don't they know what people do after a relaxing night, good food and wine? I will ask for my money back in the morning. Well, Lloyd's money back, that is.

Lloyd comes back to the bed, sits on it and says, "Charlotte, I am so sorry, truly, but there is a lady who needs a doctor. She is about to have a baby and they saw I was here."

"Why come to a hotel and have a baby? Why not go to the hospital?"

"She is staying here, and the ambulance is going to be a while. Charlotte, I am so sorry!"

I lift my head. "I am sorry, Lloyd. I will come with you, I might be able to help."

Chapter Twelve

We leave our room and followed the hotel manager to one of the other rooms where a middle-aged woman lay on the bed.

"It's too early, it's too bloody early!" she shouts at us as we enter the room.

My old nursing instincts take over, walking to the bed calmly but with authority.

"This is Dr Hughes, and I am Charlotte. I'm a nurse, so you are in good hands." I offer my hands to her.

"Let's have a look. How far gone are you?"

"About thirty-five weeks."

"OK, when did the contractions start?"

"I don't know, I had a bit of a backache earlier and came up to lie down and then, oh no, another one!" She grabs my hand and screams. "I want to push."

"No, breathe in, out, in, out, come on, breathe with me. In, out."

She starts copying me.

"OK, Charlotte, she is going to have this baby here, and in the next half-hour."

I look around at Lloyd.

"Are you sure?"

"Yes I am, it's crowning as we speak."

I look back at the lady.

"What's your name?"

"Diane."

"OK, Diane, did you hear what Lloyd said?"

"Yes, but I am scared!"

"No need to be scared, he is one of the best. He knows what to do."

"Are you sure he does?"

"I would trust him with my life, one hundred per cent. Don't worry." I stroke my hand down the side of her face to reassure her.

"Right then, Diane, with your next contraction you are going to push with all your might. Let me know when you feel a contraction."

Lloyd turns to the hotel manager. "Any sign of the ambulance yet?"

"Not at all, Dr Hughes."

"OK, I need a towel or a sheet to clean and wrap the baby in when it's born. Can you get me some please?"

"OK, I will be just a minute." The manager leaves, closing the door behind him.

"OK, it's on its way, shit, this hurts!"

"Pussshhh."

She clenches her hand tightly around mine as she pushes.

"That's it, doing great." As the contractions ease, so does her grasp on my hand.

"Oh, not another so soon, I can't take it," she cries.

"Pussshhh," I say firmly again; my hand is in a vice, for sub's sake, I will have no hand left soon.

"Doing great, doing real great. I can see the head now. Not long, Diane, and it will all be over."

Diane puts her head up and in a strong, aggressive voice, looking straight at Lloyd, she growls, "Don't you have any painkillers? Are you a real doctor, I thought you had painkillers?" Her grip tightens again.

"Push! Diane, push!" I say.

"I am so sorry, Diane, but I don't have a bag here. We are off duty tonight, we are guests here at the hotel. Nice one, Diane, now, with the next one its head will be out, I think! And after you have pushed, I want you to pant until I say stop, OK?"

"OK," she says abruptly.

The grip is tighter.

"Push, Diane. Here it comes, push. OK, pant, pant." I start to pant to encourage Diane to pant with me. "You are doing so well, Diane." I try to release her grip from my hand a little.

"That's good, next one and it should be out."

The hotel manager returns with a midwife.

"Hi, Lloyd, I didn't know you delivered as well on house calls?"

Who is she? Stop, brain, you have other things to worry about. Get control.

"Hi, Sue. I don't usually, I was here with Charlotte."

"Well, you are doing fine. I will get set up. What a lot of hair your baby has, Diane."

"Another on its way, Lloyd," I say as the grip clamps down on my hand.

"OK, last push and it will be out. Ready to take over, Sue?"

"Yes." She undoes a delivery pack with everything needed to deliver the baby.

"Pussshhh." And Diane pushes. Within seconds, we hear the noise of a crying baby. I look at Diane.

"Congratulations, Diane, your baby is here. You have done so well."

Looking at me, she smiles. "Thank you, thank you so much."

"You're welcome. Do you want to sit up a little?"

"Yes please."

I help her to sit up and by the time I have done that, Lloyd and Sue have cut the cord, wrapped the baby up and are handing it to Diane.

"Congratulations, Diane, you have a little girl."

"Oh, thank you, Lloyd. Thank you so much, and is she all right?"

"She looks perfect to me, maybe four weeks premature, but just perfect."

And with that, Diane, like so many mothers, starts cooing and crying all at the same time from so many emotions.

"Right, Diane, Charlotte and I will leave you to the midwife and your baby now. I will see if I can find you an ambulance."

With lots of thank-yous from Diane, we left the room.

Outside the room, Lloyd put his arm around me and said, "Drink or bed?"

"Drink. I think we have to wet the baby's head, don't we?"

"Yes, we sure do, let's go to the bar."

Downstairs, we went to the reception desk and Lloyd asked for a phone to call the hospital and see if an ambulance was on its way. The manager appeared with a clean T-shirt saying he was sorry to disturb him but he didn't know what else to do, and that he had got a bottle of champagne on the house cooling for us at the bar. Lloyd managed to get a hospital car response team dispatched to the hotel. Then Lloyd and I went to the toilets to get cleaned up. In the toilets, washing my hands, my thoughts went back to that perfect moment in the bedroom; such a perfect moment.

Why is it that all our moments are spoilt, taken away just like that? I bet if I was on a subbing desert island with him, I would get to that moment, and something, somewhere, would just come and spoil it, like a coconut falling from a tree and smashing straight onto his head. I finish sorting myself out and go to the bar where Lloyd is already sitting with champagne poured for us both. He picks up his glass. As I approach I notice he has a hotel cleaning staff T-shirt on, and I laugh.

"Oh, Lloyd, I didn't think you had anything to do with cleaning?"

"Shut up." He hands me my glass of champagne and I sit down next to him. He raises his glass to mine and says, "To Diane and baby Diane." We clink glasses, take a sip, looking deep into each other's eyes.

"Another moment gone then, Charlotte, don't you think?"

Oh yes, I think.

"Yes, but that is one hell of a way to lose such a moment, Lloyd, the birth of a new life."

He puts his arm around me and kisses my head.

"You were fantastic," he says softly.

"So were you."

Lloyd wants to wait for the response team to get to the hotel to ensure that Diane and the baby get away safely. Apparently there had been a very bad road traffic accident and that's why the ambulance couldn't get to the hotel as quickly as usual. After Lloyd is satisfied that maybe we could go to bed and not be disturbed in any way, off we go back to our room. We both take a shower, and somehow it just doesn't seem right to have rampant sex after such a wonderful experience of a baby being born. So we cuddle, and go to sleep. It's the perfect end to a perfect beginning.

Chapter Thirteen

Next morning, I wake up and look around the room – Lloyd isn't anywhere to be seen. A note is on the pillow next to me:

Good morning! I have put some clothes out for you to wear. I am downstairs having breakfast with Anthony and Kat. See you soon sleepy head. xxx PS: Please wear your hair up xxx

I look around for my clothes, seeing them on a chair by the dressing table: tight jeans and T-shirt. I get up and go for a shower, then get dressed. I put on my jeans, lying down on the bed to zip them up. Once zipped and sitting up I remember why Lloyd would have put tight jeans out for me. I have fresh wax syndrome; my clit is sensitive. Oh well, best get it over with then. I go down to the breakfast room; standing in the entrance I see the three sitting at a table that is nestling in a corner. I fidget as I get ready to walk over, thinking, keep in control. As I walk over, Kat says something to Lloyd and he turns to look at me. I reach the table and so far, so good – not too bad, not too many fidgets, I think.

"Good morning, Charlotte, how are you this morning?" Lloyd asks.

"I'm fine, thank you."

He pulls out my chair to sit down, and as I step to go around the chair to sit, Lloyd puts his hand on my thigh.

"Mmm I like you in jeans, I really should let you wear them more often." He strokes my leg slowly. OK, enough, I don't need touching, that will just aggravate my syndrome.

I sit on the chair and wiggle my bottom slightly. Oh God, this is going to get so hard to control as the day goes on.

"Fresh wax syndrome, Charlotte?" Kat asks.

I place both of my hands on the edge of the table and leaning forward, I scowl at her. How the hell does she know that?

"Oops sorry, Charlotte, I couldn't resist."

Then Anthony says, "Charlotte, I notice they have Coco Pops on the breakfast bar if you want to see if they have the same effect as last night."

I swiftly turn my head and look at him, my mouth dropping open as all three of them fall about laughing at me. Isn't anything sacred, for the love of a sub?

I stand up, and with an act of defiance, something I know will probably stop Lloyd in his tracks, I reach up and grab the spring clip that was holding up all my hair, pulling it out and letting it tumble, cascading down my back. I give it a toss and swing it around onto my left shoulder as I step around the chair. I bend down to Lloyd's ear, whispering, "You are the Dom from hell."

Lloyd's hand reaches out and takes hold of a strand of the hair that has fallen down to one side.

"Quick thinking, Charlotte, to let your hair down. It has created a curtain – see, no one can see anything."

I move my eyes left to look; I see nothing but a curtain of hair. Lloyd, still holding part of my hair, moves his hand to my inner thigh and starts to rub gently.

"Please don't, Lloyd!" I whisper.

"You know what that little remark has cost you, don't you?"

"What? Please don't, Lloyd."

"No, Charlotte, the one before that, and that little act of defiance is saying game on to me, don't you think so?"

"Lloyd, please let me go and get my breakfast."

With that, he lets go. I stand up, wiggle a little and start walking away.

"That really wasn't funny, you two," Lloyd says, pausing before saying, "Actually, it was." They fall about laughing again.

Why am I always the butt of their jokes, I think as I looked around at all the items on the table? Coco Pops, I will get him for that, bloody Coco Pops. I look back round at the table. Yes, they are still laughing, making fun of me. Good, there is coffee on the table, and orange juice, the less I carry the better. I wiggle my arse again just to try and stop the sensation a little. Grabbing a look at the yoghurts, I decide that will be best as they have lids on. I can't do any damage with a sealed yoghurt if I drop it, can I? I grab some grapes. Getting back to the table, I place the items I have chosen down and I sit back down. The first thing Lloyd does is hand me my hair grip that I had attached to the collar of his shirt when he had hold of my hair.

"Thank you, Lloyd." I place it down next to me on the table. I open my yoghurt and started to eat. After my first mouthful I say, "So what are we talking about, apart from me that is, as you must be finding it very boring by now?"

Lloyd chuckles, replying, "Charlotte, the subject of you is never boring, in fact we find it very entertaining and I think we always will." Anthony, Kat and Lloyd start laughing again. Scowling at them, I flick my eyes between them.

"Stop laughing at me," I demand.

"Excuse me all, but I don't think I have given Charlotte a kiss good morning yet," says Lloyd as he leans towards me, kisses me on the cheek, and says good morning. Then leaning to my ear, he says, "Shall we try again, and start afresh?"

"What, you all want to laugh at me some more?" I pout.

"My, my, Charlotte, are we feeling brave this morning? You seem to have a lot to say."

"Aww, I am sorry, Lloyd, but I think sometimes I am here for your amusement and nothing else." I wriggle my arse on the chair. I don't feel like playing these games today, not at all.

"Charlotte, you are not losing control, are you? You have done so well this weekend, so far, it would be such a shame to lose control now." He leans forward and plants a little kiss on my lips, looks me in the eye and says, "Not only have you played so well, but we delivered a baby." He smiles softly.

Oh yes we did, I had forgotten about Diane and the baby. A smile lights up my face as I turn to the others. "Did Lloyd tell you what happened last night after we left?"

"No!" they reply.

And in my excitement I say, "We had a baby!"

Well, Anthony nearly chokes on his coffee, which sends Kat into fits of laughter, and Lloyd, I think, nearly has a heart attack, sputtering, "No, no, that's not what she means! Anthony, Kat stop it!"

"No, that's right, we didn't have a baby. We delivered a baby."

The waiter comes with some cooked breakfasts and places them on the table.

"But you went to bed?" Anthony says, mopping his chin in amazement that he spilt his coffee.

I look at the big breakfast. It's the works: sausage, eggs,

mushrooms, fried slice, beans and tomatoes. And then I look at Lloyd.

"Eat up, Charlotte, you need your energy for today. We have a lot to get through."

Looking over to Anthony, Lloyd continues, "Yes, we did – about fifteen minutes after we got into our room there was a knock on the door, and off we went."

While we eat we explain how it all came about, and how it was gone two o'clock before we returned to our room.

Then Anthony changes the subject as we all finish our breakfasts. "Charlotte, are you still standing by what you said last night about you trusting everything to do with the lifestyle?"

"Yes, I am, why?"

He puts up a finger to signify he hasn't finished, and continues questioning me. "And what about Lloyd, is your trust truly growing in Lloyd?"

I look at Lloyd, thinking, what is going on? He winks at me – OK, there is something going on, but why is Anthony asking me and not Lloyd? I know, it's Lloyd, he is testing me. I turn back to Anthony and say, "I said last night that my trust in Lloyd is growing. I also said last night that I would trust Lloyd one hundred per cent—"

"When did you say that? I didn't hear you say that," Anthony chipped in before I could finish the sentence.

"I think that is irrelevant, the fact is, I said it, and most important of all I said it and meant it and I didn't even think about it – I didn't have to. So in answer to your question, I trust Lloyd one hundred per cent in everything we do, but..." I pause.

"Don't say 'but' and then not finish it, Charlotte!" Anthony demands.

"If you give a girl a chance you would find out that I was

going to finish by saying that everything that Lloyd and I do for now I trust him with, although I am sure that there are going to be times when I question that trust, but I know that my trust will just keep getting bigger and stronger now."

Anthony sits back in his chair. He looks amazed, then says, "Are you sure?"

"Yes."

Anthony looks at Lloyd, raising his eyebrows. I turn and look at Lloyd. What is going on, I ask myself?

"OK, Charlotte, I have another question for you. What is your biggest fear?"

Thinking along the normal lines of spiders, flying, closed spaces, that type of thing, I answer, "I don't have any fears, Anthony, you know that, and to be honest, do you really think that I would tell you if I was frightened by spiders and snakes? I would probably wake up in the morning to find everything covered in them."

"That's interesting, so you don't have any fears... What about coming down into The Room with me, then?" asks Lloyd.

"I don't fear The Room, not at all," I say bravely, but deep down I do. What have you done to yourself now? I grimace inside. It's OK, Lloyd wouldn't be so stupid as to take me to The Room and leave me there, would he? I can control most things now anyway, and when Lloyd is with me I trust him, so what have I got to fear?

"Well, in that case, I will take you to The Room today and have a little one-on-one time together, what do you say?"

"Yes, Lloyd!" I hold my head up high. I am not having them all laughing at me again today, it just isn't going to happen.

Lloyd leans in to me and says quietly, "You don't have

to if you don't want to – the time is now to say. I know and heard everything you have said over the last few days, but I want you to be sure of this."

"Lloyd, I have said yes!"

"It sounds like game on to me then, Lloyd," Anthony says. "Kat and I will be there too if either of you need us," he adds.

After we finish we leave the hotel and make our way back to Lloyd's. Lloyd goes into the office and I go to the bedroom while Anthony and Kat sit in the lounge with some coffee. By the time I finish unpacking the overnight bag and putting things away, Lloyd joins me in the bedroom.

"Charlotte, I know this is a big step for you but I do wonder if you are truly ready. Your last experience was not a very nice one."

"I have said that I will go down."

"You will have to keep control." He walks over to me, putting his arms around me for a cuddle. What, no throwing me on the bed for a spank, or over his knee? This isn't like him – for the sake of a sub, I called him a Dom from hell right into his ear. There is no way he should be giving me a cuddle.

"Are you OK, Lloyd?" I ask.

"Yes, fine! Why do you ask?"

"Oh, nothing, I just thought maybe you were a little tired from last night?"

"No, not really, I just want to make sure you are ready for the next step. I don't want you to go too quickly or to say something that you might be feeling brave about, but in reality you are not ready for, that's all. Anthony is very impressed with your attitude this morning but he is also a little hesitant that you may not be ready for this."

"Oh come on, I am ready, you know that. I kept control yesterday, didn't I, in the hotel?"

"Yes, but we have only been playing and now I want you to know that this is just as serious, and that downstairs you have to take control. The other users will expect you to behave like a regular sub. You know, 'Yes, sir', 'No, sir' – the very things you find so difficult to do, and you also know that if you don't you will be spanked in front of them to show that I am your Dom and that I will correct you, if needed."

"But you said you don't play with other Doms and their subs!"

"I don't, but sometimes we might be down there with friends just chatting, or at a demonstration. If you are disrespectful then something has to be done about it. Come, sit." He takes my hand and we sit on the sofa.

"I think we do need some rules for when we are downstairs, and I think we should talk them over first. Now, we can do this by ourselves or we can do this with Anthony and Kat so that you know that Kat plays with the same rules when she is downstairs. Up to you."

"Well, I trust you not to give me rules that the others don't have."

"That's the point, Charlotte – not everyone has the same rules, but we have stricter rules as we are the owners. We don't play with others unless it's a demonstration, we don't allow ourselves to be compromised in any way, so we have to keep to those rules. The only time anyone has ever seen us playing is when we are in a demonstration, and that is it. Oh yes, if it's a party for charity, we all have to come up with something to demonstrate."

"So what's the problem? You just tell the big fat Dom that is giving me hassle to back off. You have said it yourself – you are an owner and they can't take advantage of your subs."

"No, Charlotte, that isn't what I said, and the phrase 'big fat Dom' isn't going to save your arse downstairs, is it, or do you think you will be able to say to me, 'That big fat Dom is provoking me into saying disrespectful things'? No, Charlotte, I don't think so. You have seen Kat and Anthony behaving normally up here and out. But you have also seen Kat being very submissive with Anthony, up here and downstairs. You have seen her demonstrating – she does everything Anthony asks of her. She doesn't say, 'That big fat Dom has said something I don't like.'"

"But how will you know if I have a problem with someone if I don't tell you?"

"I will know."

"And will you stop them from doing whatever it is they are doing if you think they are out of order?"

"Charlotte, get one thing straight here: no one, but no one, will ever lay a finger on you if you don't wish it, and no one, but no one, will ever lay a finger on you if *I* don't wish it. I am not into sharing in any way, unless it's a demonstration, and even then you have to be one hundred per cent happy with what might be going on. That is a rule of the club, and no one will ever break that rule."

"Oh come on, Lloyd, you know that your rules can be broken and you know that things go wrong sometimes – you can't promise me that."

"I can promise that when we are in the club if you behave in a fashion that is correct you will never be spanked and you will never come to any harm by anyone else."

"But what if we get separated?"

"You know George will always look out for you, and you know that Anthony, Kat, Sophie or Nats will be there somewhere – you just have to look out for them and make sure they know you are on your own and where you will be. They will make sure you will be safe."

"Right, so no calling Doms big or fat – got it. So are we going downstairs now?"

"No, not quite, there is something else that you're not very good at."

Oh, here we go – he is going to point out every single one of my faults, as if I haven't got enough to think about.

"If for any reason you feel like you are losing control or you can't handle a situation, please excuse yourself from the room."

"What do you mean, excuse myself? I am not a child, I don't have to ask to go to the toilet, do I?"

"Charlotte, please, that isn't what I am saying here. If you were at a formal dinner and you wished to leave the table you would politely ask to be excused, wouldn't you?"

"Well of course I would, I am not ignorant, Lloyd."

"Right, so what is the problem here then? If you were to say, 'Please may I be excused?' I would automatically say yes. I would also follow you out of the room to ensure that nothing had happened I wasn't aware of, with either someone touching you or saying something to you, or if it was that you needed five minutes to yourself. If you had asked because you wanted five minutes I would know by your body language – part of keeping you safe and happy is knowing – but sometimes something may happen that you don't like. I might be deep in conversation and miss something, so you excusing yourself will tell me you need me to pay attention to you as well, but it's much nicer to do it this way than by you stamping your feet and calling me a Dom from hell, don't you think?" He raises his eyebrows as if to say, I haven't forgotten this morning's little foot-stamp.

I feel my cheeks burning as they turn red with embarrassment, and I lower my head. As always the points he makes are perfectly correct, but at the time of speaking my excellently timed comments are always perfectly correct to me too, and yet again Lloyd has managed to make me feel just inches high with a few well-chosen words and a look.

"Lloyd, is there nothing that makes you lose your temper?"

"No, Charlotte, I have worked hard for many years on controlling my feelings and my body. Loss of temper is negative and has negative results, usually ending up with either both parties or just one person getting hurt physically or mentally, and there is usually no way back to start again. I would rather work things out calmly and rationally in a language I can understand than lose my temper, shouting and screaming obscenities at another person. I like to think that I am more productive because I don't shout and lose my temper with people."

"So you would never shout at me?"

"No, not in temper. I would never do anything in temper, I have told you that."

"That isn't what I asked, Lloyd – I asked would you ever shout at me?"

"I might shout at you if I thought you were in danger and I couldn't get to you, yes, so now you know that if ever you hear my voice raised, you must listen to it." He grins. "Charlotte, joking aside I can honestly say I wouldn't hurt you, not like you have been in your vanilla relationships. If by any chance I did hurt you it would be purely accidental, nothing malicious at all."

"Well, I don't know if that is good or bad. I don't want to get hurt accidentally or on purpose."

"Charlotte, I don't want to hurt you at all – that is why we have rules, so that I don't." Lloyd looks at me, a little exhausted.

"But—"

"No buts, rules are there to protect you and me. Different people have different rules, they play differently, so it is important to remember that whatever they are, Dom or sub, they will be playing because that is what they want to do, and you have to respect their rules and most importantly their choice in what they are doing – no one is forced to do anything here."

"OK, I understand that."

He places his hand on my knee, looking at me.

"I hope you do, because you can have so much fun if it's done correctly, and safely."

"Well, it doesn't seem like it's going to be fun with all the rules, the dos and don'ts – I will be exhausted just thinking about them and making sure that I don't upset any Doms. They seem to me to be very precious."

"No, it's respect, just respect, that is all I am asking from you. No matter what happens you keep in control and you keep your respect as well. One other thing – do not do anything, and I am talking body language as well, that will provoke or entice another Dom."

He gets up, walks over to the drawers and takes out a pair of my leather shorts and a little matching leather crop top, both in powder pink. God, I will look like an overgrown Barbie doll, for the love of a sub.

"How the hell are you expecting me not to look provocative in those?"

"Charlotte, please get changed and I will see you in the lounge." With that he turns and walks out of the room, shaking his head left to right.

I quickly get changed, then go outside to the lounge. Kat and Anthony are no longer there, and Lloyd is standing holding the door open, ready to go.

I walk over to him and he takes my hand as he leads me out of the apartment to the lift.

"Ready, Charlotte?" he asks, looking at me with a slightly worried glaze on his face.

"Yes, Lloyd, ready!"

"Good," he says, kissing me on the forehead.

Chapter Fourteen

Once downstairs, still holding my hand he gives it a squeeze and he walks us to the punishment room where the nutter... I feel my body go stiff and my heart start to race. Shit, don't let me down now. I can do this, I must do this. He isn't there, I know he isn't. Lloyd is with me, I will be fine. I start to calm down.

"You OK?"

Closing my eyes and taking a deep breath, I open my eyes and answer, "Yes."

"Let's get it over with then, Charlotte." He opens the door and we enter.

My eyes are darting around the room, taking in everything. Good, no whips – everything is where it should be. Kat and Anthony are over by the window talking. Sophie and someone I presume to be her Dom are standing at the back of the sofa. Sophie is bent over holding her ankles, and her Dom is at the back of her with a paddle in his hand. This is good – too many people in here for anything bad to happen. I start to calm down.

"Hi, everyone," Lloyd announces. Everyone answers simultaneously.

"Hi, Lloyd."

Lloyd squeezes my hand reassuringly.

"Hi, Charlotte." Sophie's head pops out between her arm and leg.

Swipe – the paddle hits her arse. My eyes jerk closed and open again, and my body goes rigid.

"It's OK, Charlotte, come here and talk with me," she says. As I look at Lloyd and he releases my hand, I go over and bend down to look at Sophie.

"Didn't that hurt?" I whisper.

"No, not at all."

"Is this your Dom?"

"Oh sorry, Charlotte, I didn't realise you didn't know him. Yes, it is. Steve, hun, this is Charlotte, Charlotte, this is Steve."

I look up at him sheepishly. He is a well-built man and very tall, dressed in leather trousers with a very clingy white T-shirt, blonde hair and green eyes, and very kissable lips that smile down on me.

"Hi!"

"Ah, so you are the Charlotte I hear so much about. Hello, Charlotte, it's nice to meet with you after so long."

"Yes, and you, erm, it's nice to meet you!" I look back at Sophie. "He is very nice, very good-looking."

Swipe – he lands a direct hit on her arse, and still she doesn't move.

"Yes, he is."

"Why is he paddling your arse so hard, are you being punished?"

"No, Charlotte, I am getting ready for a charity event we are putting on. People will pay ten pounds for a paddle to swipe my arse – if they can make me go 'ouch' they will get their tenner back."

Swipe!

Not a sound, not even an eye-clench in pain.

"I don't think many will be getting their money back from you!"

Sophie laughs. "That's why I am training, to toughen me up."

"Are you tough enough for a charity paddle, Charlotte?" Steve asks.

Swipe.

No, oh shit, a thousand swarming subbing bees have just stung the hell out of my arse. I fall, crumpling, clutching my arse as I fall, muttering.

"I see not." I hear everyone laughing. No, no, that isn't supposed to happen, no one is supposed to touch me.

"For the love of a sub, what the hell was that for?"

"Charlotte." Lloyd tries to cut me off in mid-sentence.

"You said no one would touch me – what for the sake of a sub's arse was that?"

"I am glad she fell to the floor, Lloyd, or I would just have to have another go. I bet you have such good fun with her, though, I know I would."

"Charlotte, here, let me help you up!" Lloyd offers his hand. Everyone else in the room has gone deathly silent. Placing my hand in his, he helps me up. Keeping a firm grip on my hand, he leads me to a sofa.

"Excuse us for a moment, I have to explain something to Charlotte."

Lloyd sits down, looks up at me and shakes his head in a no fashion, and then over his knee I am.

"Lloyd, no!"

Slap.

"Lloyd, you said no one would ever touch me without permission, this is out of order."

Slap.

"Do you not remember the very last thing I said to you?"

Slap.

"Lloyd, I can't remember anything when you are slapping my arse so hard."

Slap.

"I think I said do not provoke or entice a Dom. Watch your body language."

Slap.

"Lloyd, I was not being provocative or enticing whatsoever. I was having a conversation with Sophie. I just think that is so rude of you."

Slap.

"I also said to keep in control and be respectful at all times, no matter what happens. So what part of that was controlled and respectful, Charlotte?"

Slap.

"That's more than five! For the sake of a sub's arse, my arse feels like a hundred bees have stung it and now you are slapping the hell out of it!"

Slap.

"That's it, Lloyd, quit. Stop, that's well over five!"

"I am not counting, Charlotte, and did I say you could count?"

"No, Lloyd, but you said a lot of things this morning and I don't see you sticking to those rules."

"Yes, Charlotte, we did talk about a lot of things but you haven't taken them in, have you?"

Slap.

"Please, Lloyd, please don't and I am not counting, I just know it's over five."

Slap.

"Charlotte, can you please try and remember the word 'respect' at all times?"

Slap.

"Lloyd!" I kick my legs up and down in an attempt to try and make him stop.

Slap.

He bends his head down and whispers in my ear, "Are you having fun, Charlotte?"

"Lloyd, you said that no one would touch me without permission, so do you think I am having fun when you allowed Steve to paddle my arse with a thousand bee stings attached to the paddle?"

Slap.

"Charlotte, you were bent over with your arse in the air. Sophie explained to you the first time we came in here that it is so tempting, provocative even, to a Dom. If I had had a paddle in my hands I would have done it myself."

Slap.

"OK, I get the picture, now will you let me up please?"

I sigh with relief.

"Yes, Charlotte, let's see how long we can go now without you changing the game."

Slap.

"Ouch, what was that for? You said you wouldn't spank me in front of anyone."

Slap.

"I said I didn't want to but I would if it was needed, and I don't think I was unreasonable to expect you to keep control and to be respectful, do you?"

OK that should be a 'no' answer, I know that, but my mouth just isn't there with my head. Oh no, I had to say something else, didn't I?

"Well, Lloyd, if you didn't have such precious friends…"

Slap, slap, slap.

"Let me stop you right there, Charlotte, before you get into more trouble."

"Ouch, Lloyd, please!"

"Yes, Charlotte."

Slap.

"Lloyd, please, I have had enough explaining."

Slap, rub.

Yes, a rub, thank the subs for that.

"Please, Charlotte, keep control of your body, mind and most importantly your mouth."

"Yes, Lloyd," I say through gritted teeth.

He flips me up and sits me on his knee, and sitting back into the sofa, he cuddles me tight into him, rubbing the top of my thigh.

"Now that your first public spanking is over with, and now that you know that I will do it, maybe you will remember more of what I explain to you. The rules are there to keep you safe. You are also responsible for keeping yourself safe, no matter where you are or what you are doing. Keep safe, keep in control. Lose control and you will always lose the argument – as soon as you start shouting, using unacceptable language, you have lost the argument. That's not only in here, it's everywhere. Keep control and people will listen to you. You have more of a chance to change the outcome. Surely you can see that, Charlotte?"

"Yes, I can, Lloyd. I used to be able to keep control, I am a nurse after all, but I don't know what has happened to me."

"What has happened to you is that you have been bullied and taken advantage of. You have your emotions muddled and you have become aggressive – it's a defence mechanism. But instead of being defensive in a controlled manner you have become aggressive – we just need to turn it all around. You are doing well, and you will get it."

Swipe.

"God, doesn't she ever say 'ouch'? They have been doing that all that time and not even an ouch?"

Lloyd laughs. "It's just practice, Charlotte. It's all control – being paddled, everything here, is just a matter of practice."

"I'm never going to get it, am I?" I look at Lloyd with sadness in my eyes.

"Yes, you will, and when you do you will have all the control you need to handle every situation you are in, whatever you choose to do."

I look over to the window where Kat and Anthony are standing, still talking, and Sophie and Steve are still swiping away, not even shocked a little or bothered at what Lloyd has just done to me. Why haven't any of them had a reaction to Lloyd and his behaviour towards me? Why haven't any of them said anything, not even an, 'Are you OK, Charlotte?'

"Why are they all so blasé about you spanking me?" I ask Lloyd.

"Because it is normal in here. If, on the other hand, and make no mistake about this, if for one minute they thought I was hitting you with anger, or if they thought you were really distressed, they would question my actions, and they would put a stop to it."

"Well, that's nice to know – so how would they know the difference? After all, I was yelling and shouting for you to stop!"

"They will know, just as you knew that Sophie was in trouble, when you entered the room and realised the man who came in wasn't her Dom."

He kisses me on the head.

"Look and watch. We shall have a little experiment. I will put you over my knee and spank you. Watch Anthony and Kat, watch what they do!"

He releases me from his grip and places me over his knee.

"Lift your head so you can see them and I will spank you after three circle rubs."

I lift my head, placing my elbow on the edge of the sofa. I prop my head up so I can see Kat and Anthony clearly. Lloyd starts to circle his hand on my arse.

"OK, I can see them."

"Cool, that's two, last one now."

Slap, rub.

They never even look up, they don't move.

"See, now I will slap you and shout at you after three again," he whispers to me.

Three smoothing rubs and…

Slap.

"Charlotte, I said NO!" he shouts.

Kat and Anthony both look around, the swish of the paddle stopped in mid-air, and both Steve and Anthony say together, "You OK, Charlotte?"

With my arm still propping my head up, I smile at Anthony and answer, "Yes, Lloyd was just showing me something. Thank you both."

Then Anthony looks at Lloyd. "Are you OK, Lloyd? Never heard you shout before."

"Yes, fine, I was just showing Charlotte how you would react if you thought she was in danger. She thought that you had behaved uncaringly when I spanked her for real, and she didn't think it was normal."

"Oh, OK." Anthony and Kat turn and carry on talking, and I hear the sound of the paddle swishing through the air and then the swipe as it hits Sophie's arse.

Lloyd lifts me back up, setting me back on his knee.

"See, you are perfectly safe – no one will ever let you

get into a situation you don't want to be in. Shouting is an act of losing control, and that does not happen here. People who have lost control are dangerous, not just to themselves but to others around them, so if you hear someone shouting there is something very wrong and someone might need help."

"Anthony said he had never heard you shout before."

"Never. No one here has ever heard me shout apart from just now. I never shout, and there are two firsts in this room today – one of them will be the first and only time, and the other, well, I suspect it will not be the one and only. I suspect that there will be many more occasions."

I look at him, trying to think what he could be meaning.

"Spankings, Charlotte, spankings are what I suspect will happen again, and not me shouting."

"But—"

"No buts. After all, you have been such a good sport so far in here." He places his hand over my mouth. "Now I think maybe a coffee for us all, and some sandwiches. Do me a favour, Charlotte, and go and ask a butler to bring some for all of us, please."

"OK, Lloyd." I get off him and leave to find a butler. I order exactly what Lloyd has told me, and then return. Once inside the room I notice that the men have sat down on the sofas and are huddled over the coffee table; they seem to be deep in conversation. Sophie and Kat are sitting on chairs next to an occasional table. I stand still for a moment, looking first at the girls and then at the men. Oh for the love of a sub, what the hell do I do now? I look back at the girls. Sophie moves her eyes to me for me to come and sit down with them. Sitting down, I ask, "What's going on now?"

"Quietly, Charlotte," Kat says in a soft voice.

"Charlotte, they are discussing things, it's all part of what is happening."

"Well, I think it's very rude of them not to include us in their little secrets," I say with confidence. I hear Lloyd clear his throat; I turn to look, but he isn't even aware of me being back, I don't think.

"No, Charlotte, they are discussing ideas, things they can come up with to make things interesting."

"But shouldn't they include us in that as well?" I ask again. Once more I hear Lloyd clear his throat. I turn, but he is still deep in conversation.

"No, not always. When they first come up with ideas they discuss them with each other and work out the pros and cons, the feasibility of how it could or would work."

"OK, but I still think that they should discuss those sorts of things with us – breaking canes, why does Lloyd keep doing that?" Lloyd clears his throat again.

"I think he is asking you to talk a little quieter maybe, Charlotte!" Kat says.

"Well, why doesn't he say so instead of that throat-clearing stuff? I thought he was getting a throat infection, for sub's sake."

"Charlotte!" I sit bolt upright, eyes open wide, looking at Sophie and then Kat. I mouth at them, That's Lloyd isn't it, he is not happy, and they both nod at me. I turn my head around to see Lloyd looking at me.

"Yes?" I smile sweetly at him.

"Did you order the sandwiches?"

"Yes, Lloyd."

"Good, I want you to eat as much as you can – maybe they will keep you quiet as not much else is working, is it?"

"Yes, Lloyd, I mean no, Lloyd, oh what the heck do I mean? Whatever the answer should be, Lloyd, that is the one I mean!" I'm still smiling sweetly. Lloyd turns around and I start to breathe again and drop the stupid smile, turning to the other two.

"I will never get this, will I?"

"Yes, you will, Charlotte, Lloyd is just tuned into you at the moment and he is finding it very hard as well."

"Why is he finding it so hard? He is the one that belongs to this lifestyle, he hasn't got to get used to people swiping at his backside."

"He is finding it hard because he knows you are not in control, so he feels as if he has to take control for you as well. He is always trying to be a few steps ahead of you, as well as everything else he has to do to keep you safe – it's hard work for him. Everything these three do is carefully worked out. I thought you knew that, Charlotte – have you still not cottoned on to it yet?" snaps Kat.

"Kat, please, I am trying. I really don't understand the rules and everything, let alone what they all do. Apart from spank arses and tie you up I don't really know what else they do, do I?"

"Right, OK, you two. Charlotte, listen – everything is planned. Your weekend, Saturday night, was planned. Kat and I had done similar things during the weeks before, trying them out, seeing what would and could happen in what sort of places. Steve and Anthony made sure we would be OK. It took weeks of planning, more than we would usually do, but Lloyd wants to make sure you have fun with very little to go wrong – he doesn't want to put you off. We can handle most situations because we can stay in control, and although you are doing better, you still have so much to learn. Lloyd is just trying to make you take control, that's all, but he has to make sure that everything is very safe for you."

"Oh, I didn't realise. I *am* sorry if I am getting in the way of your fun."

Sophie rolls her eyes. "You are not getting in the way of anyone's fun. We have enjoyed all the games that we have played while we have been test-driving the games for you, so you are not in the way, in fact, completely the opposite – you are keeping everyone on their toes with the games you are playing, or the games you don't realise you are playing, should I say."

"Charlotte, we all love you but sometimes you can be a little blonde inside that head of yours," Kat says, smiling.

"Yes, a little frustrating is the word I would have used, but blonde fits perfectly." Sophie adds.

I sigh and slump down on the chair. Everyone thinks I am some sort of blonde bimbo now, all because I don't quite understand all their stupid rules.

"Oh come on, don't sulk with us, we are trying to help you," Kat says sweetly.

The butler enters with the tray of sandwiches and coffee and serves us all – Lloyd, Anthony and Steve first, obviously, and then us.

"Well, best stuff my mouth full of sandwiches, I don't want Lloyd to think I am not doing what he has instructed."

They both snigger.

"That's it, Charlotte, back to your old sarcastic self." Kat winks at me.

"Yes, you all want to change me but I just can't change like that overnight, you know."

"No, no one wants you to change, you are refreshing and individual. We want you to take that and get it under control, that's all. We don't want you to change, not one bit, we like you the way you are, but we want you to be safe."

"Why is it you are all saying the same things over and

over? Is this all part of the great plan as well?"

"Don't you think if we are all saying the same thing it might, just might, be right?" Kat says, grabbing another sandwich.

"We came into the lifestyle because we wanted something different. You came into the lifestyle because it has chosen you, not because you were looking for it. It will take you time to get to grips with everything, but you will," Sophie says with a look of despair in her eyes, as if this might take longer than we all thought.

"I am trying to take all this in."

"We know, and it's OK that you don't get it, but you will." And Sophie winks.

I nibble at my sandwich, trying to take in everything they are saying, one minute praising me, the next telling me what I am doing wrong – or it seems like that at the moment.

"You have commented forcefully on everything you disapprove of, but the one thing I thought that you might have something to say about you haven't mentioned once."

Oh, here we go, cryptic time. OK, I give in.

"And what would that be then, Kat?"

"You haven't said one word about Lloyd spanking you with us all here, in fact you didn't disapprove of that at all. Yes, I heard you at the time but that to me was just part of the game you and Lloyd were playing. I think it's your game, Charlotte."

"Well of course I wouldn't disapprove, I like being spanked by Lloyd. It's quite sensual in a way, and I didn't notice you were all here so I wasn't bothered."

"But when Lloyd knew you had had enough, he stopped, didn't he? He didn't stop as soon as you asked because he can read you, just the same as you can read him. You knew he was unhappy with you when he called your name out, and you went rigid. You read him by the tone of his voice, you are getting it."

"But how do you know the games we play, or does he tell you every little thing like I suspect he does?" I open my eyes wide and look at Kat as if to say, See, I know.

"No, he doesn't tell us anything, in fact most of the time we guess by reading you, your reaction to things. Don't forget we play very similar games, so it's not too hard to work you out at all."

"But how? I don't understand."

"We don't know all the games you play or how many at once you might be playing, but sometimes we can say something and you will go bright red, a tell-tale sign of what you might have done," Sophie points out.

"Charlotte, Lloyd is constantly playing with you, every text, every note, all mind games of one sort or another to see what mood you are in, to see what response he will get, so he knows where he can take off from in his next game when he sees you. It's no use him seeing you and spraying champagne over you and him risking a black eye or something, is it?" Sophie says, trying to contain the sniggers as she mentions champagne.

"See, he has told you all exactly what we are doing."

"No, he was on the phone to Anthony when you did it, and Anthony was down here with us and he had the loudspeaker on. He was trying to make sure that we were all happy with the games we had tried out for you when you did it, and just for the record that was classic, but I bet he didn't let you get away with it, did he?"

"No he didn't, and I am not going to tell you what he did either."

"Well worth it, though. You give him a run for his money,

Charlotte, but I do think Lloyd would be happier if—"

"Oh come on, Sophie, he is more than happy, he is content, very content, being with Charlotte." Kat cuts in.

"Do you think so, Kat?"

"Yes, I do. He is relaxed, he doesn't spend every waking minute at work like he used to, he can't wait for the weekends for Charlotte to be staying with him. Never before has he been so comfortable with someone else."

"Now that you mention it, I suppose he is, Kat." And they both look over to Lloyd, automatically making me look at him as well.

Lloyd is deep in conversation. While Anthony and Steve speak I try to listen to what they are saying, but I can't quite make out the words. I will have to get hearing aids to spy on them, I think, then maybe I will get one step ahead of them.

Then Kat says, "So you see, Charlotte, you have a player and a stayer in Lloyd. He will not give up on you, not until you get it, and he is sure that you will be able to look after yourself. Even then I am sure he will want to take things further. So you had best start learning how to read him properly," she says, picking up her coffee mug.

"Oh, that I am doing, but..."

"But what?" Kat says with interest, leaning forward so she doesn't miss anything.

"OK, we still haven't fucked yet."

"So what is the problem with that?" Sophie asks.

"Well for one thing, it's frustrating the hell out of me!"

"Charlotte, relationships aren't all about fucking." Oh God, Kat, here you go, sounding more and more like Lloyd.

"I know we will when the time is right, Lloyd has told me that, but there have been moments when the time has been right, I know there have, I have read his body language and he is up for it to happen, but something always happens."

"Like what?" Sophie also moves closer on her chair.

"Well, we will be past the point of no return and that first rocket will have taken off and is just about to burst, to be followed by all the other fireworks exploding one by one, then it should be a grand finale of them all bursting at once, but no, not for us – the first rocket takes off and then it fizzles. And what makes it fizzle, you may well ask – it's either the time isn't right, an alarm on his phone or his beeper, or I open my mouth and say something and before I know it I am off him, he is up, going off to get more to eat or a knock on the door. We just don't get to the first rocket exploding."

"Oh, Charlotte, you are funny. It's not Lloyd, it's circumstances – or you!"

"How do you mean, me?"

"Well, I assume when you have said something you have changed the game again."

And they laugh.

"Oh, oh, it's all right for you two laughing at me, you know what games you are playing – I don't! Do you know, I have nightmares of us being on a desert island together all alone, where everything is right, and either a coconut falls on his head, or a turtle sneaks up on us and bites his ankle, and oh yes, Charlotte is left frustrated and hanging while Lloyd hops around the beach. No, no, this isn't funny!"

And with that the small laughter turns into big, bellowing laughter, as they just can't contain themselves anymore.

"Oh, that's right, laugh away at my expense, why don't you?" I snap.

"Oh, Charlotte, that is just one of the funniest things I have heard," Kat says, wiping tears from her eyes.

"Charlotte, would you like to explain your joke to us?" Oh pants, Lloyd. I had forgotten they were here, for the sake of a sub's arse.

"I thought last night and the chocolate was funny, but this is just so…" Kat says between her uncontrollable laughter.

"My, my, Charlotte, you have managed so much today." Lloyd is standing right behind me, and is talking quietly into my ear. "I asked you a question and not only didn't you answer it, but you didn't even acknowledge I was talking with you. Would you like to explain what they are in hysterics over?"

"No, Lloyd, the answer is obviously no. I would like to be excused, if you wouldn't mind. I am going to find it very hard not to contain myself in a manner that you obviously mistook for me being able to control." With that I get up and walk outside, leaving the door ajar so I can still hear them. Lloyd stays in the room with the others and I can hear the girls trying not to say what I said that had amused them so much.

They try to distract the men by saying, "Charlotte! You can't hold us accountable for the things she says, they have no relevance whatsoever!" And then Kat says, "Oh come on, guys, she is human and this is why we all like her so much, isn't it? Let her have her secrets too – now leave it at that."

Lloyd comes out to see where I am. By the time he opens the door I am sitting on a step. He comes to sit beside me.

"You OK?" he asks in a soft voice.

"Yes, but I don't know why people have to laugh at me so much!"

"It's because you make them, but they love you for it – you make them happy."

"Do I? And what about you, Lloyd, do I make you happy too?"

"Yes, Charlotte, you do. I am always happy with you for all sorts of reasons." He cuddles me. "So are you going to tell me what made them laugh so much?"

"No."

"They will not tell us either."

"Will they not? Maybe it's because it's the code of a sub not to let on what another sub has said."

"Nope! No such thing, Charlotte. It's because they are your friends, and it's the code of friendship, I should think."

"Oh what, like really friends, and not just because I am your sub?"

"Yes, I guess so, and you are not just a sub either, you are my friend, my partner, the person I trust to share my innermost desires with. You are and always will be the naughtiest sub I have ever known. You are uncontrollable, but you are working on it. And most of all, you don't ever change."

I sit astride him on the step, putting my arms around his neck. Putting nose to nose, I ask, "Do you really mean all that?"

"Yes, I do, and I am sorry I haven't told you before. I should have done, it's just the moment has been interrupted or something has happened that meant I just didn't get the chance. There are so many things I need you to understand, but this is the most important by far."

And he kisses me, a good kiss, a long and hard kiss and drop-dead kiss from heaven. I wriggle my arse as shivers dance lightly up and down my spine. It's then that I realise for the first time that my body is so in tune with everything he does, it's like my body's reactions are as one with his, and I like this feeling so much. I have never experienced such a delightful pleasure with anyone else. After we finish kissing I look him in the eye.

"Thank you, Lloyd, for teaching me and sharing with me."

"That's OK, Charlotte, the pleasure is all mine." He winks. "Shall we go and join the others again?"

I smile and nod yes. I lift myself off him and he stands up, taking my hand.

"Ready?"

"Yes." And we go back in.

Sophie and Kat are now sitting on the sofas with Anthony and Steve.

"Nothing! It's the first time since we have been down here she has had nothing to say," Lloyd says, and he shrugs his shoulders.

"Yup, these two are the same! Not a word about what Charlotte has said to make them laugh so much, and it's the first time that Kat hasn't told me something when I have asked."

"Charlotte, what are we going to do with you? Our subs are getting to be as naughty as you are!" Steve adds with a chuckle in his voice.

Lloyd leads me to the sofas and we sit down.

"Charlotte, we need to toughen your arse up with a paddle so you can have some real fun, then you will not crumple in a heap on the floor every time you have a little slap."

Steve, who do you think you are? For the love of a sub, you hit my arse and ripped its skin off, of course I am going to be a crumpled mess on the floor, I think as I glared at him in terror.

"Your face, Charlotte, is a picture." He laughs at me.

"I see, it's a joke! Ha, ha, very funny, Steve."

"No, it's not a joke, we are being deadly serious. You will get the hang of it – it's all in the way you stand. You have to keep your breathing under control and you have to relax." OK, now he wants me to stand holding my ankles with my arse up in the air while I keep breathing and relax – does he think I am out of my mind? My mouth drops open just trying to think about doing all of that while I know someone is going to swipe my arse at a thousand miles an hour – no, he must be out of his tiny mind.

I look around at Lloyd for him to save me from this very one-sided conversation, as my mouth has decided to go on a holiday.

"You're up for that, aren't you, Charlotte?" What, what, Anthony as well? You want to paddle me as well?

"Oh well, Lloyd, if you think it's OK then it must be, but if you just wanted me on my knees you should have just asked, not got your friends to pretend this is an arse-toughening exercise."

"Charlotte, there is no pretence, this is reality. Now are you going to have a go?"

"Yes, Lloyd," I answer, tossing my head away from his glare.

"OK, Charlotte, come over here and I will show you a few tricks. This will help," says Sophie.

I follow her to an open space in the room.

"Feet apart so they are in line with your shoulders, then take a couple of deep breaths slowly. That's it, nice and deep."

I breathe long and deep.

"OK, next just flop forward, let your hands and arms dangle, followed by a few more deep breaths."

I flop and dangle everything, breathing deeply. Mmm, yes, this is quite relaxing.

"Now with both your hands, grab your ankles, but still remember to breathe."

I clasp my ankles with my hands, breathing as I go, closing my eyes as I relax. This is what they must call sub yoga; I think it's very relaxing, I must say. As I relax, deep breathing slowly, I am aware of Sophie saying something about my arse – it sounds like 'wriggle your arse'. So I wriggle my arse.

Swipe.

Shit! Fuck!

"For the love of a sub!" He swiped my arse, someone has swiped my arse! I fall to the ground, still clutching my ankles, straight onto my head. Lloyd's hands come down and move my hair from my face.

"You OK?" And that soft, sweet smile he has when he is not sure of what my reaction is going to be sweeps across his face.

"Why the hell did you do that? I was enjoying subs' yoga for sub's sake, Lloyd!"

"You OK, ready to go again?" And he holds out his hand and helps me up.

Sophie is again standing upright. When I finally manage to keep my balance she says,

"You wriggled your arse, I said *don't* wriggle your arse, that means you are ready."

"Oh, that's right, just tell me half the subbing story," I mumble under my breath.

"Problem, Charlotte?" Lloyd asks as I assume the position of legs apart. Don't even answer him, you can do this, it just takes control; flop forward, breathe.

"That's it, Charlotte, good," Sophie says with encouragement. Clasp ankles, breathe – got it – and don't you wriggle your arse. I just stand, breathing, relaxing, floating away the sting of that last swipe. This is nothing like the paddle Lloyd has upstairs; his one is softer and he doesn't take a running leap at my arse with it either. Wake up, wake up, Lloyd is talking to you. I open my eyes and see Lloyd's eyes looking at me.

"Hello, Charlotte, are you OK under here?" He moves away the mountain of cascading hair with his hands so he can see me properly.

"Yes, I am fine thank you, Lloyd, just having five minutes relaxing."

"Oh good, can I help you relax more?" And his eyes light up. Devil horns, I can see you.

"And how…" Before I can say another word he raises his head and kisses me, placing one hand on the back of my head, pulling it a little closer towards him and the drop-dead gorgeous kiss. I start to melt, tingles dancing on my spine. I wriggle my arse, oh no, don't wriggle, I said don't wriggle.

Swipe.

What…what…my hands clench tighter around my ankles and my eyes open wide. Lloyd holds my head, kissing me so I can't pull away. Breaking canes, what? How did he do that? The swipe to my arse dies down as the kiss, the deep-down kiss, takes over again. Wow, this is so good, ecstasy as after the swipe Lloyd's tongue weaves in and out of my mouth. My arse wiggles again.

Swipe!

My body clenches tight and then slowly starts to relax into Lloyd's kiss.

Swipe.

Again my body tightens, but not so much. Lloyd pulls out of the kiss with a few little soft, gentle kisses on my lips, then whispers into my ear, "See, you can do it without having a smart-arse mouth." He gives me a cheeky wink, and just like that, he is gone. Oh, just like him to prove a point in such a devious way. Well, buster, let me tell you, I could have bitten your tongue off, did you have that in your plan for how to control Charlotte? I bet you didn't.

Swipe.

My body tightens. Subbing hell, that one hurt like mad. I look around my legs and Lloyd is holding the paddle with a grin on his face.

"Back to reality, Charlotte?" He holds his hand up for me to get up, and I walk towards him. My legs wobble a little but it's hard to tell if it's the swipes from the paddle or the drop-dead gorgeous kiss he gave me. He cuddles me up and I rub my arse.

"A little intense, Charlotte?"

"No, not intense, it sub…"

Lloyd waves the paddle in the air as if to say, Think before you go on any further.

"See now, you are starting to take control. With a little more help from me than I wanted or expected, I would have to admit, but hey, it's a start. The next thing we have to talk about is your fitness."

I watch the paddle, mouth open as my eyes follow it back and forth as he speaks. Fitness? I am fit!

"There is nothing wrong with my fitness," I protest strongly.

"Come and sit down, we will explain." He walks me back to the sofa and we sit. My arse is a little sore and I fidget as I sit down, trying to find a place that doesn't smart as much.

"Steve runs a gym here."

"What, there is a gym here?" I ask in surprise.

"Yes, it's important to keep fit, keep your muscles working correctly, keep supple, and Steve is just the man for the job."

"Oh no, you can't send me to another Dom for training – I am not going," I protest strongly, and I twist my head away from him.

"Charlotte, please don't. You are going to the gym and Steve is going to be your personal trainer. You need to be fit, agile and toned – it's all part of you taking control of your mind and body."

"I will not treat you in any other way than a professional trainer. When I am in the gym I am not a Dom. It's my work, just the same as I would send Sophie to Lloyd if she was ill – he wouldn't treat her any other way than professionally."

"No, no, no," I persist.

"We all go to the gym to work out, keep fit and toned, you are the only one that doesn't. I have said to you before that you need to go."

"Lloyd, I find it hard to keep up with you now, you are trying to wear me out so you can always get the upper hand."

"No, not at all, and you will go to the gym – even if I have to carry you there kicking and screaming you will go."

"Even if you carry me there kicking and screaming I don't have to do anything, do I?"

I swing my head around and look at him as if to say nah-nah-nah-nah. He looks at me in amazement – that's it, you haven't a reply to that have you, stick that in your Dom pipe and smoke it, huh!

"I am amazed that you think I wouldn't drag you down there. I would make you participate – even if I had to tie you to a machine and switch it on, you would do it."

"Lloyd, I really don't think that it says in the Dom's handbook that you can tie your sub up and leave them strapped to an exercise machine until you are happy they have exercised enough." My eyes widen as I wait for his reply.

"You are going. Steve will be expecting you tomorrow after work and that is that – I don't want to hear another word about it."

"A—"

"Not another word, please," he cuts in on me.

I slouch back on the sofa and fold my arms and legs as if to say 'this sub is closed for the foreseeable future'.

"You are not pouting, are you?"

"Nope." That's it, short and sweet.

"Good." He puts his hand on my leg and gives it a little, loving squeeze. I look around at the others; everyone looks so content and comfortable with their partners, cuddling and chatting.

"Lunch gone down now, Charlotte, ready for the next round?" Lloyd sits forward to see my face.

"I don't want to do any more paddling, thank you, Lloyd," I announce assertively. That will get him, I will spoil his little games.

"That's good because we are not doing that this afternoon." What? Oh pants, I walked straight into that.

"What are we doing, then?" I ask, looking straight into his eyes.

"We are going to another room, just me and you." He winks at me. That's a playful wink; good, it must mean we are going to the fire and ice room, just him and me. It will be so nice to have some gentle, relaxing touching. I smile as if to say OK. With that he's up off the sofa, grabbing my hand and giving it a little squeeze. Game on. We say goodbye to the others and leave.

Chapter Fifteen

In the hallway, instead of going up the stairs as I anticipated, he pulls me towards the stairs that go down.

"Err, Lloyd, you are going the wrong way!"

"No, Charlotte, I am not going the wrong way."

"I think you are, the fire and ice room is this way." And I try to turn and walk to the other stairs.

"Who said we were going to the fire and ice room?"

No, no, no, I didn't clarify what we were doing, no, no.

"So if we are not going to that room, which room are we going to?"

"We are going to face your fears." His grip becomes tighter and he starts the descent of the stairs.

"But I have already said I don't have any fears, we have had this conversation already today."

"In that case, you have nothing to worry about then, do you?"

"If you think locking me in a cellar with spiders is going to make me lose control, you will find out different, Lloyd."

Reaching the bottom of the stairs, Lloyd turns and pulls me towards him. He looks into my eyes.

"Who has said anything about spiders, Charlotte?" He kisses me on the head and returns to leading me along the passageway, then down some more stairs.

"We are here. This is also a practice room, so please keep in control."

He opens the door and pulls me inside, closing the door behind me. I hear the key turn and the door lock as I am looking around. For the love of a sub! I turn, but Lloyd is standing behind me.

"Have your fears caught up with you?"

"Lloyd, this is not funny, let me out, please."

"No, I will not let you out. You said you had no fears and you are not going to have by the time I have finished."

"I really don't want to be in here, why have you brought me to this room?"

"To face your fears. I will ask you again what your fears are."

"You know full well I can't do this, for the sake..."

"Keep control, breathe deep breaths please. Now you have been saying all weekend that you trust me, more than trust me – now is the time to prove it." He puts his arms around me and cuddles me up. "I know this is very hard, but you do have to get a grip on this, I will not hurt you, you know that."

"I really don't want to be here, I want to call time out."

"Time out isn't for things you just don't want to do, it is for when you feel unsafe."

"Well, I feel unsafe."

"And why do you feel unsafe?"

"You know why."

"There isn't anything here that will hurt you, other than yourself, that is. Now let's walk into the middle of the room and then you can open your eyes and look around. I want you to take in as much detail as you can." He walks with me, still cuddling me up in his arms. When we reach the middle he releases me.

"Now look, what do you see?"

I open my eyes to an array of coloured silk scarves hanging on the wall, so many of them, just like a rainbow.

"See, not so bad, is it?"

"Well, scarves are not the problem, are they?"

"Why not?"

"Because they are soft and silky." As I speak I notice that my voice is echoing around. My eyes automatically follow my voice as it bounces off the walls; the walls are stone. As I look up to the ceiling I notice there are chains; following my eye along the chains, there is one end attached to the wall with a giant hook. I follow it back up and it passes through a giant eyelet in the ceiling and then another, before starting its descent to a spreading bar, which has manacles and chains attached. As the line of my eye follows from the chains to the wall behind me, I catch sight of the whips – so many of them, so many sizes. I freeze, my eyes fixed, my body tense.

"Charlotte, how can they hurt you? They are hanging on the wall."

I can't talk.

"Look, this is your biggest fear – whips!" He puts his arm around my shoulders and turns me around so I am facing them.

"Lloyd, I don't know why you have brought me here, you know I don't ever want anything to do with whips, ever."

"They are your fear, your biggest fear. To be in control you have to face your fears, you have to be able to control your reactions, you must be able to show no fear even if you are terrified. This afternoon we are going to play in here, and we are going to get some of that fear turned into a positive. I am going to show you there is nothing to fear. By the time we have finished in this room you will be able to use a whip, every whip, and you will be able to control the way you react with them." He pulls me closer and I lean my head on his shoulder.

"I don't think I am ready for this, Lloyd."

"You are ready. This is your limit, and you can look at them with a small element of calm, and by the time we have finished I am not going to say that you will like them any more, but you will understand them, and the way they are used."

"I don't understand – there are all these whips here, but over here there are silk scarves?"

"Yes – extremes, Charlotte, soft and harsh extremes. Just like fire and ice, it's just a new level or limit."

"But why is this room not decorated? It makes everything echo."

"It is decorated, it's a dungeon, and the echoing is there for effect, to add a little authenticity."

I look down to my feet; we are standing on what I can only describe as play mats. Soft and spongy.

"So why the mats?"

"Well, I have changed that part just for you, to stop you hurting your backside when you fall on it." He laughs.

"Lloyd, I have had enough now, can we go? And please don't laugh at me."

"We are not going anywhere. You are going to play with me today, in here, now."

"Lloyd, I don't want to." My eyes flash across the whips.

"Well what if I promise to leave the whips where they are? I will not touch them."

"Well, your promises aren't holding very well today, Lloyd. They seem very empty."

"My promises are good, it's the way you interpret them. Do you trust me? And it's a yes or no answer, Charlotte."

"Yes," I say, knowing I am not going to win this argument.

"Good, let's play."

He turns to the scarves and takes two down from the wall.

"Here is yours and here is mine. Now I want you to close your eyes and relax. Hold your scarf in both hands so it stretches across your thighs with the rest of the scarf dangling down the sides of your legs." He widens my feet with one of his feet so they are shoulder-width apart. He pulls the top part of my crop top down over my arms, revealing my shoulders.

He whispers softly into my ear, "Right, Charlotte, this is the same as fire and ice, hot and cold sensations, observing the way your body reacts to sensations. I promise you there will be no whips whatsoever." Then he kisses down my neck, sending goose bumps all over my skin, waking up every sense my body has. I then feel the silk scarf drag over my shoulders and slide down my back, soft and gentle, and then back up the other side onto my other shoulder. I feel my hands relax, loosening my grip on the scarf I have hold of.

"Don't drop your scarf, Charlotte," he whispers in my other ear. I clench up the scarf again; now I feel the scarf being drawn across my chest and one end being draped over one of my shoulders and cascading down my back. I feel the other end of the scarf being drawn the other way across my chest, then up onto my shoulder and that also cascades down my back. I feel the excess of the middle part of the scarf rise up towards my neck, and my muscles tighten.

"What's the matter?" Lloyd whispers.

"You are putting the scarf around my neck, I don't like it."

"What do you want to do?"

"I want you to stop."

"So you want to change the game?"

"Yes."

"Relax, you know the scarf isn't going anywhere now. Let your body feel the scarf, and if I have hold of it."

"How do I know if you have hold of it? My eyes are closed."

"The scarf will feel different. Feel the differences, it's all about sensations. You assume I am putting the scarf around your neck, when in reality it's just your mind telling you that's what I am doing. I don't have hold of it at all – open your eyes."

I open my eyes and Lloyd is standing about three feet in front of me, his hands behind his back.

"But you were standing behind me, how did you get there without me knowing?"

"You were only paying attention to the scarf, you weren't paying attention to anything else. You must use all your senses – hearing to listen to everything that is going on. Smell – you can smell where someone is or if someone else has entered the room by their perfume. Some people are very good at smelling things, but some not so good. You are very good at sensations and things that touch you normally, but now you have to get control of everything else, it's just as important."

"I just start getting the hang of things, then you tell me something else I have to get under control. I don't think this is ever going to stop, is it?"

"Yes, but it's important that we learn all the time, not just take it for granted that we are always safe.

"Now your turn. I want you to do the same thing to me, exactly the same, but I want you to watch my reactions, and I mean every reaction, however small you think it might be." He leans forward and takes the scarf from my neck, slowly letting it drift across my skin; my eyes close momentarily with the sensations he causes.

"Change places, Charlotte."

I move as he stands where I was standing. He stands, holding the scarf in his hands, the same as I had done.

"That's not right, I can't pull your T-shirt down like you pulled mine down."

"OK, take it off then."

I step towards him, and releasing one of his hands from the scarf, I then put my hands under his T-shirt. Rubbing my hands up from the top of his leather trousers I can feel his six-pack, then I slowly run my hands around to his back, easing his T-shirt up as I go. I have learnt over the weeks that I get a better reaction from Lloyd if I do things slow and sexy with sensual touching, and this will be no different. I raise his arms with mine and pull the T-shirt up and off his head. I take one step back as I let it fall to the floor. He does have such a fine body; looking at it, he could be a Roman god with that six-pack. I step forward to place the scarf back in his hand, the way it was before removing the T-shirt.

I move my head to his ear and whisper, "I want you to close your eyes." As I lean up to his ear I make sure that my foot is in between his, and tap his feet to make him stand the way he made me stand, but with one difference: I am sure that the top of my hip made contact with his groin. I step back again, looking at his face. It looks so restful and calm. My eyes wander down to his six-pack. There are more fitting things I would like to do with him right now than to run a scarf over him; I wonder if I could get away with anything else?

"Charlotte, the instructions were only to do what I did to you."

"Yes, Lloyd," I reply, startled at him talking and guessing that I might not be following what he had said. My eyes dart over his face and body as I try to quietly walk around him to start tantalising his body. I notice his eyes under his eyelids moving and following in the direction I'm stepping. I stop, and his eyes stop. I move back to where I was and his eyes follow me again. Huh, it must be because I have shoes on; he can hear them. He hasn't got shoes on, I notice, looking at his feet. I kick my shoes off quietly and Lloyd smiles slightly. OK, again this time I will step one way, then the other to see if he knows where I am. I step, his eyes are with me; I step again and they are still there. OK, he has very good hearing, I knew that anyway. But I didn't realise it was as good as this. As I get further around his left side he moves his head slightly, just slightly; if I wasn't watching I wouldn't have noticed. OK, so I am on his left side, he is expecting me to touch his left side.

I raise the end of the scarf in my right hand and slowly move it around the back of his neck, careful not to touch him. He moves his head slightly to his right, then with my left hand I raise the scarf and slowly draw it down his left shoulder from the front to the back. His initial reaction is to move his head back to the front; his skin shivers with goose bumps. I then lay the scarf on his right shoulder; the reaction, just a small shiver. I let the scarf cascade down his back and nothing, or nothing that I can see, anyway. I move around to his back and then to his right side; he again moves his head with me as I turn around his side. I drape the scarf over his shoulder, then walking slowly to his front, I draw the other end of the scarf over his chest; he draws in a deep breath. As I do this, placing the scarf over his shoulder with the middle draping down his chest, I move back around his right side to the back of him, giving both ends of the scarf a small tug. The scarf starts to tighten and draw up to his neck. I try to walk quietly and quickly to the front of him but oh no, splat on my knees. For the love of a sub.

"Charlotte, I told you to watch every reaction. In your haste you missed the fact that I had moved my foot." Lloyd looks down at me, holding his hand out to help me up.

"That was a little below the belt, don't you think?"

"No, not at all." He pulls me up and close to him. "But you did very well, you read me very well. You noticed my head, and I think you noticed my eyes?"

"Yes I did, that was the first thing I noticed. But why move at all when you can't see?"

"No, but if I need to open my eyes I will be looking straight at what I can hear, and I listen also by moving my head to keep any noise as close to my ears as I can. So now I have shown you that and you have calmed down a little, are you ready for the next game in here?"

"Yes, I like these soft games, very sensual, isn't it?"

"Yes it is. Stand here." He goes over to the scarves and takes down another. Then he picks up an eye mask and returns.

"Right, no peeping at all." He places the eye mask on top of my head.

"It's no use asking what we are going to be doing, is it?"

"No, Charlotte. Hands behind your back, I want to tie them up."

I place my hands behind me, and using the scarf I had, he ties up my hands.

"Right, this scarf is a little thicker than the silk ones and it gives different sensations. It's satin."

He takes it off his shoulder and runs it down my chest; it is just as soft, but heavier.

"Right, you ready? Remember, keep control."

I nod yes and he lowers the eye mask.

He moves in front of me, slowly at first. I can hear him,

and I feel the scarf on my leg. I jump – I wasn't expecting that.

"Stand still, Charlotte."

Turn around; he is behind me.

Whip!

What was that?

Whip.

Whip.

I feel the slight rush of air whipping past my legs. No! No.

"Lloyd, no, you said you wouldn't use a whip, you have a whip?" I start frantically moving.

"No I don't. Stay in control and stop moving."

Whip.

Shit, that hurts.

"For the sake of a sub, you just whipped my leg, you have a whip?"

"Charlotte."

Whip, whip.

Straight on my arse. And then he rubs my leg, where he got me the first time.

"It's OK, you can take that out of what you owe me."

"Lloyd, I don't think this is good, you are using a whip. I can't think, you are scaring me."

"I am not using a whip."

Whip. I feel the air rush again across my legs.

"Lloyd, you will hurt me very much, it will mark me for life."

"It will not, I am not doing it that hard. Stand still, take control. I am not using anything different to what I was before."

I twist with his voice, following him, or I think I am. Then a boom of sound as my name echoes around the room.

"Charlotte, Charlotte." From every corner I can hear

his voice. I have lost all sense of direction. I stand stock-still, trying to hear, but I can't hear anything other than the echoing of Lloyd's voice. I spin around frantically, trying to see where he is.

"Where the sub are you? Don't, Lloyd, this is not the game we are playing."

"Yes it is; sensations, keeping in control. You have to keep in control of everything. Use what you have to keep in control."

Whip.

Whip.

"Ouch." Straight on my arse with pinprick precision. I try to release my hands from the scarf, but it just gets tighter around my wrists.

"Breaking Doms' canes, you made me a promise no whips, and you have broken your promise."

"No I haven't, I have told you it's what your brain perceives because you are letting yourself lose control of everything. Now take control."

Whip, whip, I feel the air rush past my knees.

"I hate you and your stupid subbing games," I snap.

Whip, whip.

Again, another direct hit to my arse.

"Ouch, Lloyd, it hurts, do I have a subbing target on my arse?"

"No, but that could be an idea. Thanks, Charlotte, you are very good at coming up with things, maybe I should get shorts made with bullseyes on them, then we can have proper target practice." All the time he is moving, and I am just spinning around and around, trying to keep up with him.

Whip, whip.

Again, direct to my arse.

"Stop now, please, I feel like the donkey."

"Donkey, Charlotte, what donkey?"

"The donkey you pin a tail on, what other donkey is there? Now subbing stop!"

Whip, whip.

"Shit, Lloyd, you are well out of order."

"Take control." The word 'control' echoes around the room loud and fast; my head starts spinning.

"Lloyd, please," I shout, and that starts echoing as well. I start to panic, and I feel like I want to run as fast as I can.

"Take control of this, you can do it," he whispers into my ear. He is next to me, and I kick out in the direction that I think he is in.

"Tut, tut, Charlotte, I'm not there and kicking isn't in the rules, now take control."

Whip, whip.

"Well, I might be able to take control if you didn't keep whipping me, the very thing I hate the most, the very thing you know will bring me to my knees, Lloyd. Why do you have to be so hard on me?"

"I'm not hard on you, you are being hard on yourself. Now come here, come to my voice."

I move towards his voice, and he lifts the blindfold off my eyes.

"Now look around you – is there a whip? Is there anything in my hands that I didn't have when we began?"

I look at his hands, then quickly to the wall with all the whips hanging on it – they are all still there, every single one, and none of them are moving or look like they have been moved.

"I have told you, it's what your mind perceives. At the moment you are just thinking 'whips' because you think the worst. Well, this is going to change the way you think about everything, and it is going to help you with your control."

I look back at him.

"What were you doing?"

He puts his hands behind my back, and holding me tight, he unties my hands.

"Here, sit on the floor and I will explain."

I sit down.

"I don't understand any of this, Lloyd, not at all."

"I asked you to keep control, you lost your control – your perception was lost as well as your sense of direction. You were panicking, and your mouth was going dry. How am I doing so far?"

"Well, if you knew all that why didn't you just stop?"

"Charlotte, I knew because I was in control, I was still reading your body language, your reactions, and I knew you were safe."

"So you knew I was safe, well, I could have fallen over my shoes and broken my neck for all you would have cared." Holding up my hand, I point to where I left my shoes.

"No you wouldn't, I moved them." Lloyd points in a completely different direction. I follow the line of his hand, then do a double take and flick my head around to where I left my shoes. Yep, the Dom from hell moved my shoes. My mouth drops open.

"How do you do it?"

"I bent down, picked them up and placed them out of the way."

"Not my shoes!" I roll my eyes. "How do you keep such control always? How do you see things that might happen, to eliminate them out of the equation?"

"I have practised for years, I keep telling you, but it's important to me, Charlotte, that you keep control of everything all the time."

"But it's easy for you, you are the one who invents the

games, you know what is going to happen."

Lloyd laughs, tilting his head back.

"Charlotte, if only that were true. I would love to know everything that happens beforehand when I am with you, that's what makes you special – I never know what you are going to do until moments or sometimes split-seconds before, and the reason for that is because *you* never know what you are going to do."

"Am I to read between the lines there, Lloyd, and think that you think I am difficult just because I don't think quickly enough for you?"

"Not at all."

"But you were hurting me with whatever you had."

"No, again, that was your brain thinking it was going to hurt – you have leather shorts on, your brain heard the little creak and assumed that it was going to hurt. There was only one that caught your skin on your leg, and that was where you moved straight into it. I rubbed it for you to take the sting out, look, not even a red mark, just a little pink."

I look down at the mark on my leg – a little line, slightly pink; it looks like I had scratched one of my nails across my skin. In fact I had worse damage from my nails when I first had them put on than from the mark on my leg.

"Ready for the next part of this afternoon? Have you calmed down enough yet?"

"But you didn't tell me what you were doing."

"No, I haven't. It will spoil my fun for the next time we play this little game." Kissing me on the forehead as he stands up and helps me up as well, he walks me over to the whips.

"Charlotte, whips, whips, Charlotte. Now you have been properly introduced, maybe you can become friends. Touch them, Charlotte, they are objects like any other. They are not to be feared when they are like this, they are not to be feared when they are to be taken off the wall, they are not to be feared when being used correctly. The only thing that makes a whip dangerous is the person using them, and a lack of respect by others when they are being used. That said, let's take down your faithful friend, my bull whip."

"Erm, I don't think so, Lloyd."

"Oh, I think so, Charlotte. I have just told you they are not to be feared, big or small, but respected. Now, do you remember the rules, the ones I first told you?"

"Yes."

"They still apply down here. Don't panic, don't lose control. I am going to show you now how to use a whip correctly, how to stand, how to hold it, then how you get on will determine what we do next." He reaches up and lifts down a bull whip.

OK, breathe, I have to breathe deep, long and hard. It can't hurt me, it will not hurt me. I look at it in Lloyd's hand, curled like a snake; he takes my hand and leads me back to the middle of the room. He stands behind me, puts his arm around me and cuddles me, resting his chin on my shoulder. The hand with the bullwhip manoeuvres my other hand to be at my side; he releases the coils of the whip from his hand and gives it a little flick so it is straight out in front of us. I freeze. I go rigid.

"Relax, Charlotte, breathe, it will not hurt you at all."

"It's OK for you, Lloyd, you are the one holding it."

"OK, you take it, just like you would hold a hairbrush." He places the whip in my hand and I start to shake.

"Do you think this is such a good idea, Lloyd? After all, I am not in control."

"I know you are not, but I am." Placing his hand on mine, he holds it tight.

"But how is this going to help me?"

"You will get used to it – the noise, the way it moves, and most important, the way it can be moved, and by the time I have finished you will be as good as me with one of these."

He moves his hand up and down in turn, taking my hand, making the whip snake to the tip. I hold my breath in anticipation of a crack, an echoing crack. Subs' arses, I want to go home.

"That's good, now breathe, please, before you pass out."

I gasp in air as if I have just been swimming underwater.

"Well, that's good, Lloyd, I have done it, now can we go?"

"Not yet, you are nowhere near relaxed enough yet. You are still very tense and you need to get rid of that fear you are holding."

"What about you, what do you fear? Or don't you fear anything? I bet you don't, you're a big toughie."

"I have fears, everyone has fears, it's normal, but it's the way we approach our fears that counts." He continually moves my hand as we talk.

"Well, come on then, what is your fear?"

"Well right now my biggest fear is you. I fear you breaking out of my grip and losing control, running around like a whirlwind, waving the whip in whatever panic you are in, like you did when we were playing with the scarves. You were so funny, bent over with your back straight, stretching your head out as far as you could to see if you could hear me. At one stage I thought you were going to turn into the Tasmanian devil, and not even I could keep out of the way of you and an uncontrollable whip, doing an impression of Tassie." He laughs.

"Now who's being personal? That isn't nice, comparing me to the Tasmanian devil, is it?"

"No more, Mrs Personal, than calling me the Dom from

hell. Oh yes, I still owe you for that this morning, but it will wait, thanks for the reminder."

"I wasn't reminding you," I said under my breath.

"What's that, Charlotte, I didn't quite catch it?"

"I didn't quite throw it!"

"Let's get a little faster." He starts moving our hands faster, and now instead of the end of the whip snaking, it's bouncing up and down.

"Careful, Lloyd, it's getting out of control!" I say with concern as my eyes bounce up and down with it.

"Nope, not yet, Charlotte, you are standing still here in my arms – as long as you are here nothing will be out of control. Now you need to give your wrist a little flick as we reach the up position with our hands, so you need to relax your arm and wrist. I will let you know when we are going to flick, OK?"

"Yes, so what do you really fear? That wasn't a real example."

"Yes it was a real example, but if you are asking what my greatest fear is it would have to be losing control."

"What, you losing control? Never, Lloyd."

"Well, that's not strictly true. There are a lot of factors to take into account. The biggest one is other people."

"So if I can't control people and you fear other people taking control away from you, why are you so hell-bent on me taking control?" My eyes bounce fast as he moves our hands faster; watching the end of the whip is making my eyes feel like they are on a trampoline.

"That's not exactly what I was saying. You can't control people, that is true – all you can do is take control of situations. By keeping yourself in control and taking control of situations you can then usually gain control of the people within that situation, like you did when Diane was having the baby. You took perfect control of the situation, and by doing that you managed to keep Diane focused on what she had to do."

"Aww, I wonder how they are doing?"

"Ready, flick your wrist after three. One, two, three, flick." He raises my hand upwards slightly, and I flick my wrist. As Lloyd lets go of my hand I watch the wave that I created in the whip zap down to the end. As it cracks I impulsively let go of the whip and it falls to the floor; as the crack echoes around the room my eyes dart and follow it around, trying to see where it will end up. I feel Lloyd's arms tighten around me.

"There you go, nothing here to hurt you, and your very first whip crack. Not a big one, but nevertheless a crack to be proud of. Just one thing, though."

"I know, I know, breathe."

"Well, that as well, but if you ever drop one of my whips on the floor again you may not like the consequences" he warns, holding me tighter and kissing the back of my neck.

I start to relax again, wanting, willing, needing him to carry on all the way, imagining what he will kiss next.

"Right, OK, let the fun begin now we are over that hurdle. You feel OK?"

"Yes, I'm fine," I say sleepily, a little in my own moment.

"Good, let's get cracking, you have a lot to learn still. It's going to take weeks." With that he lets go of his grip and slaps my arse. "Snap out of your moment, and pick up the whip. Your turn on your own – keep control and don't drop it!"

All afternoon we crack whips, with Lloyd showing me how to keep it straight and how to control it. So much to remember, but he is very good at instruction, he keeps calm all the time, even when I hit him – by accident, that is. It's a good job I can't crack it properly yet, but I did get a few good ones out.

Then we sit on the floor and have a cuddle before Lloyd says, "I have some work to do, and you, Charlotte, have been through a lot this weekend and I think you should go and get some rest. You have a busy week next week with work and the gym."

"Oh, but Lloyd, this is so nice."

"Charlotte, I do have a lot to get on with. I have all my notes to write up from last week and I have to go to the practice to check on things there. Do you want me to drop you off at home on the way?"

"Yes, OK, that will be good." It's strange how quickly things change from playing to reality.

He gets up and puts his hand down to help me get up from where I am sitting on the floor. A thought jumps into my head. No, let's not go, I want to play some more. I take his hand and giving it a sharp tug, I lean backwards and Lloyd is on top of me.

"Let's finish what we left last night, Lloyd," I whisper in his ear, then rolling him over, I am sitting on top of him.

"Charlotte…"

I place my index finger on his lips, bending down slowly and kissing him on the lips, a slow, lingering kiss. He grabs my hips and slowly starts gyrating me on him, then he rolls me over and he is sitting on top of me, holding both my hands above my head. He bends and kisses my lips, then he nibbles on my ear.

"Do you think you are that much in control that you can control this situation?"

I move my hands and we roll again, with me sitting on top of him.

"I know I am in control of this situation, and all I am asking for is a little controlled sex to finish off the afternoon right."

I run my index finger down his chest, followed by little kisses. He takes a deep breath, grabs my hair and lifts my head.

"Are you sure you have everything under control, Charlotte, sure that you haven't left something out of the equation?"

"Oh, I am sure, it's just you and me – the door is locked."

"OK." He slips his hand under my bra and starts to tease my erect nipples. My eyes close and I run my hands slowly over his chest, and he rolls us over again, pushing his groin into me. I roll us quickly again and start kissing his chest, teasing his nipples with my tongue. He runs his fingers through my hair as he lifts his hips in rhythm.

I kiss his ear and whisper, "This has been such a sensual weekend, Lloyd, I feel that my body has woken up."

I kiss down his neck.

"Lloyd, you have fifteen minutes to get to the surgery. I have left you and Charlotte some clothes outside the door."

I lift my head abruptly, looking at the door and then around the room as George's voice echoes around. Where is he? The door is still closed! Where the subbing hell is he?

"So it looks like I am still in control then, Charlotte, and that maybe you are not in control after all?" Lloyd grins up at me.

"What, how, where?" I spluttered.

"PA system. I asked George to give me a shout if I wasn't out so I wouldn't be late – it's so easy these days for me to lose track of time when I am with you, Charlotte. Come on, I have to go, I am going to be late." He pushes me off him and gets the clothes that George has so kindly left outside for us. George is slowly creeping up on my list of things that can happen when I want sex with Lloyd. We get dressed and hurry out.

Chapter Sixteen

I find it hard to sleep as my brain runs over and over everything that has been said, and the games we have played. They were good games, and I must admit, a turn-on. I have noticed lots of things this weekend: the way that my body reacts, how sensitive my body has become when I am with Lloyd, the different ways he looks at me, talks to me, touches me – all get a different response from me and my body. Depending on what situation I am in, my body reacts in different ways as well now. It's making me more confident, both when I am with him and when he is not with me. Everything that everyone has said is right, I can't really argue with them. I do need to control my brain and mouth more, but it is hard, especially when someone is taking pot-shots at my arse like Steve was doing. Yes, that was Steve paddling my arse, I know it was, but it wasn't so bad with Lloyd kissing me, in fact it was a turn-on, in a strange sort of way. It's also strange that I am only so argumentative with Lloyd when we are playing, but when it comes to reality and our day-to-day lives I just accept everything he says, without question, and he listens to me and what I have to say. I have noticed that the clear boundary never gets blurred.

And sex, what can I say about that? Yes, my orgasms are getting stronger and longer and the more I control them the better they seem to be. Being sexed up is just so heavenly, and although I do still want him inside me so much, it's not a big problem. And food, well, who would have thought food was so erotic? I have always liked chocolate, but never have I had such a good experience as the one this weekend, just by eating a little good chocolate, although I think it was a combination of being sexed up and my imagination running wild, something else I really have to learn how to control when I am in public.

When I finally fall asleep I start to dream. I'm in a game on Dom TV. The compère announces, "For your next challenge in How to Get Laid by Lloyd, you must eliminate everything that can go wrong on a desert island." I spend the rest of my sleep chasing turtles and putting them back into the sea, but the pesky creatures just keep getting out, and then when I think I have that done it's coconuts, and I'm trying to climb trees to pick them but then I keep falling out. I'm frantically trying to throw sticks, stones and anything I can find to knock them out of the tree, and all the time Lloyd is saying, "Take control, Charlotte, just take control." Meanwhile Kat, Sophie, Anthony and Steve are saying, "Come on, Charlotte, you know you can do it."

Then as my frustration grows the radio comes on, playing Eva Cassidy's 'Somewhere Over the Rainbow'. It feels like I have only just got to sleep. I sit bolt upright, my bed-mess hair falling down my face. I haphazardly try to brush it away. God, I need coffee and I need it now. I get out of bed and walk to the kitchen for the much-needed big boost of caffeine, and as I walk through the lounge Anthony is there.

"Just made a pot, Charlotte. How's your arse?" Oh no! Oh God! I had forgotten he was there, for the love of a sub. I feel my cheeks burning as I walk straight past him, not saying a word. I get my coffee and return to the lounge.

I sit down, take a few sips of coffee and glare at Anthony before saying, "My arse is delightful." I'm still trying to get my hair under control, like you do with bed-mess hair.

"Good, you look a little rough this morning."

"Don't ask. I can do without you laughing at me this morning too," I mutter under my breath. "I will get those bloody turtles, that's for sure."

"What was that, Charlotte?"

"Nothing."

"Are you feeling the strain of the weekend?"

"No, Anthony, not that you would notice!" I complain.

"Oh."

"No, sorry, I didn't mean that the way it came out. I just didn't sleep very well, and then when I did get to sleep it was time to wake up. I enjoyed the weekend, I learnt lots about myself."

"You amaze me. You have taken everything so well with the lifestyle considering you didn't know anything about it, and you seem to play with Lloyd so well. You have grown together so naturally, I have never seen it before – well, that's to say a total vanilla with a hardened player like Lloyd. Oh, by the way, he has just phoned to ask me to remind you about meeting Steve at the gym."

"Well, he wants to watch out I don't harden too much, as I don't like gyms and I don't like all that stupid 'bottom down, tuck your tummy in' rubbish, I hate it. Does he not think I get enough exercise chasing around the salon and then being chased by him when we are together?" I sip my coffee – God, it's good.

"That's his point – the more exercise you do, the more you will be able to do, and Lloyd now wants you to get your body fit, and as you work on your body's fitness, your mind will become a little more in tune, and I think Lloyd wants you to be equal to him in mind and body – it makes for better playing."

"Ha, ha! Well, that is never going to happen, is it? I am never going to be equal to him, or haven't you noticed, Anthony? He is a man and I am a woman – we are made completely differently. I have tits – he doesn't."

"I am so glad about that, Charlotte, as I would have to start questioning Lloyd's behaviour towards you, and yes, I have noticed the differences between you both, the main one being that you are both very, very, happy. I haven't seen you so happy for years, and Lloyd, well, he has a spring in his step again. He has a new zest for life."

"What do you mean, again? I have never known Lloyd any different."

"Maybe you haven't, and it's not my secret to tell you."

"What secret, what are you on about?"

"Charlotte, I didn't think about the words I was using, I forget your brain is finally starting to wake up again. Just forget I have said anything, please."

"Anthony, if there is something going on I have the right to know, don't you think?"

"Look, Charlotte, it was a long time ago. We all have pasts and there they should stay – in the past. It has taken Lloyd a long time to get over it but now he has, so let's leave it at that. I am sure when he thinks the time is right he will tell you."

"Anthony, I am getting so fed up with the phrase 'when the time is right'. I feel that every time I want to know something that I think might be important to me all I get is that phrase." I give him my lost-little-girl look.

"Oh, OK, but not a word to anyone, do you understand me? Not even Lloyd!"

"OK, I promise."

"You must also promise that you will not change your feelings or the way you act towards Lloyd."

"I promise."

"OK, Lloyd and I were roommates at uni, and we were no different to any other boys who had escaped from home for the first time. We had total freedom, and our hormones were racing. We happened to fall upon a club one night, not a normal club, but it was dark and dingy and thinking of only the end product, of filling our boots, we watched some of the most gorgeous girls we had ever seen go inside, all very scantily dressed, so we decided it would be a good place to try our luck. We thought at first it was a strip joint, but then a guy came over and asked us if we were in the lifestyle. Curiously, I asked what he meant and he explained to us in great length what the club was all about. That's how we found the lifestyle. The more we got into it and understood it, the more we wanted it.

"Well, Lloyd met Lucinda, and they played together for about four years, to cut a long story short. When we graduated, Lucinda decided she and Lloyd would live together, and moved in. They continued in the lifestyle, playing and working hard. The more that Lloyd learnt about control, the better he became at being a doctor and a real nice person. Lucinda on the other hand was into real risky stuff, a little extreme for me, but Lloyd seemed to be able to keep her in control most of the time. One day he had finished early and he went home to surprise her, but it was Lloyd that got the surprise – she was at home with another guy, who took off as soon as he saw Lloyd. By all accounts, Lucinda started shouting and lost the plot with Lloyd, saying it was his fault, he had made her look in other places for what she needed because he was just too scared to do things she liked. Then she left. As she left he said to her that he wished he had never met her, and he wished she were gone forever.

"About half an hour later his hospital beeper went off and he was called back to Accident and Emergency. He arrived at the same time as the ambulances were arriving. Taking control of the situation, he organised everything in A&E and then set to work, as if nothing had happened. Lloyd is good at doing that, putting things on hold until another time or day, and he never forgets anything – I don't know how he does it. Well, the ambulances just kept coming, with more and more people. By the time he had finished one, there was another person to take their place. Then a nurse came in and asked him to pronounce a death on arrival. He followed the nurse and she pulled down the sheet that was covering the face and body. He barely recognised that it was his partner, as she had been through the windscreen. A tattoo on her shoulder confirmed it, a small whip that she had had done to show her undying love for him. He pronounced her dead, then got back to work." Anthony gets up, takes my coffee mug and gets us a refill.

"That's awful."

"That's not the end." He continues, handing me the coffee, then sitting back down. "He carried on working, saving lives and patching people up, and then he was asked to pronounce another death. This time he was told that the police thought it was the other person's husband or partner as they were in the same car together. Apparently the nurse continued talking to Lloyd as he just looked at him, lying there dead. Apparently she was driving and went straight out onto the motorway. They don't know how fast she was going, but she went right in front of the wheels of a coach full of people. They didn't stand a chance. Later on he learnt that they had both been drinking and were well over the limit. Coupled with Lloyd finding her with another man and her loss of control, she flew down the slip road at about a hundred miles an hour. It took Lloyd a long time getting over it. None of it was Lloyd's doing and he knows that, he has always been one to say that you choose your own destiny, and the control you have over your life is what helps you choose that destiny. The thing is, he realises that for one split-second he lost control and said that he wished he had never met her and he wished her gone forever. He can't get those words out of his head…or he couldn't until you, Charlotte."

"Oh my God, that is so awful, so sad for him."

"Yes it was, but you made promises, Charlotte. Please keep them."

"Of course I will. I will never let on about them at all. Is that why Lloyd is always on at me, do you think?"

"Partly yes, partly no. I do know he will not let you go until you have complete control of your mind and body, but what you do after that is completely down to you. The thing is, she had lost control in the extremities of the lifestyle – the riskier the games, the better. Then they had to become dangerous as well, it was like a drug to her. And then when Lloyd wouldn't play the games, he didn't quite know how to stop her and make her take control. He was in the middle of trying to work out how to sort it when he found them both in the apartment, so yes, he doesn't want you to end up hurt or worse because you are out of control like she was. And I know that because he said that yesterday was the first time that you had realised he had reached his limit with you, even though you sat pouting. That was something that she never realised, that Lloyd had limits, so he knows you are getting there."

"So how does he know it wasn't me reaching my limit on the subject?"

"Oh, I am sure that we all know you will have more to say on the subject. Lloyd is fully expecting you not to go, and trust me, he will do what he said he would do if you are not there. You know from now on he is going to get harder on you, don't you?"

"What do you mean, harder? Wasn't yesterday hard enough for him?" I frown at Anthony.

"Yesterday was just a taster, to see what would happen if you could keep it together, and the short answer was no, you couldn't."

"What do you mean, no? I thought I did very well indeed."

"You may have done in your eyes, but in the eyes of a Dom – nope, you still have a long way to go."

"Oh hell, you Doms are all the same, give you an inch and you want a mile from me. How the hell do you expect me to do this if you are always changing the goalposts? That's what I want to know."

"We are not changing anything, we have started you off slowly, that's all, but now it's time for you to change from a baby sub into a grown-up sub."

"Oh hell, look at the time, Nats will kill me, I'm late!" With that I jump off the sofa to get showered and ready for work.

I get to work just in time. I had to run, well, walk as fast as my heels would allow me to. It's almost a run for me. Just as I arrive I feel my phone in my pocket vibrate – well, no points for guessing who that will be. Too much to do; I'll get in on time, but he will have to wait five minutes.

"Hi, Charlotte, good weekend?" Nats says as I dash past her to go and put my bag and things in the office.

"Good morning, and I had a fantastic weekend, thanks, Nats."

"I thought you might have done." She giggles to herself.

After putting everything in the office and grabbing two coffees, one for Nats and the other for me, I head back out to the desk.

"Everything OK here at the weekend?"

"Yes, fine, went like clockwork, thanks to your organising skills."

"What do we have to do?"

"Well, we have a few Doms coming in with their subs and they are trying a few new looks, makeovers and new hairstyles. One or two of the girls are already here setting up for them so it's not going to be a heavy day today, and by the looks of you it's a good job it's not."

"Oh, I didn't sleep very well last night, that's all." My phone vibrates again in my pocket. I take it out.

"Don't tell me you haven't said good morning to him yet!" Nats says when she sees the phone flashing in my hand.

"No, not yet I haven't, I was talking with Anthony about the weekend and we didn't realise the time. That's why I am bang on time instead of being early as I usually am." Looking down at my phone and opening the messages while speaking to Nats, I realise I have three, not just two, messages from Lloyd. Oh for the love of a sub, he must have sent one while I was in the shower and I didn't hear it; not only that, I didn't look at it either. I read the messages; the first one is:

Good morning, Charlotte. I trust you slept well? Lloyd xxx

The next:

Ah good, you have made it to work OK. Lloyd xxx

The next:

Was that brisk walk your attempt at training for the gym tonight? Lloyd xxx

I look around frantically. Where is he hiding? He has to be here somewhere. How does he know that I have just got to work, and how does he know I was walking very fast, well, almost running? No sign of him anywhere.

"What's the matter? What are you looking for?"

"Oh, Nats, sometimes Lloyd freaks me out. How does he know I have only just got into work, and how does he know I was practically running to get here on time? I sometimes think he is watching me all the time."

"Think about it – was Anthony at home when you left for work?"

"Yes, he was."

"Right, OK, you talked with Anthony about things you did at the weekend, correct?"

"Yes."

"Well, Anthony would have phoned Lloyd to tell him if you were OK or not about things, and he would have said you had just left."

I sighed and relaxed.

"So he isn't spying on me?"

"No, not at all, it's easy when you look at the picture. Take in all the elements and then you can come up with rational conclusions and not half-baked ideas. Pep talk over, let's get sorted out and answer him, for God's sake, or he will be ringing me to see if you are really here."

No sooner said, her phone started to ring.

"Hello, Lloyd, ears burning are they… No, nothing, I will pass you over. Make it snappy, Lloyd, the first are due in any moment…" She hands me the phone.

"See, he doesn't know for sure." She winks at me; today's eye colour is yellow.

"Hi, Lloyd, I am sorry I haven't answered, I was just about to when you phoned Nats."

"You OK? This morning Anthony said you didn't sleep very well."

"No, I didn't but I will be fine, no worries. I'm on my third coffee now so hopefully I will be OK when I have finished it."

"OK, you take care today."

"OK, I will do, Lloyd. Talk later, bye."

I hang up the phone. He didn't mention the gym to me; I wonder why he hasn't done that? Maybe he has forgotten.

The rest of my day is spent like all other Mondays when I work, pampering Doms with tea, coffee, sandwiches and cakes. God, they are so precious – everything with their subs has to be correct all the time. The right shade, the right length – one of them had a ruler and made Nats measure the exact length he wanted his sub's hair to be. That to me is just too much. I sometimes wonder how Nats does it, and how she doesn't tell them where to go. All day my feet don't touch the ground, back and forth with this and then that, just nonstop. At five we see the last customer go, and it isn't until then that I realise Lloyd hasn't sent me a text since the morning. Strange, I usually have a text or two from him.

"What you up to tonight, Charlotte, anything good?"

"No, Nats, nothing good, just the gym. Lloyd says I have to…" I turn my nose up at the word 'gym'.

"I guess you don't like the gym?"

"You guess right, but Lloyd has been most insistent that I go so I will try, and I must go now or I will be late, so see you tomorrow, Nats." I grab my things and off I trot as fast as my feet can take me.

As I rush out, Nats says, "Yes, OK, Charlotte, have a nice evening. See you tomorrow!"

Chapter Seventeen

I arrive at The Room and ring the doorbell. George opens the door.

"Good evening, Charlotte, how are you today?"

"Oh, I'm just pumping to go, George, and a good evening to you too." I punch the air with my fist and enter. "Erm, is Lloyd here?"

"No, he isn't."

"Oh, I need him to show me where the gym is. He hasn't shown me yet so I'll just go upstairs and wait for him."

"No, Charlotte, he gave me express orders that I was to take you straight down and show you where to go."

"OK, well I will just go in here and have a cup of coffee." Anything just to not go down, and the cup of coffee seems to be the right get-out-of-jail card to me.

"Hmm, let me think… OK, I have thought. The phrase Lloyd used was 'straight down'. I don't think that having a coffee is straight down, do you, Charlotte?" He offers his hand towards the stairs for me to go that way. As I pass him I give him a sideways glance of disapproval. I can't even count on you for a coffee then, can I, George? He takes me downstairs, around and around till we reach the gym, and takes me inside.

"Ah, Steve, Charlotte is here."

"Oh good, thank you, George."

George turns and leaves without another word.

"OK, Charlotte, have you got any gym stuff with you?"

I screw my eyes up – oh no, in my panic this morning I forgot to pick it up. Never mind, I will not be able to do it, then. Good thinking.

"Oh dear, Steve, I have left them at home, I forgot to bring them this morning. Well, I will see you next week and I will remember to bring them with me next time." That's it, good, now turn and walk away.

As I start to turn Steve says, "Ah, it's OK, Charlotte, Lloyd brought you some new stuff today for the gym. He dropped it off at lunchtime for you." He hands me a holdall.

"Oh, lucky me, for a moment I thought, how sad, I can't do it tonight, but how lucky I am to have Lloyd thinking of everything for me."

"Yes, you are lucky, Charlotte. Now, the changing rooms are over there. I will see you when you get out, and don't be too long, will you?"

"The world's fastest changing sub, that's me, Steve!" I go to change. I'm not going to get out of this, am I? Not at all, and oh yes, lucky, lucky me, Lloyd has packed everything in here: red shorts, matching red joggers, white T-shirts, trainer socks and a pair of white trainers with red trim. In the bottom of the bag there's a note from Lloyd.

Glad to see you have made it this far, Charlotte. I don't think I have forgotten anything! Love Lloyd xxx

As if you would forget anything, Lloyd. Your head is like an elephant's. You never forget anything when it comes to me, so why would you think you might have done? OK, I'm ready, breathe deep breaths before I go outside and face

Steve. You can do this, Charlotte. I go outside and Steve is waiting for me.

"That's better, Charlotte, you look like you mean to do some training now. I think we will do some stretches first." He walks to a clear area in the gym, and I follow him.

"Just follow me. We will warm up your muscles and then set to work." What, does he think I have been doing nothing all day and that my muscles aren't already warm? Subbing cheek of the man. "Twist your arms this way, Charlotte. Now like this, good." He thinks I am a contortionist, but I can't get them right around my back like that. Look at him, he could cuddle himself all night long.

"Right, I think that's about it, we have stretched most of them by now. So, first machine, treadmill. I will set you off on a slow jog for fifteen minutes. You should be able to do that."

He takes me to the treadmill and makes me get onto it. He shows me how it works and the emergency stop button. Then he sets it going.

"It will start you off walking and slowly get up to a jogging speed, OK, Charlotte?"

"Yes, I think so!" And off it goes. OK, this is OK, I can do this for fifteen minutes. This is easy, I think to myself as the treadmill starts. Oh no, slow down, my little feet are running so fast to keep up with it. No, no. I don't do running this fast, I am not a one-minute-mile runner. I start panting as it gets to the speed that it is set for. Please stop, I don't know what he thinks I am.

"OK, Charlotte?" Steve asks just after it reaches the speed he has set.

"No, no, I am not," I pant. God, I can't even talk to him.

"What's wrong?"

"It's too fast. I can't do this. Please stop."

"Not yet, Charlotte, you are doing fine. Don't forget, I am monitoring your heartbeat and everything and your heartbeat is nowhere near a good level yet. Just you keep going."

God, I feel like Forrest Gump: he ran and ran and when he ran out of roads he ran some more. Now I know he was on a treadmill.

"I will be straight back, I just have to check on someone." Steve disappears.

This is hell, no, it's worse than hell. I can't breathe now and he has left me. I could have a heart attack or something. I feel my legs getting weaker and weaker as I run so fast. I have been here for hours. Now he has left me for hours, I look around for someone to come and rescue me but there is no one around. I feel like I have duck's feet now, they feel all flat and awkward as I lift them and place them back down.

"OK, Charlotte. How you doing? Well, your heartbeat is doing great, just as it should."

"Please, Steve, I have been here for hours. You forgot me when you went away and I really can't run for much longer. I need a rest."

"Charlotte, you have been on this machine for four minutes, that's all." No! How can he say such a thing, it's been hours, I know it has.

"Please, Steve, I beg you, let me get off now!"

"No, Charlotte, now keep going and I will go and get you some water for when you have finished."

Oh no, oh no, don't go away again, I really need to get off now. I watch him disappear through a door. Right, that is it, I am getting off. Remembering what he said about the emergency stop, I hit it hard, stopping the machine. I get off and head for the door. I run out and manage to make it to the lift. Phew – I call the lift and get in. I put in my key and off I go, leaning one hand on the wall of the elevator and the other hand on the side of my stomach, trying to catch my breath. I'm still panting by the time the lift doors open. I look out of the lift and Lloyd is standing there. Double subs' arses, I thought he was still at work.

"Hello, Charlotte, that was a quick gym lesson!"

"No, Lloyd, it wasn't, I have been on a treadmill for hours, he just left me there for hours," I pant, still trying to get my breath.

He puts a key into the wall outside the lift; then he leans up against the door of the lift and places one of his feet on the other door. That's great, I can't get out now even if I could walk.

"Charlotte, I know your gym session has only just started. I also know that by the time you had done warm-ups and Steve had set you on the treadmill you would have probably done no more than five minutes on it." He folds his arms and looks down to his foot on the opposite door.

"No, Lloyd, you have that all wrong. Look at me, do I look like I have been for a gentle five-minute stroll? I don't think so. No, just look at me, I am still panting."

"Charlotte, I am not going to give in on this one. You are going to go back down and finish your gym lesson – one way or another you will go down."

"No, Lloyd, I can't, I will have a heart attack. Please, Lloyd."

The lift buzzes. "Oops, Charlotte, you have about five minutes before Steve gets up here and he will take you back down to finish your gym lesson. So you can do this the hard way or the easy way, your choice."

I place one of my hands on my hip, looking at Lloyd, a little smug.

"Well, Lloyd, I hate to spoil your little party but don't you think that Steve will have a problem with getting up here?"

"Why would that be, Charlotte?"

"Because your foot is leaning up against the lift door so he can't use the lift either." The smug grin on my face gets bigger.

"Charlotte, do you think this is the only way up here?"

"Yes, it is, I remember when Kat first brought me up here, she said this was the only way."

"Yes and no."

"What do you mean, yes and no?"

"There is a service door, that one over there. How do you think George and everyone get here with food and everything? They don't always use the lift, you know."

What? I have never thought about it before. I look at the door. I have never even been curious about the door before, not even given it a second thought. My heart falls along with my mouth and my hand off my hip.

"No, Lloyd, no, don't let him get me, I will be no good for anything after he has finished with his torture."

"Charlotte, you are going back down."

"Lloyd, I am not a hamster, I don't run. He has got me on a machine that goes nowhere like a hamster's wheel. For the love of subs, don't make me go back down with him – I will not go down with him." I protest strongly by standing up straight and putting my hands on my hips.

"Charlotte, how much do you want to bet, or should I say *what* do you want to bet, that you will not go back down, when I am saying you are going back down?"

"Oh, that's right, Lloyd, bet on Charlotte when she is at her weakest. That just isn't cricket. It would be like betting on a dead horse."

"Oh, so are you saying you are going back down? You have probably got about one minute left before Steve gets here." He looks up at me, and I place my hand back on my hip.

"No, Lloyd, I didn't say that at all and you know that isn't what I was saying. I am saying I have had enough of the gym. I have tried it for you and I don't like it. He is trying to kill me."

Steve appears at the service doors.

"Hello, Charlotte, I thought I would find you here. Do you realise if you had stayed downstairs you would have finished by now? The treadmill, that is."

"Lloyd, please stop this."

"It's not my call, Charlotte, I have told Steve whatever it takes, and I have also told him I will stay out of it so he can give you the best training he has to offer. That was the deal I made. You wouldn't want me to go back on that deal, would you?"

I drop my arms down to my sides and raise my head to the gods.

"Why did you do that? I feel like you have betrayed me. Please, Lloyd, don't do this."

"Sorry, Charlotte, but this is important for you, and you will do it."

"OK, Charlotte, I have had enough. Excuse me, Lloyd, please." Steve gets in the lift. "Now, Charlotte, are you going to take yourself down or do you need some assistance?"

"I don't need assistance anywhere. I'm not going, this isn't right, is it – you are both ganging up on me..." With that I am flung over Steve's shoulders and he carries me out of the lift and through the service door to another lift. I start to protest very strongly.

"Please, Steve! Put me down, I don't want to go with you." I try to push myself out of his grip but I can't.

"Now, Charlotte, with the right training you would be able to get away from me very easily." He laughs.

"For the sake of a sub's arse, put me down," I demand.

"Yes, Charlotte, I love a sub's arse and I have a nice sub's arse just here." He taps it.

"Oh no you don't. Lloyd wouldn't like it if you slapped that arse, it's not yours to touch." I try to kick my feet but that doesn't work either. I try and punch his arse but it's like a rock.

"Now, Charlotte, that's not very nice is it? And although you need a spank in my eyes, and Lloyd has given me permission to spank you if you do give me too much of a hard time, I will leave it to Lloyd. Now we are nearly back, do you think you can refrain from your temper tantrum just for a few minutes, please?"

"Just put me down, I don't want to do this. No I don't, and treating me like a child isn't helping, is it?"

"Charlotte, you have put more effort into trying to get away from me than you would have doing the treadmill, and as for treating you as a child, try behaving like an adult, then maybe we can all get on with our jobs and not chase after someone who is behaving like a spoilt brat."

We enter the gym and he takes me into a room that has soft mats on the floor. He sits me down on a chair.

"I am not spoilt at all!"

"Oh, so you are admitting you are a brat then, Charlotte?" What is it with these Doms? They are all the same, twisting everything you say.

"No, I am not and you can just stop twisting everything. I just don't do gyms. Now let me go back upstairs," I demand once again.

"Now don't move, Charlotte, if you want to fight me that's fine, we will fight."

"Oh yes, I want to fight you, you don't scare me, not at all."

"Big words, Charlotte, from one so small. Are you sure you want to do this?"

"Oh yes, bring it on, if it means I don't have to come to the gym anymore, bring it on, OK."

He grabs some boxing gloves and puts them on me, tying them up tight.

"I will give you an advantage – I will wear sparring pads." He holds up two round pads that look like small red cushions. "OK, Charlotte, I think we are ready – come into the middle of the room. Let's get this over with."

I get up and move to the middle of the room. Oh yes, I am ready for you, mister. I will show you what I can do.

"OK, put your hands up, Charlotte, let's get going." I raise my hands and using the pads, he pushes them backwards with all his might.

"Time out, I believe your safety word is, is that right?"

"Oh yes, that's right, but I don't think I will be needing it." I grit my teeth and take a swing at him; he leans back as my glove swings past him.

"Good try, Charlotte, try again." I swing again, stronger and faster; he leans to his left and I spin around a little and I feel his foot push my arse. Oh no, oh subbing no. I fall down. Subbing hell, that wasn't supposed to happen. I get up quickly.

"That was a little below the belt, don't you think?" Swinging again, I miss again.

"Why, Charlotte, am I not allowed to defend myself? Seems a little one-sided to me?" This time he sweeps my feet from beneath me and I fall, slap, straight on my arse.

"I have never done this before, but I will knock you out." I get to my feet again.

"So much anger, Charlotte. Where does it all come from?"

I swing upwards again; he moves out of the way and pushes me in the chest. I stumble backwards but manage to stay on my feet.

"It comes from arrogant men like you, who get right up my nose."

"Come on, Charlotte, I thought you would at least have made some contact with me by now, even if it was by accident."

I swing again, still missing, and he taps me on the head.

"Oh, that's right, give me brain damage while you are at it, why don't you?"

"Charlotte, I thought you had more in you than this?" He offers his chin and I swing for it, but still he gets out of the way, and he trips me up again. "Lloyd is right, you know: you need to get rid of this anger and you need to take control."

"Well if you and Lloyd weren't such subbing bullies, then maybe I wouldn't be so angry right now." I make two swings left and right in quick succession, but he still gets out of the way. "You should have been called Jack." I move back quickly so he can't knock me off my feet.

"Now why should I be called Jack?"

"You know, Jack be nimble, you are so fast at moving."

"Why thank you, Charlotte, I will take that as a compliment."

I swing again and miss him again. I am on my arse.

"Come on, Charlotte, you are not putting up much of a fight. Get up. Now I will put both my hands up. When I wave my hand like this, hit it as hard as you can." He raises his hands, gives his right hand a little wave. I hit it with my right hand and he sweeps my feet away with his left foot. Bang. I am on the floor again.

"Wrong, Charlotte, get up. Now hit it as hard as you can with your right hand." I hit it with all my might.

"That's good, Charlotte, and again – watch for the moving hand and hit it." His left hand moves, I hit it with my left hand, and he sweeps me off my feet again.

"No, you can't keep knocking me down, it's not fair!"

"What's fair about a fight, Charlotte, and what's fair about you losing control, and what is fair with you having so much anger? Now get back up. Do it again, come on."

I get back up. He waves his left hand and I hit it with all my might.

"Is that all you have got? Barely felt it."

"Well of course you don't feel it, you have those stupid cushions on your hand, for sub's sake."

He waves his right hand and I hit it with my right hand. Bang, on the floor.

"Wrong, get up. Would you prefer I take them off if you think it will make a difference?"

"Yes, take them off if you dare. That will show you how hard I am, punching your hand."

"OK, so come on, Charlotte, why are you so angry, why can't you let go of it? After all, you don't find it hard to let go of your control, do you?"

He takes off the pads and throws them onto the floor.

"I have told you I am fed up with idiots taking advantage of me."

"That's better, Charlotte." He waves his left hand and I hit it with my right.

"Good one, Charlotte. Idiots who take advantage of anyone aren't worth losing control over." He waves his left hand again; I hit it with my left hand. "Wrong."

As I tumble back to the floor, this time some of my hair cascades down the side of my face.

"Get up again. So why don't you go and be angry at them?"

"Oh, what a dumb question."

"Why is it dumb?"

"Because they always win, that's why."

"Change hands, Charlotte. They always win because you let them." He waves his left hand; I hit his right hand. Down I go, hitting the floor, and some more of my hair falls loose.

"Wrong – don't change my hands, change yours. Get up. Come on, you are never going to knock me out sitting on the floor."

I get up.

"I will knock you out, and this is the one." I launch myself at him and he moves right out of the way, kicking my arse as I go through. I fall onto all fours.

"Get up, Charlotte. Come on, don't just sit there. So much anger still, what are you angry at now?"

I get up and I look at him with determination and grit. I will get you, I will.

"I'm angry at you because you will not stay still long enough for me to land you one."

"Good, what else?" He waves his right hand; I hit it with my right hand.

"I'm angry with Lloyd for letting you carry me off the way you did. He could have stopped it but oh no, he is just showing me that he can do whatever he wants." Left hand waves and I hit it with my left hand.

"Making progress, Charlotte, change hands. What else are you angry at?"

"I'm angry at subbing turtles!"

He waves his hands in quick succession, with me making contact every time. He lowers his hands and I pull back, panting and glad for a little rest.

"Turtles! Why are you angry with turtles?" He looks puzzled.

"I just am."

"OK, be angry with turtles, but I don't see why anyone would be angry with a turtle! But I suppose it's progress." He puts his hands back up, shaking his head. "When I say change, you change your hands." He waves his hand and I hit it. This goes on for a while, with him sweeping me off my feet every time I get it wrong or if I say something he doesn't like.

"OK, Charlotte, I think that's it. You have made good progress today. I will see you here tomorrow, same time."

"What? What do you mean, tomorrow, and that we have made good progress?"

"Well, your anger changed the plan I had for you, but that's OK. I have learnt a lot from you today. A little one-on-one contact is good for releasing some of your anger. It's a much better release than a treadmill or cycling machine, and you have had a better workout too. So I will see you tomorrow and we will carry on. Get rid of some more of that anger, I think."

"No, no, no, you don't get away that easily."

"Charlotte, your muscles will be very tired now. You need a bath and you need to relax, and if I were you I would go before I do change my mind. Here, let me take off your gloves for you."

I hold up my hands and he unties my gloves.

"I am very intrigued though, Charlotte – what do you have against turtles? Everything else you said made sense, but the turtles, that just seemed very random."

"Oh, nothing really, I don't even know why I said it!"

"Charlotte, you know if you start controlling things, your anger will start to disappear. It's normal to have anger.

It's all part of fight-or-flight. We are conditioned with it, it's all part of our makeup. The problem is you have had so much adrenaline floating around your body for so long without being able to release it properly, and that's why you get angry and that's why you lose control."

"OK, so why couldn't I get angry like that at idiots?"

"Because you were scared and now you feel safe. You are letting go, but you are letting go with the wrong people."

"Look, I have Lloyd for therapy and tying my head up in knots. I thought you were a personal trainer?"

"I am, Charlotte, and your attitude and where your mind is at is all part of it. A positive, controlled mind gives you a better understanding of getting fit the right way. An uncontrolled, negative mind and you are throwing your punches into mid-air, and you will never hit anything. Didn't you notice when you started to calm down you got more hits right, and the more you got right, the more controlled you started to become? You started to turn that negative energy into positive energy. You did well, and, Charlotte, you will be here tomorrow," he demands. "Right, go on, upstairs with you. I am sure Lloyd will want to know everything you have done. Get a hot bath. I took your stuff up earlier."

"Thanks." I go to the lift. Standing waiting for it, I think, do I really want to go upstairs and have Lloyd quiz me and bounce my head around? I'm too tired for that. I walk up the stairs, slip out of the front door and walk back to mine. When I arrive Anthony is there.

"Hi, Charlotte, wasn't expecting you just yet!" he calls.

"Erm, no, I thought I would get an early night for a change. I'm just going to have a bath." I go straight into the bathroom as I don't really want Anthony quizzing me either, as I really have had enough for the day.

*

238

I submerge my head underwater. Bliss – not a sound. I can't hear anyone saying do this, do that, take control – nothing. Just me, I am all alone. After about forty minutes I get out of the bath, wrapping a towel around me. Still feeling very tired, I walk to my room.

"Do you want anything to eat, Charlotte?" Anthony calls.

"No thanks, I am going to bed, I am so tired."

"OK, night."

"Yeah night, Anthony." As I close the bedroom door I lie down on my bed and that is the last thing I remember.

Chapter Eighteen

I wake up in the morning with the towel underneath me on top of the bed. My body aching from the workout, or should I say my attempt at boxing, means I still feel very tired. I get up and sort myself out for work. My hair is a little bit of a mission as it's just all over the place where I fell asleep on it wet. There's no sign of Anthony, just a note.

> Lloyd has taken your bag and phone to the salon for you. Have a good day. Anthony x

Pants, I left it all at Lloyd's. I get a coffee before leaving for work. When I arrive my bag and phone are already there. There is a text.

> How's my little Mike Tyson this morning? xxx

Well, if he is referring to me I feel crap so I am not going to answer him. I put my phone back in my bag and get on with work. The day just seems to be so long; it's dragging. My muscles ache in places that a girlie shouldn't have muscles, I am sure.

*

At five-thirty on the dot I am at the gym. As I enter I really don't feel like doing this all over again. Steve is standing by his desk.

"Hello, Charlotte, nice to see you on time."

"Hi, look, I feel so tired, every muscle hurts."

"Charlotte, let's cut to the chase: next you will tell me you haven't got any things with you because you forgot your gym kit." He leans down behind his desk and lifts up a bag and holds it out for me.

"Lloyd?" I look at the bag in amazement.

"Yes, Lloyd."

"Well, of course, who else would it be? After all, I don't have a fairy godmother, do I, because if I did she would have taken me away from all of this by now." I snatch the bag from his hands and make my way to the changing room.

"Glad to see you still have some anger to work out," Steve says.

I don't answer him. I can't be bothered, to tell the truth.

When I come out Steve says, "Right, I am going to teach you kickboxing. You seemed to enjoy it yesterday. Now every time, and I mean every time, you come in, you will do your warm-ups like I showed you yesterday. After that, I will show you everything you need to do, from standing correctly to punching correctly."

"But I really feel so tired."

"It will pass, now go get warmed up."

After an hour and a half of punching and kicking air, which I really can't see the point of, when I am literally on my knees, he finally says, "Right, Charlotte, see you tomorrow. Now go and see Lloyd!"

"Tomorrow? Can't I have a day off?"

"No, Charlotte, you can't."

"Well, good job that I can't wait for tomorrow then,

Steve!" I curl my top lip with disapproval.

I go and get my bag; I don't change again. I go to the lift and press the button to call the lift. Then turning, I walk up the stairs, sneaking out of the door. I go home for bath, bed and sleep.

The rest of the week is the same routine – I hardly have the energy to work. Every evening Steve says the same thing to me when I leave, which is to go and see Lloyd. But every night I just feel I can't see him, I am too tired. Besides, he would just run me ragged, twisting my mind to give my brain a workout too. My brain has had enough of a workout trying to stay on the hamster wheel, and Steve is still badgering me about what makes me angry, so I just leave.

Friday's session at the gym it's same thing, only after we finish Steve says, "Why haven't you been to see Lloyd? I have told you to go and see him. Are you still angry with him?"

"No, I am not angry, I am just so tired. When I have finished here with you I just feel like I can't see him only for him to mash my brains as well. I need something to be normal for me."

"Are you going to go and see him tonight?"

"No, I am going home to bed, as I have done every night this week. I ache, and I am just so tired I can't do anything other than sleep, work and work out. What does he expect? I told him if I did this I would be no good for anything else. I am not a sporty person. Why don't any of you get it?"

"Charlotte, you are eating, I take it? And taking care of your body isn't sport."

"Yes, I am eating! And what is it, if it isn't sport?"

"What are you eating? Talk me through what you eat and drink every day."

"Well, I have coffee in the morning, then coffee when I get to work, a sandwich at work, usually salad, washed down by more coffee, and a coffee before I come here."

"What about dinner, Charlotte, are you eating in the evenings?"

"No, I go home, have a bath, go to bed, sleep. I told you, I am too tired."

"Charlotte, you must eat every mealtime. One of the reasons you are feeling tired is because you are not eating properly. Now I want you to go up and see Lloyd."

I go out to the lift, press the button, turn, walk up the stairs and sneak out of the door. I go home and get in the bath, get out, go to my room and lie down, feeling so depleted of energy. Why do they all think that I am Rambo? If I carry on with this, there will be nothing left of me. I even noticed the skirt that I had on today was too big for me, and it kept spinning like a hoop around my middle. And that is the last thought I have before falling asleep.

The next thing I know, Lloyd is sitting on my bed.

"Charlotte, wake up please." He is stroking my hair away from my face. I open one of my eyes and look at him.

"I'm sorry, Lloyd, I am just so tired I can't see you in the evening as well as do the gym every day."

"I know, but I need you to get dressed to come and have some dinner with me. It's the weekend and you are supposed to spend it with me – those are the rules."

"Oh, Lloyd, can't we make it lunch tomorrow, please? I promise I will be there."

"No, we can't. You have the weekend off and tonight is Friday, and you should be with me. That's the deal. Remember?"

"Oh, Lloyd, I will. Move over and you can slip in here

– Anthony will not mind." I attempt to move over but I am so tired I just can't move.

"Anthony might not mind, but I need you to get dressed and come for dinner with me, and I need you to be at mine this weekend."

"Oh, but Lloyd, I am so tired, please."

He sits me up and I flop just like a rag doll, hair tumbling everywhere.

"Come on, here is some strong coffee, Charlotte, that will help get you going a little. I have put some sugar in for you." He hands me the coffee mug and I take a sip.

"But I don't take sugar, Lloyd." I screw up my nose at the sweet coffee.

"You do in this one. Now drink."

"But it tastes so sweet."

"Drink, then you can get dressed. I will help you."

"I think, Lloyd, you have got something wrong," I say, sipping my coffee.

"What have I got wrong, Charlotte?"

"You said I have the weekend off but I don't. That was last weekend I had off, not this one. I am working tomorrow so I need to get some sleep."

"No, Charlotte, Nats has been trying to phone you this evening to say she doesn't need you this weekend, and as you have worked so hard all week she is giving you the weekend off as a bonus."

"Oh, that's nice of her."

"Yes, so let's not waste any more of our time together. Let's get you dressed and back to mine for dinner."

"Are you sure you wouldn't prefer to stay here, Lloyd?"

"Quite sure, Charlotte, come on." He helps me to get dressed and takes me back to his flat in a taxi he had waiting for us outside.

Chapter Nineteen

The table is set with loads of food. We sit at the table and I just look – I really am too tired to eat anything, and I feel a little overwhelmed with all the food. I look at Lloyd.

"I'm sorry, but I really can't eat anything right now. I am too tired."

"Eat please," he says curtly.

"But Lloyd!"

He picks up a strawberry and dips it in chocolate, wiping the excess off on the side of the bowl. He lifts it to my mouth and God, it smells so good. I take a bite and it tastes just as good as it smells; my tummy rumbles with anticipation of what is to follow.

"Now eat. The reason you are feeling so tired is because you haven't eaten enough all week – so eat. You can't work and work out on one salad roll and five coffees a day."

"How do you know that?"

"Well, when you didn't show up again this evening I phoned down to Steve. He said that he had sent you up ages ago. I then phoned Anthony to see if he had seen you, but he said he was at Kat's. I then went down to the gym and couldn't see you on the way down, and Steve told me you hadn't been eating all week. We looked around the club, couldn't find you, and I eventually found you at home."

He picks up a glass full of something and hands it to me. "Drink this!"

I look inside the glass; a green, milky liquid is inside. I look at him.

"What is it?" I screw my nose up as I hand it back to him.

"A protein shake."

"No, Lloyd, I don't do health food, you know that."

He pushes the glass back to me.

"Well, this week you haven't done any food, now drink." I look into it again. Green slime, probably radioactive. I take a sip and it tastes like... I don't know, but it is horrible.

"No thank you, Lloyd, it's horrible. I just don't like it."

"It's either drinking that or eating oysters, Charlotte."

I didn't see oysters on the table. My eyes dart around all the food. Phew, no oysters, I am saved.

"I can get some, Charlotte. Drink it down, Steve made it especially for you."

I take another sip, waiting a moment or two to see what happens. Nothing yet. I take another sip and wait again. That's good, I haven't grown a third eye yet in the middle of my forehead.

"Charlotte, just drink it down,"

"I am making sure it isn't poison, there is nothing wrong with being curious, is there?"

"Drink it now, please."

"Oh, can I not have a glass of wine please?"

"No, no wine for you tonight."

I look at the glass. Oh well, he isn't going to give up so down it goes. Watch out, stomach, here it comes.

Gulp, gulp, and gulp.

"Yuck! That is the most disgusting thing I have ever drunk." I place the glass on the table, not letting go of it, and my head follows to the table too and lands on the plate.

"Can I go to sleep now, Lloyd?"

"No, eat some more, come on, sit up and eat."

"This is the exact reason I haven't come up here all week, because I knew you would bully me somehow, I just knew you would find a reason."

"I will bully you, as you put it, if you don't eat for a week. I want you fit, not anorexic. Now eat before you forget how to."

"Please, I just want to sleep," I say wearily.

"Sit up, come on, you will start feeling better soon. I promise that shake will start working and you will have a little more energy."

I sit up and Lloyd feeds me another chocolate-covered strawberry, which instantly takes the taste of radioactive green slime away.

"You may hate me as much as you like, but all the time I like you, Charlotte, you have nothing to worry about. I will look after you, I will make sure you are safe, if you are with me or not, but I will not give up on you and I will not let you get sick." He feeds me another strawberry followed by a spoonful of cream cake. I take a proper look at the table I hadn't noticed when I quickly scanned for oysters that it's all cream cakes and chocolate; puddings everywhere, nothing but puddings. We are having a girl's dream meal: pudding for starters, main, and dessert.

"Lloyd, how many of these puddings do you think I can eat?"

"I don't know and I don't care – you can eat as much as you like, but not as little as you like. Sometimes to eat unhealthy comfort food is just so good and puddings are the perfect way to tempt most people, don't you think?"

"Well, I don't think I can eat much more right now,

I am starting to feel a little full. Can we sit on the sofa and have a cuddle for a while to have a break? That milkshake is swishing a little."

"OK, yes, for half an hour, then we eat something else, deal?"

"Yes, Lloyd." I smile at him.

We go and sit down on the sofa. He puts his arm around me and cuddles me. It's now that I realise how much I have missed him all week. His smell, a clean, fresh smell like a spring day. The warmth of his body, so cosy; his strong arms holding firm but not tight, so comforting and loving. The feeling of wellbeing and security, just like a cuddle from your mum and dad when you are a kid. I forgot that my mum, and dad, when he was alive, always had a cuddle for me, no matter what. Naughty or good, the answer was always a cuddle and they cuddled a lot too. It was very important to them. It must have been.

"I have missed this, Lloyd, cuddling up with you. All week I have missed you."

"Have you? Well, they have been here waiting all week for you to come and claim them, but you haven't come for them. That was your choice." He rubs the top of my leg.

"I was just so tired, and I thought you would give me a hard time about what I was or wasn't doing in the gym."

"I wouldn't do that at all." He moves his head and peers down, trying to see my face. "I thought you knew that. I said I wasn't getting involved, that Steve had asked me to keep out of it, and I had promised him I would. He also said that what went on in the gym was between him and you, and he wouldn't tell me anything all week. I have been here worrying about you, if you were OK and if you were cross with me."

"I wasn't cross with you, Lloyd, I was just tired, so tired."

"You were very angry with me last time I saw you."

"I think, truth be known, I was cross with myself because I couldn't do it."

"Now I know you are ill."

"What makes you say that?"

"Well, usually I am the Dom from hell for ages afterwards, now you are admitting that you were cross with yourself – something not quite right there, Charlotte."

"No, Lloyd, when I tell you that you are the Dom from hell I mean it and you are, but did I once insult you the other evening? I don't think I did. I knew you were right. I just didn't want to do it or sort it out, so I got angry."

"Wow, Charlotte, you sound so different. Are you finally getting things in boxes up there? I am impressed. What a difference a week in the gym has made."

"No, Lloyd, I have had so much stuff flying around in my head all week that I can't see the boxes, let alone put things away."

Lloyd laughs.

"That's the Charlotte I know and love." He kisses me on the head. "Right, something to eat now, I think. What would you like?"

"Oh, I don't know, surprise me."

"OK." Jumping up, he releases me from the cuddle. Returning, he has a big plate with strawberries and a slice of death by chocolate cake. Sitting back down, he lays my head in his lap, and while he feeds me a strawberry, dipping it in chocolate, he says, "You know, Charlotte, it was the hardest thing I have done with you so far this week."

"Why is that, Lloyd?" I munch through a strawberry.

"Because I didn't like to see you so upset with me, and then when you didn't come back up I wanted to come and find you."

"So why didn't you?"

"Well, I must have picked up my keys a thousand times, walked to the lift, then turned back again, since all of this started. I just didn't know what was going on in your head."

"So why didn't you phone me and ask?"

"I have phoned you hundreds of times and you haven't answered me. I have texted as well. Anthony and Nats have been letting me know when you are at work and if you are home." He feeds me some death by chocolate. "I didn't know what to think, Charlotte. No contact from you, nothing. I was going to come over to see you Tuesday but Anthony said no, in fact everyone said no, to leave you to let you work things out. I thought about it and they were right. You had a very intense weekend followed by Monday and my being very hard on you, so my decision was that I wouldn't come, but that I would be here for you every night in case you did want to see me for something. I asked Steve every day if he would ask you to come and see me. I stopped ringing and texting on Wednesday in case it was driving you mad."

Oh shit, the phone. I put it in my bag Tuesday and forgot about it. It probably ran out of battery long ago and because it hasn't bleeped or rung I haven't even given it a thought.

"Oh, Lloyd, the phone is in my bag. I have been so tired that I haven't even thought about it all week until now."

"Well, I just guessed you were trying to work things out, and if you were you didn't need me confusing your head any more. That's why I have stayed away, no other reason, and I am telling you this now because I want you to know that no matter what has happened during the day, there is always a cuddle right here waiting for you, and I think that you have forgotten that."

"No, I hadn't forgotten, I just felt so tired I just didn't want the next round with you after a round at the gym, that's all. I couldn't face it," I say, with the biggest mouthful of cake and strawberry that Lloyd could fit in my mouth. I think he is trying to keep me quiet with food.

"Right, OK. First rule for me and you, and yes, I am going to make you stick to this one, is that at the end of every day, no matter what, we have a cuddle before we do anything else. We sit, chat and cuddle just like this."

"Mmm, oh good, will the rule include the chocolate cake as well when we cuddle?"

"Hmm, no, Charlotte, all these goodies are here for you as a special treat to make you eat, and to pick up your energy levels quickly."

"Oh well, I suppose that's a very good rule to have, and an excellent one to have first for our contract."

"Contract, Charlotte, who said anything about a contract?"

"Well, I think that we should have a contract soon, Lloyd, don't you?"

"Oh, Charlotte, I think you are still very tired."

"Why do you say that? Don't you want a contract with me, then?"

"There isn't anything I would like more, but I really don't think you are ready just yet for such a big step. I think you have a lot to think about and you have a lot more gym sessions to go to before we can talk about it. I said six months, and it hasn't been six months yet."

"But I have thought and I am starting to get it, I know I am. I can see why you have sent me to the gym and why you have chosen Steve to be my trainer. It is also probably the hardest thing I have done since all this started as well, and I am glad of it. If I wasn't do you think I would have gone every day, even though I was so tired I could barely stand up, and I have to go tomorrow morning as well? If I am not there he will come and get me, and I really don't want to go through all that again."

"Is that the reason you have been going every day, because you didn't want the same thing to happen as what happened on Monday?"

"One of the reasons, yes, but something else happened on Monday." I pause.

"What else happened?"

"I don't think I should tell you because you will say it was a blatant loss of control, and yes, you would be right."

"What happened, Charlotte?"

"I had a fight with Steve and I am not talking verbally, I mean a real fight. I wanted to knock him out and trust me, I tried, and I will tell you this, if I had made contact I would have bloody killed him." My eyes started to well up with tears.

"Hey, Charlotte, why are you crying?" he asks, wiping the tears away from my face with his hand.

"I am crying because that isn't me. I have never before been so angry. I am not a violent person, I hate violence – everything on Monday night was just so wrong with me, I hated everything, just everything!" I put my hands over my eyes and face.

"What did you hate?"

"I just told you, I hated everything."

"Like what?"

"I hated you, Steve and turtles, I just hated everything."

"Turtles, why hate turtles?"

"I just do, OK, but most of all I hated myself for being like that. I really don't know what came over me, and when Steve got me downstairs he put on some boxing gloves, and said if I wanted to fight him go ahead, and I did."

"Charlotte, I can promise you this, you wouldn't get near to killing Steve. He has been a boxer and he knows exactly what he is doing. When he is sparring he is one of the best."

"Yes, well, that's beside the point. He made me so mad, and he kept pushing and pushing, until I became so angry that I couldn't think straight at all. I didn't like it, and that's when I decided I would keep going even though I have tried every night to get him to say, 'Go on, Charlotte, you go home tonight, you deserve a rest,' but oh no, he has just kept pushing me all week."

"Steve has said he is impressed with you, that tonight he got you on your hamster wheel for ten whole minutes before you left. That is over a hundred per cent improvement, and he said that you were learning kickboxing, and that you were very good at it. But that's all he has said. Now come on, dry your eyes. None of this is worth crying over, Charlotte."

"But, Lloyd, I still hate myself!"

"What else do you hate?"

"Nothing...well, almost nothing, that is."

"Why almost nothing?"

"I hate turtles still."

"Charlotte, what is it with turtles that you don't like?"

"I just don't like them at the moment."

"OK, strange but OK, so you don't hate me or Steve anymore, then?"

"No, that had gone by the time I had finished falling on my backside every two seconds when I was trying to fight Steve." I sob into my hands.

"Oh, Charlotte, please stop crying!"

"I can't, I don't really know why I am crying. I think I have wanted to cry all week but I just didn't have the energy to."

Lloyd lifted my hands off my head.

"Come here, let me cuddle you up. Now, Charlotte, you are tired and you are lacking energy and that's why you are emotional – that's fine, we all need to release sometimes." He sits me up and cuddles me as I sob on his shoulder.

"Don't tell Steve, but I quite like kickboxing."

"That's good, he says you are really quite good at it. That reminds me, you need a drink now!" He pushes me up off his shoulder and smiles. He goes and gets me a glass of water and a large coffee, and a coffee for himself. By the time he gets back I have managed to contain the tears and have wiped my face.

"Thank you, Lloyd."

"That's OK, do you feel a little more awake now?" He places the drinks on the table.

"Yes, a little."

"Shall we have these drinks and you can have a little more to eat? Then we will go to bed, cuddle up and just sleep in each other's arms. Tomorrow you will feel fine, Steve's magic shake will have well and truly kicked in."

"OK, but do I have to go to the gym in the morning for nine?"

"You don't have to if you don't want to."

"No I will go – you made a deal with Steve and if I am not there he will just come and get me. I'd much rather just go."

"Well, can we see how you feel in the morning before saying for definite? And if you don't feel up to it I will talk to Steve."

"No, Lloyd, if I don't feel up to it I will go and talk to him – you made a deal with Steve to keep out of it. You have put trust in Steve to do the right thing and I have to trust him too. It's about time I started trusting, and I mean really trusting other people again, and not just you and Anthony."

"That's me well and truly told."

"It's not you well told at all, Lloyd, it's what you have agreed to, and I don't want to let you down, especially in front of others in the lifestyle."

"Thank you, Charlotte, but make me a promise – if at any time you don't feel well you will come back up here and rest."

"Yes, Lloyd, I will, I promise."

Lloyd makes me eat some more cake and strawberries; then we drink our drinks and go to bed.

Chapter Twenty

"Wake up, Charlotte!" Lloyd is standing by the side of the bed with a tray. "Here, I have breakfast for you."

I sit up and Lloyd places the tray on the bed. There are bagels, a bowl of cereal, toast, butter, jam, two large mugs of coffee and a glass of orange juice.

"Oh thanks, Lloyd, I am starving."

He sits down next to me and picks up a slice of toast and starts munching. I pick up the plate with the bacon bagel on it and take a bite.

"How do you feel this morning?"

"Erm, fine," I say as I bite into the bagel again.

"Good, it's amazing what a bit of food can do, isn't it? Don't you ever do that again, Charlotte, don't you ever not eat."

"I did eat at lunchtimes, I had my roll." I wash down the last bite of bagel with a large gulp of coffee.

"Well, it's a good job you had that, it's a wonder you haven't collapsed. None of us know how you have done it, in fact none of us realised you weren't eating properly, we all thought you were just acting as if you were so tired just to try and get out of going to the gym, so everyone just ignored you. If Steve hadn't realised last night I wouldn't have come for you, and who knows what might have happened?"

"I know, Lloyd, I am so sorry to you all, but today I feel full of energy. My muscles aren't aching like they were, I feel great. Last night felt like the first time I have slept all week. Even though I have fallen asleep where I have landed every night, I haven't felt like I have slept at all. My head feels clear for the first time, but I am sure as soon as I get into the gym it will cloud up with Steve pushing me to do better. I don't know what he thinks I am, really, but I am not a fit type of person, I have always hated sports." I lean forward to give him a kiss.

"Charlotte, did I hear you right, your head is clear?"

"Yes, I don't have loads of stuff flying around, I feel like a big weight has been taken off my shoulders."

"You are broken. I have broken you, you don't sound like Charlotte anymore – no insults, no smart-arse mouth. I usually have at least one excuse to give you a spanking by now."

"There is still time yet."

"I will have to call in some of those you owe me if you carry on being so correct. It's a good job I have kept count."

"You know you can spank me anytime, you don't need an excuse."

"But, where is the fun in that? Where is the play?"

"Ah, but you wanted me to fix my head, and now you don't like it?"

He leans forward and kisses me on the lips.

"I love it, and I am sure that the other Charlotte will put in an appearance from time to time. Right, shower. I will put your clothes out for you. You don't want to be late."

I have a shower, get dressed and while we wait for the lift to arrive Lloyd gives me a drop-dead gorgeous kiss, the first one for a week. When the lift arrives he peels me off him and puts me in the lift.

When I get to the gym Steve is on the phone; he puts his finger up for me to wait. Saying goodbye, he puts the phone down.

"Hello, Charlotte, how are you feeling this morning?"

"Fine, thank you, Steve, I feel buzzing in fact."

"Good. No argument or excuses today as to why you shouldn't be here?"

"Nope, none whatsoever."

"Here is your protein drink." He pushes a glass towards me.

I look inside the glass: green slime. Yuck, for the sake of a sub's arse, no, I can't.

"I have just had breakfast with Lloyd, I am totally full. Thank you but no thanks," I say politely.

"Charlotte, you will drink it, and every time you come there will be one here for you, and before you do anything you will drink it."

"I really don't care for them that much and I really don't think I need it, thank you."

"Charlotte, it is not up for debate – you will drink it." He crosses his arms as if to say subject closed. God, stressed Doms, I hate them. I pick up the glass and raise it to my lips. It smells awful and looks even worse up close. I try to tip it into my mouth but I just can't, remembering what it tasted like last night.

"I'm sorry, but I just can't. See, I have tried it, it just will not come out of the glass."

He laughs, leaning back slightly. "Oh, Charlotte, one day you will surprise us all and that day will be when you don't have something to say. Drink it."

"Now look, I have eaten this morning – do you think Lloyd would let me come down here and not have breakfast?"

"Oh, I know you have had breakfast and you are very lucky that you haven't ended up seriously ill, and from now on you will have a shake before every session, and when you leave you will take a shake with you that you will drink either if you feel very tired after getting home, or in the morning for breakfast, or should I say *with* breakfast. I will know if you haven't drunk it. And I have prepared a diet sheet for you to take, which you will also keep to."

"Oh no, I don't diet, I don't believe in diets. I am drawing the line on that one." I scowl at him as I divert the conversation from the drink.

"It's not that type of diet, Charlotte, it's one that will give you everything you need, but as you showed us all last week that you can't control your eating, you will do it. Now drink."

I raise the glass to my lips again and take a gulp.

"Aww no, it's even more disgusting than last night. It's radioactive, please don't make me drink it, Steve, I promise I will eat properly from now on, I have learnt my lesson."

"Drink, Charlotte. I can stand here all day waiting for you to finish but you are not going to do anything until you *have* finished, which means you will not leave here for at least an hour after you have drunk it."

My eyes widen; he is blackmailing me now, and he never gives me a break.

"All I have to do is phone Lloyd and he will come and get me."

"Not gonna happen, Charlotte – drink!"

I take another gulp of radioactive liquid; as it hits my stomach it seems to bounce back up into my throat.

"Please, it's trying to escape! I have taken over half of it, Steve."

"Charlotte, you haven't even drunk a quarter of it yet – drink."

I look into my glass. Breaking canes, it's multiplying; it seems to have more in it than I started with.

"Oh I get it, this is a magic cup – the more I drink, the more there is in the glass." I try to discreetly put the glass down on his table.

"Charlotte, I can assure you that it isn't a magic cup. Get on with it, down in one, and don't put it down." He looks at me trying to put it on his table.

I raise the glass again – watch out stomach, here it comes. One, two, three, gulp, gulp, gulp. I shiver in disapproval at the flavour; I still can't work out what it is.

"Good, now we can begin. I hope that is the end of being disagreeable Charlotte today. We have a lot to go through."

I spend the next hour working out with Steve until I drop and he sends me upstairs to Lloyd, and this time I do go.

When I arrive Lloyd is talking on the phone. I collapse on the sofa and curl up. I'm tired and I feel drained again. I thought that the protein drink was supposed to help me feel better, give me more energy? Lloyd finishes on the phone and comes over to me, crouching by where I'm lying.

"You OK, Charlotte?"

"No I am not, that gym isn't deep enough!"

"What do you mean?"

"It should be right down as far as it can go. It's hell, and Steve is the Devil himself. Did you know he has radioactive solutions down there? It's a health hazard – I am sure if Environmental Health came you would get closed down. I can see the headlines – DEVIL POSING AS A DOM FEEDS SUBS RADIOACTIVE DRINKS SO HE CAN CONTROL EVERY ASPECT OF THEIR BODY, MIND AND SOUL!"

"Hello, Lloyd." Steve enters the room.

"Oh God, he is here, isn't he? He heard, didn't he?" I whisper to Lloyd, and Lloyd nods his head.

"Afraid so, Charlotte!"

"Oh, for the love of a sub!" I roll my eyes.

"Yes, Charlotte, I heard, and as we are not in the gym I will not have to kick your subbie little backside around, I can leave that to Lloyd. You forgot your radioactive solution, so I have brought it up for you. I have also brought up extra in case you need it later on."

"Oh joy, there is no escaping, is there?" I roll over on the couch with my back to them both. I'm not even going to talk to them now, I will ignore the two of them.

"Make sure she drinks one now. She will be OK, she has worked hard again today – she has even broken her record on the treadmill. She is now on just over half a mile in ten minutes." Yes, a result; he is happy with the hamster wheel. If I can just keep that up, he will be a pushover next week.

"OK, will do, see you later."

"OK, Lloyd, bye, Charlotte. Oh yes, I will see you in hell next time, Charlotte." He laughs as he leaves us alone.

"Oh, what joy. Bye, Steve," I mutter into the sofa.

"Here, Charlotte, drink this for me please."

I roll back to face him.

"Lloyd, as I was saying before the Devil arrived, he has made me drink that stuff already before I started this morning and quite honestly, it doesn't work. Look at me, I am exhausted. He made me work so hard he will not let me sit down for a minute. Work, work, work, that is all I do down there, and the hamster wheel is not what it seems either – he has me generating electricity for him, I am sure."

"Charlotte, you will get the hang of it, it just takes time, so drink. After the weekend you will feel better again, and tomorrow you can rest."

"No, Lloyd, I have to go to the gym every day. You don't understand, there is no hiding now I have drunk his radioactive drink. He can find me anywhere, like he just did."

"Strange, he doesn't usually work on a Sunday – the gym is closed!"

"Well, now he has me I am sure he is making exceptions to the rule – devils do that, you know."

"Charlotte, trust me, he isn't working in the gym tomorrow, you have a day off. Now drink, and in an hour you will feel better, I promise. Then we shall have a relaxing weekend, just you and me."

Chapter Twenty-One

It's been four weeks since Lloyd made me go to the gym. I have started to enjoy going, I look forward to it, though Steve ups the pace every day and I have progressed from the hamster wheel to a rowing machine, another device that is made for generating electricity, I am sure. I have also been allowed to join everyone else with kickboxing. It's more fun, but hard work. The weight training, well, that's another story. I always end up stuck under the weights; they are so heavy I just can't push them back up. One day Steve left me there for over an hour, saying that even I could raise eight pounds. I have pointed out that us girlies' muscles are not supposed to look like a man's, all bulging and highly formed, and that I wasn't sure about the muscle groups of a devil but I thought they would be superhuman, and if he was a girlie he would know that eight pounds was very heavy, especially when lying on your back, and if he didn't unpin me I would have to kick his Dom devil arse all over the gym. Not the right thing to say to a devil, not at all. When he did unpin me an hour later he put on the boxing gloves and my feet didn't touch the ground, him telling me that respect was the most important thing to have, especially where he was concerned, and even if I was a vanilla person he would still treat me exactly the same.

Apart from that, most of my training has gone like clockwork. I have found that I have more energy than ever before. I still have to drink radioactive shakes, but he hasn't noticed that I leave a little in the bottom of the glass. Lloyd and I talk more and spend more time together, and even though I didn't think it was possible I appreciate him even more than I did. I am starting to read him better; his body language, his voice and his texts are all very clear now. I can keep control for most of the time, although my sarcasm is still there; I don't think I will ever lose that and I don't think I want to – after all, spontaneous is good, isn't it? And it's part of what makes me, me.

Oh yes, the baby we delivered. We went to her christening last weekend. We had such a good time, and to our surprise they named her Charlotte Lloyd-Jones, giving her a double-barrelled surname so they could include Lloyd's name. It was such a humbling experience for both of us. They are going to send us photos of her every month, and we have said we will visit them as well. Lloyd is such a natural with babies. I watched him for ages, cuddling baby Charlotte and talking with her. No, I have no chance of being pregnant. Yup, you guessed it, we still haven't got around to doing it yet. Same old thing: the time isn't right. But foreplay? Well, ladies, I can honestly recommend it. Fan-subbing-tastic, all the way. And yes, I still hate turtles. That dream is recurring, especially when I have had a good playing weekend with Lloyd and he leaves me a little frustrated. I still can't get rid of the turtles.

It's Thursday and I have decided to get a wax without Lloyd. How brave is that? Well, not really, the reason is so that I can make as much noise as I want without him giving me a hard time on what is and is not acceptable. Also, it will calm down a little before the weekend and I won't be fidgeting as much over the weekend. I have told Steve I will be a little late getting to the gym and he is fine with that. I have just finished work and gone into one of the waxing rooms. Lying on the table, eyes closed, I have been doing some deep breathing and bracing myself for what is to follow. I haven't been here five minutes when:

"Hello, Charlotte."

"Erm, hello, Lloyd." Lloyd? What? For the sake of loving Doms. My eyes open wide. "Lloyd, what are you doing here?"

His head bends over mine. "I have come to meet you from work."

"But you didn't say you were meeting me?"

"No, it's a surprise, and what are you doing here? Having a crafty sleep before gym, are we?"

"Well, err…"

"You are not having a wax on your own, are you? You of all people should know that you don't do that without me saying you can."

"It's like this – I thought I would save you the time, you have been so busy all week."

"No, you know that I would have arranged this for you if you had asked. It wouldn't be that you thought you would get away with not having me here and that you would be able to make as much noise as you liked, would it?"

"How did you know I was here?" I ask, changing the subject.

"I didn't."

"How did you know I was having a wax?"

"I didn't. I mentioned to Nats yesterday that I would meet you from work today. When I left the gym Steve said you had informed him that you were going to be late in this evening because you had something to do at work. I thought, good, Nats has made an excuse to keep you here for me. When I arrived Nats told me you were down here somewhere and I looked in all the usual places and couldn't find you. Then I realised that all the other doors had engaged signs on them and this was the only one that hadn't. So, my dear Charlotte, it was elementary, the powers of my deduction are amazing, don't you think?"

"So no one had tipped you off, then?"

"Not at all – all coincidental."

For the love of a sub. I roll my eyes.

"We best be going then, Lloyd. I will get up."

He places his hands on my shoulders.

"I don't think so, it would be a shame to waste such a perfect moment, and when we get back we can discuss this further." He rubs the palm of his hand. I still haven't worked out what is wrong with his hand; I will have to ask him, I think.

I have the wax done with Lloyd present and I manage to bite my tongue for most of it – well, two strips in I do, and Lloyd has to remind me that he is there, and even if he isn't there he would know what I'm having done. I bite my tongue again, along with my fist and arm. I can feel the beads of sweat running down my forehead.

After it's finished Lloyd says, "There now, wasn't that better without all that fuss?"

"No, it hurts the same as it did the first time I had it done," I snap.

"You are not losing control now, are you? The hard bit has finished."

"Lloyd, a girlie can lose control when it comes to severe pain down there, I have pointed this out to you before."

"Can I assume, then, although you are getting to grips

with control, you think that if you have severe pain it's OK to lose control? Am I to assume if anyone inflicts pain on you, you will lose control?"

"Why, Lloyd, who is going to inflict severe pain on me to find out?" I cross my arms and stand up tall.

"No one that I know of, Charlotte, I am just interested in how far your control has come and where your limits are. That's all, it's a valid question."

"Lloyd, you don't have valid questions without seeing them to the end result. To see how far you can push me or whatever you think you are doing. You have something up your sleeve, I know, and I know you know I don't do severe pain."

"And you also know I will never do anything that would hurt you. Now come here and give me a kiss." He grabs hold of me and kisses me; then he places his hand down on my arse and rubs it. I feel my skirt getting caught up in the rubs, and he places his leg between mine and pulls me closer. God, this is nice, I love this so much. I could stay here all day just kissing; my body dances with sensation and he kisses me more.

Knock, knock.

Nats pops her head around the door.

"Come on, you two, I need the room!"

"Just coming, Nats, sorry," Lloyd replies. "Come on, Charlotte, I have forgotten why I have come to get you from work." He grabs my hand and we rush past Nats in the corridor.

"Bye, Nats," we say as we rush by her. Lloyd grabs my gym bag from the desk and we leave.

"Where are we going, Lloyd?"

"You will see."

"But I have to go to the gym or Steve will find me."

"No, he is expecting you to be late, don't worry."

"But he isn't expecting me to be this late, and I have the radioactive slush he calls protein drink in my bag, so he will find me."

"It isn't radioactive and he will only find you as I have told him where we are going."

"Oh, I see, the little Dom circle is at work again, everyone knows where Charlotte is except Charlotte."

"No, not at all."

"Yes, well, you tell everyone else but me. I am starting to think I am just an afterthought; I am only told things on a need-to-know basis."

"You are told everything you need to know."

"Exactly, and nothing more. That is my point."

"If I told you what we were doing all the time I wouldn't be able to surprise you, would I?"

"I suppose, but everything just lately is a surprise. The games we play, the dungeon – that's always a surprise when you take me down there, cracking whips every time I get a day off. You make out that we are doing something else and before I know it there we are."

"What are you saying, you don't like surprises?"

"No, of course I do, I just don't like the element in some of your surprises."

"You will like this one, I promise."

"You always say that."

"Well, don't you like cracking whips? You have got so good at them, you are almost as good as me now."

"Yes, I do, strangely, but that is all we have done for the last four weeks. It would be nice to have some time off from the gym and cracking whips."

"You have time off this weekend." He laughs. "Right, we are here."

"Aww, what is it?" A dirty-looking building in the middle of industrial warehouses with a small door and windows.

"You will see." He opens the door and we walk in. There are rolls and rolls of materials in racks, and a desk and tables for cutting material on. It smells like cotton inside. There is a lady sitting at a sewing machine with her head down, sewing.

"Hi," says Lloyd.

"Hi, it's all ready for you, Lloyd. I can't stop, just go in." She continues to sew, not even looking up.

We walk across the room to a big old wooden door.

"Come on." He opens the door and allows me to enter first, following behind me. "There's a light switch here somewhere, there you go." The light comes on and reveals a smallish room, a little damp-smelling for my liking, and a shiver runs up my spine.

"This isn't very nice, Lloyd." There are some full-length curtains hanging on the wall opposite. I walk over and pull them.

"No, but she is a good dressmaker."

"No windows, how strange."

Lloyd walks around the room, putting on some little lights on tables. "No, but she does try to create a little ambience in here."

"I don't like it, it gives me the chills, and what was it before, do you know?"

"I'm not quite sure but this building dates back to the Victorian era. I must admit it's not one of the prettiest buildings they ever built, but she has said it was some sort of ventilation and pump shaft for underground tunnels – the Victorians were keen on building tunnels."

"So this is my surprise? You said I would like it, Lloyd."

"Not quite, look on the sofa." I look around to the sofa

and on it there is a pile of black clothes. I walk over and pick them up.

"Come on then, Charlotte, I can't wait to see you in them."

"What, I have to try them on here?" I turn up my nose.

"Yes, if they don't fit she will sort them out now for us."

"But it's so nasty-feeling in here."

"Oh, it's OK, Charlotte, just the Victorian pump house ghost, I suspect." He laughs.

"OK, but I really don't like it in here, I'm just letting you know." I start to get undressed, as Lloyd watches my every move.

"Here, let me help you with that, Charlotte." He comes over and helps me get into the new clothes, then stands back.

I look in the mirror that is fixed to the wall – wow, it's beautiful. A black silk corset with a lace-up back and front; the front laces are more for decoration, with bones to emphasise the shape of my waist and chest, pushing my breasts up as far as they can go. Fine black lace edges the top, and at the bottom is a very soft, short tulle skirt that tucks under the corset, just fitting over my hips, with teardrop lace trimming the bottom edges. Silk seamed stockings, which are held up by the suspenders which hang from the inside of the corset, just finish the look.

Lloyd stands watching my twisting and turning as I look at every aspect of the outfit.

"Mmm, very nice, but there is something missing."

"What's missing?" I ask with surprise. I know there isn't very much of it, but it all looks very complete to me.

He reaches down to the side of the sofa and pulls out a box.

"These?" He opens the box and takes out a shoe. He bends down, placing the box on the floor beside his knee; lifting up a foot, he places the shoe on my foot. Taking the other shoe out of the box, he does the same. He gets up and I look down: black satin high heels. I turn my foot to look at the heel in the mirror. Then I spin around with my back towards the mirror, feet together. I twist my head and upper body around to look at the reflection of the shoes; they have diamantes running from the bottom all the way up the heel; then onto the back of the shoe to meet the seam in the stockings. They are to die for, every girl's envy.

I look at Lloyd, who is taking great delight in watching me, taking in every little detail of the outfit.

"Do you like it, then?"

"I don't know what to say."

"Not like you to be speechless."

"No, it's beautiful. It's my first sub outfit, a proper sub outfit. I never knew it would look so beautiful on me."

"Well, I thought you should have one. You can't keep going downstairs in shorts all the time. And this weekend is the charity spank – you said you would take part, so I thought as you were being so brave I would get you this made."

"Thank you, it's stunning. Thank you."

Walking towards me, he places his hands on my hips.

"Do you really like it?"

"Oh yes, I do."

"Does it feel comfortable?"

"Yes, very. It fits like a glove as usual – you get my size just right every time you buy me something."

"The bones aren't too high or poking in you?"

"No, not at all."

"And you are right, it is stunning. It makes you look stunning, it's perfect."

I shiver and turn my head.

"What's wrong?" He moves his head to try and look in my eyes.

"I just felt…no, it's silly."

"No, come on, Charlotte, what is wrong?"

"I felt like someone was watching us, and got a feeling like someone had just walked over my grave."

"Aww, I expect it's the ghost, liking what he sees too." He laughs.

"See, I told you it was silly, but there is a draught, don't you think?"

"Maybe a little one, Charlotte, but it's just an old building."

"Yes, I suppose so." I look back at Lloyd.

"You are very beautiful, Charlotte!"

"Thank you."

"Let's get you changed – no wait, let me look at you again."

He stands back, looking at me up and down, thinking.

"What's wrong with it?"

"There is nothing wrong with it, but your key for the lift is around your neck. It just doesn't look right; I will have to come up with something for you."

"Oh, OK, but does it matter?"

"Yes, it matters, every little detail matters, you know that, Charlotte. Up until now you have worn T-shirts and I haven't thought about the key because I don't see it that often, but now I see it I don't like it there, so I will think and get something sorted for you."

"OK, but I don't see that it matters."

"Here, I will help you get undressed. Steve will be here soon if we don't get going."

Lloyd helps me take off the clothes and while I quickly put my others back on, he places everything into a carrier bag that has been left under the clothes, putting the lights out on the tables as we move towards the door. Glancing back around the room, I realise I haven't closed the curtains.

"Lloyd, the curtains, I will close them, hold on."

"OK." As I start to close the curtains Lloyd turns off the main light, plunging the dingy old room into darkness.

"Whooo, I am the ghost of the pump house, whooo."

Goose bumps shiver through my body. "Lloyd, please don't, turn the light back on," I demand.

"OK, Charlotte." Lloyd laughs.

My head turns, looking at him as I pull the curtains shut.

"I don't think you are funny, Lloyd."

"Come on, quick, you are late for Steve now with your games you are playing."

"I am not playing games, Lloyd, I think that is you, as usual."

He opens the door and lets me go first, which I am grateful for; I don't think I would like to be in that room by myself. He follows me out and I shut the door behind him.

"Everything OK, Lloyd?" comes the voice from the machine that is still tapping away as it sews.

"Yes, thanks, a perfect fit as usual. I will leave your envelope here. Are you sure this is enough?" Placing his hand inside his jacket pocket, he takes out a white envelope.

"Yes, love, it's fine, just glad I could help. Your stuff is in the bag on the table as well." She never looks up. How can you have a conversation and not look up?

"OK, thanks." Lloyd places the envelope on the table and picks up the bag. "We are off now, bye."

"Doesn't she want to check her money? I know I would if I had worked so hard on something, I would want to know that every penny was there." I whisper quietly.

"You take care and have fun now."

Once outside, I am relieved. "What a strange woman."

"Why do you say that, Charlotte?"

"She never stopped what she was doing, not once all the time we were there. She never looked at us, or checked her money."

"Oh, she is OK, she is just very busy. She is always the same, and she is the type of woman that doesn't want to know anything about anything. She isn't interested in anyone either, that's why we like her – she is very discreet. But she is one of the best dressmakers I know. Her work is spot on and a lot of your corset she would have sewn by hand. She is very skilful."

"But she must be making a packet, so why doesn't she get nice premises?"

"I suppose she doesn't want to, maybe she is happy there."

"But if she got nicer premises she would attract more custom."

"I think she has enough. She is always working, I don't think she needs any more."

"How about a coffee before we get back?" Lloyd says, dragging me into a coffee bar.

"OK, but do I get any say in this?"

"Not really."

"What about Steve, did you tell him you were having coffee as well on the way home?"

"He will be OK, and I am feeling impulsive today."

"You are living dangerously, Lloyd. Careful now, you don't know what dangers are lurking inside a coffee bar, do you?" I snigger.

We sit down. Lloyd sits in a chair facing the window and not next to me, which is a little strange. He always sits next to me.

"I am sure that there are no dangers in here, Charlotte.

Besides which, I am thinking of letting you have the evening off from the gym, I can't quite decide."

"What is there to decide, Lloyd?"

"Can I help you?" the waitress says. My eyes look up at her, a young girl with her hair up in a ponytail, holding a pad and pen poised, waiting to write down *two cups of coffee*, looking so bored, as if she would rather be anywhere else than here.

"Yes thank you, two coffees please," Lloyd says.

"Anything else?" she asks as she scribbles on her notepad.

"No thank you."

She turns and walks away, still scribbling. What is she writing? I know, she is writing *tight git, he can't even be bothered to buy his girlfriend a cake to go with her coffee*. She looks the type to do that.

I look at Lloyd and he is looking out of the window, deep in thought.

"What you looking at?"

"Nothing, just looking."

"What are you thinking about?

"Oh nothing, just thinking."

"Are you working out how to run as fast as you can to get away from me?"

"No, never, Charlotte." He looks at me.

"That's better, I was wondering if you had some sort of space attack going on."

"No, just thinking about the weekend, and I think I am a little tired, I have been very busy at work today."

"Anything I can help you with?"

"No. Besides, you help me every time I see you." Stretching across the table, he takes my hand in his.

"Two coffees."

Lloyd lets go of my hand and the waitress puts down the two cups of coffee on the table.

"Thank you," I say, looking up at her as she turns, walking away without another word.

I look back at Lloyd. He is again deep in thought, gazing out of the window. I place my hands around my cup, looking into it at the froth still swirling around on top of the coffee. Then I look back up at Lloyd.

"That's one hell of a decision, you don't usually take this long deciding what horrible fate lies ahead of me."

"What? Oh sorry, Charlotte, I just thought I saw someone I knew, that's all, it took me back a little." He smiles at me.

"Who did you think it was you saw?"

"I couldn't have seen them, just a trick of the light. I have made my decision – no gym tonight or tomorrow. You are staying at mine tonight and tomorrow night also."

"Now I know you are ill or something – no gym, are you sure? And what will SS devil Steve say about that, then?"

"I will sort it. I want an evening for two, just you and me, relaxing and talking." He looks down at his coffee and turns his nose up at it. I look at mine; the foam has broken down, revealing a dark, muddy liquid beneath it, and we both look up together.

"Nah," he says, taking out some money and placing it on the table. "Let's go, Charlotte, I can't drink that!" He picks up the bags and heads for the door.

Chapter Twenty-Two

Back at his apartment he phones Steve and tells him I will not be there for the rest of the week, but he adds that he wants to see Steve in the morning for a chat. I put away the things we have just got and sit down on the sofa. Lloyd makes us both a cup of coffee and sits down next to me, putting his arm around me.

"Do you know what Anthony is doing tonight?" he asks.

"No, I didn't see him this morning, he was gone well before I got up."

"OK, I will phone him and let him know I want us to be alone this evening." He leans forward, releasing me from his cuddle, and picks up his phone off the coffee table, at the same time picking up my coffee and handing it to me.

"Thanks."

"Hi, Anthony, what are you and Kat up to tonight?" He pauses for the answer. "Oh, that's good, can you meet me in the gym in the morning with Steve, please, after I have taken Charlotte to work, that is?" He pauses again. "See you then." He hangs up. He was very to the point and short, compared with the way he usually talks with Anthony.

"Is everything OK, Lloyd? That wasn't the usual way you talk with Anthony – no little Charlotte joke to tell him tonight?"

He puts his phone down and picks up his coffee, sliding back onto the sofa and replacing his arm around me.

"Everything is fine." He sips his coffee.

"Why the secret meeting tomorrow after I am at work?"

"Oh, you know, just a little Dom meeting." He kisses my head.

"So what are we going to do tonight, then, now you have got me here?"

"Just relax, I told you, talking and relaxing."

"Gee, this is hard work tonight, Lloyd. OK, I will play your little game." I roll my eyes. "What are we talking about?" I say.

"What do you want to talk about?"

"I get to choose the subject?"

"Yes, anything you want."

"Anything, are you sure?"

"Yes, Charlotte."

"OK, what's going on?"

"Now, Charlotte, you know if there was something going on I wouldn't tell you anyway, it would spoil the surprise, but there isn't anything going on at all so there isn't anything to talk about on that subject – pick another."

"Tell me about your childhood and your mum and dad."

"Really?"

"Yes, really, I would like to know something about them."

"What do you want to know?"

"Anything you want to talk about – what sort of people were they?"

"As you know my mum raised me alone, and my dad was nowhere to be seen so I don't know anything about him, really. I never met him, and as I got older I didn't want to know him anyway. Mum is the world to me, as you know."

"How did they meet? Why didn't they get together? Surely your mum has told you that?"

"The time is right for you to know my family's deepest, darkest secret, the secret of the missing father." He gives a ghoulish laugh.

"Stop it, Lloyd, I am being serious."

"I will start at the beginning, and I am only telling you this because…" He pauses, deep in thought again.

"Because of what?"

"Just because I like you. Mum was a freelance photographer. She travelled the world, getting photos of everything and anything – pop stars, natural disasters…you name it, she did it. That's when she met my father, an American, tall, dark and handsome, she used to say. They met first in a bar in the centre of New York – Mum was covering a story on The Beatles, and was hoping to get some good snaps of them. She was waiting for them to arrive when he started to talk with her. He made my mum laugh. He asked her how long she was staying and if she would have a date with him the next night, and she liked him so she said yes. The next night she met him for dinner and had a fantastic time, but the next day she knew she had to leave, so after dinner she told him she was going, and that she had enjoyed his company. He gave her his phone number and said if she ever came back to ring him. Are you sure you want to know this?"

"Yes, if I am to have the next generation of Hughes I need to be able to tell them where you came from!"

"The next generation? Charlotte, are you sure I have anything to do with that?" He glances at me sideways.

"What do you mean? I hope you will have something to do with it, if I am to have the next generation."

"But Charlotte, we have never spoken about babies, we haven't even spoken about moving on from here, where we are now."

"Lloyd, we both know one day it will happen, and when it does eventually happen then I think we both know where it is going to end up, don't you?"

"We have so much to talk about before we even get to the subject of having babies."

"I didn't say right this minute. I said *if* I am to have, not I *am* going to have – big difference, Lloyd, don't you think? And anyway, I was only using it as a metaphor so you would finish the story."

"Are you sure, because if you have a baby in there I know I have nothing to do with it."

"Lloyd, you are protesting too much and I don't have a baby in there whatsoever – and you call yourself a doctor. Now can we get on with the story, please?"

He looks at me.

"Well, just to let you know these are my mum's words, what she used to tell me whenever I asked about my dad."

"OK, now can you get on with it?"

"Only if you go and get into bed, and I will get some wine." With that he bounces off the sofa and he is gone.

"Why in bed?"

"Because that's what my mum used to say, that is, apart from the getting the wine bit – for me it was milk and biscuits." And he laughs.

I go and get into bed and he comes in moments later with a bottle of wine and two glasses. After getting undressed he jumps into bed, pours out two glasses of wine and passes me one.

"Ah, this is nice," he says, sipping his wine.

"Yes, the wine is always nice," I reply.

"No, not the wine, this: me and you in bed, with a nice bottle of wine."

"Story, please finish your story."

"OK, but put down your wine and give me a cuddle first."

"I think you are trying to stall."

"Not at all, this is my mum's story and this is how she told me, except I had PJs on, but I think we are too big for PJs, what do you think?"

I slide down the bed a little. He takes my glass away from me and I snuggle down under the bedclothes; he snuggles next to me, putting his arms around me.

"Now are you going to finish the story?"

He looks me in the eyes.

"After this!" He kisses me. Mmm, my body twists as his hands slowly move down my back towards my arse and give it a squeeze. He rolls me over onto my back, places his leg between mine and parts them. His hand moves over my body, first my breasts; then to my hips, softly tantalising me, making me feel soft inside. He kisses down my chin and neck onto my chest; a little teasing of my breasts and nipples and his tongue moves across my skin like silk. Then he moves slowly down, kissing as he does so. My breathing gets deeper with every kiss, every touch; I feel goose bumps popping onto my skin as I get more aroused. He reaches the top of my hips, and placing his hands under my arse, he lifts it slightly and continues to kiss. My heart is beating faster and faster with anticipation. I feel his tongue on my clit just slightly; it feels so sensitive. I feel it swell and he teases it. I wriggle my arse and give a little moan, at the same time clenching my hands on the pillow.

"Oh, Lloyd, don't stop," I whisper. I feel his tongue getting faster and faster; my body twists and turns and he slows down, giving it a little kiss before starting his way back up my body, still planting kisses and licks, finding my G-spot and sending my body twisting and turning with ecstasy as he goes.

"Oh, Lloyd." He lies on top of me and I wrap my legs around him.

"What, Charlotte?" he whispers into my ear.

"I think you are trying to distract me from your story," I whisper to him.

"What, do you want me to stop doing what I am doing?" He pushes down on me and I feel his manhood throb – he is so hard and big!

"No, Lloyd, but I think you have anyway. Why change the habit of a lifetime?"

"Exactly, Charlotte." And he rolls off me and gets my glass of wine. "Sit up then, Charlotte, and I will continue."

I sit up, have the usual little fidget, and he hands me my wine. He gets his own wine and he leans back on the pillows.

"I will begin."

"I am most certainly sure, Lloyd, that you are ad-libbing some of this story." I look at him.

"OK, but I thought you would appreciate a little sexual teasing rather than tickling."

"Ah, right, so you are improvising, not ad-libbing."

"Absolutely no ad-libbing for me. Now if you are sitting comfortably, and if you can stop fidgeting, I will give you a cuddle and continue."

"OK, I have stopped, I am ready."

He puts his arm around me and restarts his story with my head between his arm and chest. God, this is going to be difficult with nothing to look at but his chest, I think to myself.

"Here we go. The next time she was in New York she didn't ring him as it was a stopover just for a few hours – she was on her way to Niagara Falls, so didn't see the point. She went to the bar for a drink and something to eat and sitting down, she heard a voice – 'I thought you were going to call me next time you came over?' The voice was that of the man she had met the last time she was in New York.

He sat down at her table, and asked how long she was there for. She explained she was only stopping over for a couple of hours and that was why she hadn't rung him. That she was on her way to Niagara Falls. He said that he was on his way there too for work. They discovered by chatting that they were both on the same plane, so they ended up flying out together. They decided that they would spend some time together after they had finished everything that they needed to do for work, and arranged to meet by the falls somewhere, I don't quite remember where. When they met he said he had a friend who had a boat and they could use it. To cut my mum's very long, flowery version short, they had a cuddle under the falls – that is where I was made."

"Oi, that is cheating, you can't just skip bits you don't like."

"I haven't, it's just I don't want to know the slushy parts of him kissing her and eating dinner on a boat, it's a little, well, you know, things you don't want to know about your parents."

"Oh, OK then, I will let you off."

"More wine before I continue?"

"Yes, please." I hold out my glass and he moves to reach the wine. He pours some into my glass, placing the bottle down; he then takes my glass from my hand and snuggles down, kissing my head.

"This is so nice, why haven't we done more of this?"

"Maybe because you can't finish a story?" I say, frustrated.

"I can finish a story and I will finish it, but first I want to talk with you."

"What, now?"

"Yes, this weekend is such an important one for me as well as you. I want everything to be perfect. And I am sure it will be, but before we get caught up in any moments I want you to know that as far as you taking control of things are concerned, you have done so well, and you have taken control as much as you can. I want you to know you don't have to do this weekend to prove to me that you can do it, or to prove it to anyone else. I don't want the weekend to be about that, I want the weekend to be about you and me, and the start of a life which you are happy to join, a new adventure just for us. I want you to think long and hard about if you really want this lifestyle. I don't want the answer tonight, but if you are not sure about the weekend tell me now, although on Saturday night I will ask you again if you are happy to join me in the lifestyle if you are ready for it."

"Lloyd, I am completely happy with the sponsored spanking. All the time you are there I know I will be OK."

"Well, promise me this, Charlotte: you will not push your limits at all just to try and prove a point. If you get hurt you will stop, don't carry on. If you think you are losing control, then time out long before you do, you haven't got to carry on just because you think you have to."

"I promise I will not go any further than I feel comfortable with."

"I don't want you to get spaced out, your adrenaline will be rushing."

"OK, I will not get spaced out. You know I know when

to stop – you have seen me and the way that I can calm things down now. You have taught me how; I will be fine."

"And you know I am going to tease you for the next few days just to keep you on your toes. Erm, I have had an idea." Devil horns, I can see them. He grins.

"What is your idea, or dare I ask?"

"I might get the remote control love egg out for you on Saturday night as well."

"Lloyd, no, please don't."

He laughs. "No, I won't, you will have enough to think about this time. Mind you, I don't know which one of us is going to find it hardest."

"Why do you say that?"

"I think I will find it hard watching others spank you, and it's your first time really playing. I didn't think you wanted anyone else to touch you, so it will be so hard for you, but most of all I think I already feel jealous."

"Is this what it is all about, that you are feeling jealous and you think you will lose control?"

"I will never lose control, Charlotte, I am just saying I think it will be very hard on us both, but all the time you are happy doing it I will not stop it. This is your call, and it's healthy to have feelings of jealousy, you know that."

"Now we have cleared that up, can we get on with your story? Sounds so romantic, having a night on a boat at Niagara Falls."

"Yes, well, she got caught up in the moment, didn't she?"

"And if she hadn't you wouldn't be here, would you?"

"I know that. Anyway, the story. Right, got it. After their few days together, I hasten to add she only slept with him the once. They parted a few weeks later and she found out she was having me, so she decided she would get a flight and go and see him. So she phoned him and told him when she was going to arrive. When she got there, he was waiting for her at the airport and he took her for something to eat. After they finished eating she told him. Now do you want the flowery version for children or the real version?"

"I suppose the real version."

"He wasn't best pleased. He wrote her out a cheque and told her to get rid of me. She said that wasn't going to happen and that he could keep his money. She wasn't there to try and trap him and she didn't want his money. She thought that he had a right to know that he had a child on the way and to give him a chance of being in my life, not just for him but for me too. He then told her that he was already married and that he wanted no more to do with her or me. As far as he knew she could be sleeping with loads of men all over the world, and how was he to know he was the real father? My mum got on the next plane and left.

"She never contacted him after that, but when she was in New York about two years after having me he was staying in the same hotel as she was, by chance. They spoke and she showed him a photo of me. He said I looked just like him when he was a kid. He asked my mother if she needed anything, and she said no. She also added that I didn't want anything from him either. He told my mum he was going through a bad patch with his wife, that he had found out his daughter wasn't his, and that he was going to get a divorce and cut them out. And if she wanted, he would pay for her and me to move to America and they could try and see if they could have a relationship. My mother told him she would never want a relationship with a man who couldn't even acknowledge his son's existence, a man who was so cold at heart. She said that she and I were happy the way we were, and she didn't want her son to end up like him, cold and bitter."

"Aww, that was harsh of her, but I must agree you haven't ended up cold and bitter."

"No, she was right, because he said he would fight her to get me away from her. He would have the best lawyers that money could buy. But she laughed and said, 'You don't know where I am, you have never supported him', and that he would never find me. He did find Mum several times, sent her letters saying he wanted a paternity test but she just said no, because without that there was nothing he could do. Mum wasn't going to give me up to him, never, and quite honestly I am glad she didn't. And then he died."

"Weren't you curious about him?"

"No, I wasn't. I trusted my mum, she has never lied to me, and why would I be curious about a man who never really wanted to know me? I don't really know why he wanted to take me away from my mother – what sort of person would want to do that?"

"I suppose. Are you not sad he is dead, and about not getting the chance to meet him?"

"He never wanted to meet me until his life with his family had finished. Really, he just wanted me, not my mum as well, so why should I be sad about someone I had never met, someone who used my mum, and didn't even care about what happened next?"

"That could explain a lot."

"What do you mean, Charlotte, could explain a lot?"

"The respect you have for women, for me, the way you treat me."

"Maybe, but I treat everyone with respect."

"I'm not talking about everyone, I am talking about the respect you have for me, about the way you have to make sure everything is just right before taking things further."

"I suppose, but I wasn't always like this."

"What, you mean you have done mindless fucks, Lloyd?"

"Yes, Charlotte, I have. I was a teenager but to be honest I didn't enjoy them. I enjoy the whole package, with a few little extras, if you catch my drift."

"You have surprised me. I thought you were born in control."

"Talking about born and control, do you take the pill?"

"It was a metaphor. Don't worry, I will not have a baby just yet. Anyway, we need to actually do something before that happens and the way we are going we will never get that far."

"Charlotte, I am being serious. I only ask as I have never seen you take anything and I was just wondering so that I know."

"Yes, I take the pill, I pop it every morning after cleaning my teeth. It's not something I shout about, you know."

"How long have you been on the pill for?"

"What's this? You sound like a doctor."

"I am a doctor – tell me how long have you taken the pill for?"

"Ever since I was old enough. My mum took me to the doctor and had me put on it."

"Haven't you had a break?"

"I really feel uncomfortable talking to you about this, and no, I haven't. Do you really think I wanted to have a kid with anyone I have met so far?"

"Why don't you have a break now? You should go and see your doctor and discuss your options if you feel uncomfortable talking with me about it."

"OK, Dr Lloyd, I will go and see what she thinks, now can we stop talking about it?"

"Yes, we can, for now."

"Good. I don't even know how the subject came up of

me taking the pill," I said, puzzled, still trying to make the link.

"Your turn for secret stories from your family closet, Charlotte."

"I have told you about my mum and dad, loads of stuff."

"What do you miss about your childhood?"

"I miss my dad, of course, what else would I miss?"

"I suppose you would, Charlotte. I am sorry, I didn't think."

"I miss him for loads of reasons. I miss his smile to tell me that everything is OK, his smile that says he is so proud. I didn't get that when I graduated because he was still so ill, he died shortly after. I miss the way he always took charge and sorted out what would be the best thing to do. In fact, I think he was a lot like you. He always had good control, and he never argued or got cross, with either my mum or me. He always had a cuddle for us. I miss that. When he died I tried so hard to do everything. I knew Mum wouldn't be able to and I had to show her how to do everything – she had never done anything other than look after me and the house."

"Did you ask your mum if she knew how to do these things or did you assume she didn't?"

"I don't know, I think I just knew she didn't."

"I think you might have underestimated your mum a little. I am sure that your mum would have had just as much control over things as your dad did."

"What makes you say that? And if she did, why didn't she say to me she knew?"

"Maybe she thought it was your way of dealing with your loss. That you needed to do it for your dad."

"Oh my goodness! Do you really think so, Lloyd?"

"Maybe, I see it a lot when I do bereavement consultations."

"My poor mum, what have I done to her?"

"I'm sure she has got over it, Charlotte, and you say your mum and dad never argued?"

"No, they didn't, they just had a great love for each other. Mum still hasn't been out with another man since Dad. She just says there is no one that would come close to Dad."

"Never say never, that's what I say."

"Look at your mum. She never found anyone else, did she?"

"That's because she never found anyone that she thought would be right for both of us. She never had love and I am sad for that. She gave all her love to me, but true love for another she hasn't found yet. There is still time for her."

"I feel like you are analysing me again."

"Not at all, I have wanted to know all there is about you and I want you to know about me, too."

"Tell me more about your childhood."

"I went to boarding school as Mum was away working all the time and she wanted me to have a good education, not to be dragged around the world, and that's it."

"Is there nothing else?"

"Nope."

"That's quite sad, that you didn't have a childhood home. I don't think I would have survived without my mum and dad being around all the time. I would never be able to leave any child of mine at school alone for weeks on end. Would you want to do that?"

"Nope, I would want Mum at home while I take care of everything, and when I come home from work I want the house full of laughter and love."

I snuggle into him and he holds me close.

"Sounds perfect to me, so how many perfect little moments would you want to share this love and laughter with?"

"Maybe three."

"Oh, I would want four, two boys and two girls."

"That's a tall order, Charlotte!"

"How do children fit into the lifestyle?"

"Much the same as they fit into a vanilla lifestyle."

"That easy, you think?"

"I don't think, I know for sure." He kisses my head.

"This has turned very serious now."

"It all started with finding out about each other."

"Yes, I know, but you are not usually so serious about the way you find out about me. Usually it's more fun."

I know there is something on his mind but I just don't know what, and it's not having babies. I also know if I ask him he isn't going to tell me. He will skirt around it; this lifestyle seems to mean I have to tell everyone everything and no one tells me a subbing thing. It can't all be about their next evil plan, can it?

"What are you saying, Charlotte, that you would prefer me to spank it out of you?" He props his head up on his hand.

"That isn't what I am saying at all, I was just stating a fact."

I run my finger down his exposed chest; across his abs, slowly down I go.

"It looks to me that you are bored with just talking."

"No." My eyes start following the line of my finger as I move the sheets off him.

"What are you doing, then?" He watches me remove the sheet.

"I thought I would give you a nice, relaxing, smooth rub." My eyes look at his manhood – so erect, so perfect.

"Cool, Charlotte, I would love a massage!" And he bounces onto his front. No, it's gone! Not a massage, for the love of a sub, not a back massage, that isn't what I said and isn't what I meant.

Stunned, my mouth open. I couldn't speak.

"Come on then, I am ready." With his head on his folded arms, he continues. "Oh yes, there are some oils in the bathroom."

And that is our evening. Lloyd becomes a little more playful, but every time I seem to get a little too close he changes the game, keeping me at arm's length all the time. I am sure he is finding it hard to resist me, well, at least I hope that is what it is, and not that he has someone else.

Chapter Twenty-Three

In the morning he takes me to work, and all the time he seems to be a little preoccupied with something, looking around him all the time. I watch him leave the salon and again he looks both ways before starting on his journey back to the club. I follow him out and stand on the pavement, watching him walking away.

"Penny for your thoughts, Charlotte?" Nats says as she joins me on the pavement.

"Nothing, I am just worried about Lloyd. He seems to be so preoccupied with something, I am not quite sure. Look, he is looking everywhere, what is he looking for?"

"He's all right, you're just reading too much into things. It's all this taking control, maybe you have never noticed before. Now come on back in – we have work to do, and I have some very important phone calls to make," she says, stretching her neck to see him.

"Yeah, OK, but he is being very strange, I know he is."

"He is probably worried about the weekend. You know what he is like, everything has to be so perfect. I know that he is a little worried about you and the sponsor night, and he has been working very hard lately, and I think that is all there is to it."

"No, I don't think it's that. Take last night, for instance, we talked about normal things from parents to having babies – that's not like him at all, not a spank in sight."

"That's just him trying to give you a little bit of Charlotte and Lloyd time. We have all told him that he is being too hard on you as of late, with training in the gym every night and every spare minute he is training you with whips and self-defence. We have told him that you need time out for being you, so that's what it is all about."

Well, if Nats knows what's going on she isn't going to tell me either. I don't buy her story of Lloyd and me time at all.

The rest of the day flies by very fast. Things are very busy, with the single subs coming for their makeovers and the latest hairstyles. Single subs, I have decided, are more particular than Doms with their subs, and that is saying something. And tomorrow is pamper day for the Doms and subs, so this shop is closed to the general public. I am working in the morning; then Lloyd will be here for the afternoon making sure everything is right for me. I do like pamper days – they are hard work, but when you see the subs all ready to go it's worth it to see the transformation from their everyday look to their lifestyle look.

Lloyd, as promised, comes to the salon to pick me up. He's about an hour early and I'm not even nearly finished, but he sits watching me working while he drinks coffee. He seems a little more relaxed than he has done over the last twenty-four hours. Maybe Nats was right; maybe I was reading too much into it.

The evening is just the same, me and him and not a spank in sight. Even when I say to him my arse will get soft and I will be no good for the sponsored spank he just says it will be fine. I even ask him if he's turning vanilla, to which his reply is never. It's a little like drawing blood from a stone, trying to get a response from him. I have enjoyed the last few days of just chatting and cuddling, but I have also missed the fun side of Lloyd's lifestyle.

Lloyd has pampered me this afternoon. My hair has been done wavy and loose, make-up perfect, he has helped me dress in my corset and skirt, and now he is painstakingly making sure that the seams of the stockings are running straight and lining them up with the diamantes on the heels of my shoes.

"Got it, let me see." He gets up off the floor and stands back.

"Are you sure now that they are straight, Lloyd? After all, it has only been half an hour of you twisting them."

"I do hope you are not going to be sarcastic all night, Charlotte?"

"Me, Lloyd? Never!"

"Yes, perfect, turn around."

I turn around and face him.

"Oh yes, take off your key from around your neck, please."

"But why? I might need it."

"Just take it off, it just isn't right for you."

I undo the chain that is around my neck holding the key. It seems strange not to have it there after so long. I place it down on the table.

"Lloyd, are you going to be with me all night if I am not to have my key?"

"Yes. I have told you I will not be far away." He puts on his leather trousers, zipping them up, and then a leather T-shirt, not too tight. "I have something else for you!" He picks up a little box and hands it to me.

"What's this?"

"Open it, have a look."

I open the box and inside there is a mini set of handcuffs.

"It's a key ring – I thought that you could put your key on one side and the other side we can attach to your corset where the suspenders attach."

"They are lovely, thank you, Lloyd."

"Come, let me put it on for you." Taking the key, he attaches it to one of the cuffs; then getting me to hold up my skirt, he attaches the other cuff to my corset. "There, now you have your key back again."

"Thanks." I kiss him on the cheek.

"Tonight is going to be fantastic, full of surprise and mystery for you, Charlotte."

"Mystery, Lloyd?" I look at him quizzically.

"Yes, mystery, and that's all I am going to say for now. I have a mask here somewhere."

"Yes, I put it on your bedside cabinet, but why are you wearing a mask?"

"Just so that people don't realise it is me. Really, I don't want to put people off from spanking you!" he says, laughing as he says 'spanking you'.

"But they will know it's you, you will be with me."

"I will be there with you, but I will be sitting away from you. I will be able to see everything all the time and you will be able to see me, and Steve will be making sure no foul play takes place, so will be very close to you and Sophie. We don't want to crowd people."

"OK."

"Right, have you remembered everything you need to do and say?" He pulls the mask over his head, pulls the straps at the back and velcros them shut.

"Yes, Lloyd, you have run all the dos and don'ts past me for two days. Now I think I have it. I don't like that mask, it's not very pretty, is it?"

"It's just a normal leather gimp mask, but I can get out of it quickly. Usually they are buckled at the back but I got it changed to Velcro in case I need to take it off quickly. And the left side of it is red, so you know it is me. I am pretty sure that there will be others there with masks, so I had it made like this for you."

"I will rip it off you as soon as we get into the lift when everything has finished. I don't like not being able to see your face at all."

"Oh, will you now?"

"Yes, I will."

"Let's go." He grabs my hand and leads me out of the bedroom to the lift. "Remember, no talking to anyone unless I say and nod my head. If for any reason I am not in the room and you need something, Steve is your first contact, then Anthony, Nats, and then George."

"But where will you be? You said you wouldn't leave me."

"I might have to go for a pee or something, that's all. Do not lose control just because I have left the room, please."

"OK." We enter the lift, and as it starts going down my heart starts to race.

"Breathe, Charlotte, don't forget to breathe!"

I take a sharp intake of air, and Lloyd stops the lift.

"You OK? You don't have to do this, you know that."

"Yes, I will be fine, I just feel a little nervous, that's all."

He puts his finger under my chin and lifts my head; looks deeply into my eyes. Kissing me, he pushes me up to the wall of the lift and lifts my arms above my head, holding them with one hand; the other hand he runs down my side to the top of my stocking and strokes the skin between my stockings and my panties, black, soft, lacy panties that seem to move slightly with his hand, sending a tingling warm sensation across my body. I relax back onto the wall as we kiss for what seems like a lifetime, his tongue playing with mine. I can feel every sexy spot on my body getting aroused by his touch and his kiss. He pulls away slowly from the kiss.

"You sure?" he says quietly.

"Yes."

"Let's do it then, if you are ready?"

"Yes, I am ready now." Well, who wouldn't be after that kiss?

He starts the lift again, and just before the doors open he looks at me, winks and squeezing my hand, steps out of the lift with me following.

Chapter Twenty-Four

We enter the room where the spanking is taking place. All the sofas have been moved around to the sides of the room so spectators can sit and watch. Small occasional tables have been placed close by the sofas for drinks and suchlike. All the spanking subs are either standing or bent over in the middle of the room. So many pretty costumes, all along the same lines as mine: corsets, little skirts and stockings, but all different colours. The male subs have leather trousers with holes cut out of the rear, exposing their arses for spanking. I see Sophie first; she is wearing all red, and very lush and lovely she looks.

"There is Steve. Go on." Lloyd swings me forward in the direction of Steve, slapping my arse. "Enjoy your play, Charlotte, I will be right over here." He points to a sofa just to one side.

"Hi, Steve, I have made it," I say as I approach him. He too is dressed in leather trousers, but instead of a T-shirt he has leather straps and belts across his body.

"Hi, Charlotte, glad to see you have, and you look very stunning and spankable!"

"Thank you, Steve, I will take that as a compliment because you don't usually give me any. And it's nice to know you do think of me as something else other than just a gym slave!"

"Now, now, Charlotte, I don't think of you just as a gym slave, you know that!" He winks at me.

"Hi, Charlotte, your shoes and stockings are amazing," says Sophie, who is bent over holding her ankles.

"Thank you, Sophie, you look fab too!"

"Thanks, I might get to see the rest of your outfit sometime tonight, if I am lucky!" And she laughs.

I look over at Lloyd. He is sitting where he said he was going to be. I smile at him, but I can't see if he's smiling back at me. Subbing masks always get in the way.

"You ready, Charlotte, or are you just going to stand there looking at Lloyd all night?"

"Err yes, ready, sorry, Steve."

"Have you warmed up with Lloyd?"

"No, we didn't." I wonder why he didn't warm my arse, he must have just forgotten.

"Let's get started then." He raises his paddle and starts waving it! "Here we go, how much is the first bid for warming up this nice fresh subbie arse?"

What? Wait, I'm not a sub yet! How dare he! For suggesting it, I place my hands on my hips and glare at him. He looks back, smiling.

"She is very high-spirited, look, she dared to glare at me with her hands on her hips, and I'll soon knock them off." Before I know it he has taken one step back and the paddle has swung down, straight onto my arse. For the love of a sub! The sting swats straight through my lace pants as my hands immediately fall to my backside, and with a few hops I start rubbing furiously. I can hear everyone laughing at me; I even catch a glimpse of Lloyd throwing his head back as he laughs. Oh yes, so funny, the joke of the Doms' world, Charlotte, that's me.

"I give you five," Nats says, waving her finger at Steve

and then giving me a little wink.

"Ten," says someone else.

I look in the direction of Lloyd. He is talking with someone. Isn't he going to bid for me, then, I wonder?

"Fifteen," Nats adds.

"Thirty," comes a voice from the sofas, but it isn't Lloyd. Maybe he is waiting for the bid to get higher.

"Come, come, people, she is worth more than that, after all, she is a virgin at this, so to speak."

My mouth drops open. Don't tell them that! Why tell them that? I spin around and Lloyd is still laughing at me, along with half the room. Don't just sit and laugh, Lloyd, this isn't very funny at all. *Bid!* I want to shout out to him.

"Thirty-five." From Nats.

"Forty from the doorway."

Lloyd looks over at the doorway – maybe he is seeing who it is bidding on me.

"Forty-five." Nats.

"Fifty." From a big fat Dom standing next to Nats. She looks at him, I look at him. My heart drops – please, no, what if someone I don't know wins me? I don't want them paddling my arse, Nats, please don't let him get it. For the love of a sub. I look at Nats with pleading eyes.

"Fifty-five," she says, and smiles at me.

"Fifty-five for such a fresh subbie arse, come on now, it's worth a lot more than that, isn't it?" Steve says.

I swing around. What, what's with all this? He is being very personal here. I open my mouth to say something.

"Here you go, she has something to add, I think."

That stops me dead.

I just look at him when someone says, "Seventy." I spin to try and see who said it, but by now there's quite a crowd forming in the room.

"Seventy, more like it, but not good enough yet. I think the fresh sub has stage fright, I don't think she wants to say anything after all."

Oh yes, I will say something, being auctioned off like this and Lloyd having nothing to say about it. Just one of the many things I suspect he has neglected to tell me about. Him and his surprises and mystery! The panic of actually being sold to just anyone has finally sunk in. I didn't think it would be like this. Surely Lloyd didn't mean it when he said he would just sit in the sidelines, did he? He led me to believe it was a charity spanking, ten pounds a spank, if the sub says ouch they get their money back.

"Seventy-five." Nats. That's good, Nats, keep it up, I will pay you back every penny but don't let these big fat Doms get hold of me, for sub's sake.

"Eighty." Nooo, don't, please, don't keep bidding. That is enough – Nats, say something!

"One hundred." Who the subbing hell said that? I frantically look around the room but I can't see anyone who I think might have said it. I can also see Lloyd looking, but I don't think he has worked out who it was either.

"One hundred, what a good start, but the record for a sub warm-up was two years ago and that warm-up was five hundred and fifty pounds, so nowhere near yet! Do I hear one ten from any of you?"

What? I have to stand for this humiliation for another four hundred and fifty pounds? I roll my eyes, then look back at Nats; she winks.

"One ten." And then she smiles. Good one, Nats, now keep it up.

"One twenty." From the fat Dom.

My eyes dart at him and under my breath I say, "Wish you had a gimp mask on with a zip on the mouth that would sh—"

Slap! My little feet dance and my hands rub furiously before I can get another word mumbled out.

"See, I told you she is so feisty and fresh she doesn't always hold her tongue. At this rate if we don't get this bidding going I will have warmed her arse up for you, Doms." And everyone roars with laughter.

No, no, no, this just isn't what I thought. The humiliation of it all, they didn't mention that did they.

"One thirty." Way to go, Nats, that will stop him.

"One fifty." Fat Dom.

One fifty? Where are you packing one fifty? You don't look the type to have deep pockets. The humiliation of being bought by a fat Dom, how will I ever live it down... I look at Lloyd. He is looking straight at me – oh yes, you know and even a gimp mask can't hide those devil horns you have. You will not get away with this, I can tell you that, and if you were in earshot I would tell you what sort of Dom from hell you really are.

"That's getting there. Come on, look at her arse, it's very firm, and how do I know?"

"Coz she is your sub and you practise on her," someone shouts from just outside the door. Again the laughter rolls around the room. OK, I will sort him. No one practises on my arse. I take a step forward and Steve takes hold of my hand, swinging me back.

"Careful, Charlotte," he whispers as I swing round. "I can see we are in for a fun night with this sub – look at her, she is ready and waiting to go. One fifty doesn't seem anywhere near enough for ten warm-up spanks."

What the hell?

"Ten warm-up spanks? Get out of here, Steve." Oh no, out loud, out loud.

"Yes, you are right, that's nowhere near enough. Shall

we go for fifteen… No, let's make it a round twenty."

I glare at him. What are you doing to me? You know I am new at this. Again the roar of laughter bellows around the room.

"Well, in that case, Steve, I will make it two hundred." Nats, you are the God of subs. Thank you, I will pay you back but at this rate it will be all my wages for a week. I will still have my tips.

"Two fifty." Fat Dom alert. Now I know you are not packing two fifty, no way.

"Three." A voice from the sofa shouts, someone sitting next to Lloyd. Oh yes, just like him to get someone else to bid for him. I am on to your little game.

"Three hundred, sounding good, but not five fifty yet, I want at least five fifty for this special specimen of a sub, and trust me, she is special, OK." Where the hell does he get all this garbage from, calling me special? I can't believe the things he is saying about me. I look at Lloyd: he is sitting with his legs crossed, sipping his wine with no care about what Steve is saying about me, or that a big fat Dom might be beating the hell out of my arse.

"Three fifty." Fat Dom, right, I will call time out if you win me, that's for sure. I am not going to let you anywhere near my arse. That will get them all.

"Four." Nats, thank God for that, she is still bidding and long may she bid, that's what I say. At least I know she cares. Not like Lloyd.

"Four from Nats. Keep those bids coming, remember it's for charity, and if any of you are worried that her feistiness might get out of hand, I have a pair of handcuffs here to handcuff her hands to her ankles for your protection." Steve puts his hand down on his belt and unhooks a pair of handcuffs, and holds them in the air. My mouth drops as

I look at the handcuffs dangling from his hands. Oh, that will be something else Lloyd has neglected in his duty of telling everything, then.

"But you know me, everything has a price for handcuffing the sub. The next bid has to match the record bid or better."

"You give me those cuffs," I say, and I start bouncing to reach them.

"See, she is so eager to get them on she can't wait."

Swipe.

Not again. Dancing and rubbing.

"Stop, Steve, I don't think you are funny, I am not ready yet."

"Such a spirited sub, someone must have the handcuff bid up their sleeves for such a sub."

I look at Lloyd, who is still laughing. Well, I am glad you are finding this so entertaining, Dr Hughes.

"Four hundred and…" Nats pauses.

"Get on with it, Nats, put me out of my pain, please." No, no, not out loud! My body stiffens with fear from the thought of being shackled by handcuffs on my wrists and ankles.

She winks.

"Five hundred and forty-nine pounds and ninety-nine pence, as it's for charity I will up my last bid."

You did that on purpose just to get me in a stew, for paddle's sake. Everyone laughs again. Yes, go on, laugh at my pain.

"Nice one, Nats, but we still haven't broken the record yet. And the handcuffs go back on my belt for now, but you never know, she might forget herself again and I can always take them back off."

I swing around and glare long and hard at him.

"Five fifty." The cheapskate fat Dom has only bid a penny more. That's it, you are definitely not having my arse.

"Five sixty." The person sitting next to Lloyd.

"Yes, and we have a new record for the fresh sub's arse. Let's see how high we can get this, now you have all woken up."

"Seven hundred." Anthony, where have you been all this time?

"Wow, seven hundred, that's a hefty bid."

"Yes, he is my friend," I say proudly.

"Oh, come on now, we can't let her go to friends and family, can we?"

"Don't do that, Steve." Oh no, what's going on, mouth, keep shut, for the love of paddles.

Swipe.

"Any yet? Another one for a delectable arse such as this?"

I am going to get very upset with you, Lloyd, if you don't stop this right now or if you don't come and help me, I think as I rub.

"And as we have all seen, she loves a little rub after every spank. What more do you want from a fresh sub?"

"Seven fifty." Fat Dom, just go and get your own sub.

"Come now, newbie sub, I am sure if you smile you will get through that one thousand mark."

I look at Steve. Smile? You think I am happy being auctioned off like a piece of meat? I stand with my arms crossed. I am not going to smile.

"Eight." The voice from the sofa; well, that's better than the fat Dom, I suppose.

I look at him; then to Lloyd, still sipping his wine.

"I like a sub with a little stroppiness in her," Steve adds. "A little strop, but I think this one has a little more than that." Lloyd tips his head back as he laughs. Oh yes, you are enjoying every paddling moment of this, aren't you?

"Eight ten." Fat Dom.

Oh come on, Nats, Anthony, why are you not bidding anymore? I will pay you back every penny, I promise, I will even if it takes me a year, I will pay every penny back. I look at them, frantically willing them, just one of them to bid.

"Eight fifty." The sofa Dom. If I find out that is you, Lloyd, I will not be happy with you doing this to me.

"Nine hundred." Fat Dom. I roll my eyes with the agony of him bidding on me yet again.

"Another hundred and we will be at the one thousand mark. Who is going to make it one thousand? Come on, let's round it up."

"Nine fifty," says the sofa Dom. Yes, leave it there, I prefer him to fat Dom as everyone else has stopped.

"Come on, we can't stop there, surely she has got to be worth another bid or two to get up there to the thousand?"

"Go on then, one thousand, not every day I get to beat the arse of an employee, and it might make her work harder than she already does." Nats laughs.

"Nats is on the thousand mark, thank you, Nats. Who is next?"

"Don't ask such questions, Steve. You know someone will say something, even if cheapskate fat Dom puts on another penny," I mumble under my breath. As I look at Lloyd I can't see what he is thinking with that mask on, not at all. I bet that is why he is wearing it.

"And fifty." From the sofa.

"One hundred." Fat Dom.

"That will be one hundred more. I have waited a long time to spank her and by God, she has asked for it over the years." Anthony chips in.

I roll my eyes; then glare at Lloyd.

"Now come on, gentlemen, I do believe that this one is mine, one and three," Nats says, laughing.

OK, Lloyd, you can bid now, there aren't going to be that many more, surely. Nope, just sitting the same as before, sipping at that endless glass of red.

"OK, is that it? Is this arse going to Nats for warm-up spanking?"

"Just one question – if we make her say 'ouch' when warming her up, do we get our money back?"

"No, no, no, that does it…"

Swipe. Paddling arses, why does he just not stop doing that? I rub my arse, glaring at Lloyd.

"I think the sub has answered that for us."

And a ring of laughter hits the room.

"Going once…going twice…going three times to Nats. Congratulations, Nats, you have one of the feistiest subs I have ever had the pleasure of!" And a cheer as Steve takes my hand and hands it to Nats.

"Ta, Nats," I whisper as she takes my hand.

"That's OK, someone had to save you from the madding crowds of overexcited Doms."

"I don't know when I will be able to pay you back."

"Pay me back for what?"

"For saving me. I was sending you thoughts so you would bid on me. I said in my thoughts I would pay you back every penny."

"You haven't got to pay me back. I would have donated two thousand anyway."

"OK, thank you anyway."

"That's fine, Charlotte, it's a pleasure."

"Lloyd didn't explain to me about being auctioned, I thought people would pay ten pounds for a slap with a paddle."

"I guessed he didn't by your reaction. It's just a bit of fun for new subs, an icebreaker to try and make it easier for new wannabe subs like yourself. There is no way any off us would let a new sub go for warm up with someone they don't know or feel comfortable with, although there is no one here that would take advantage of a newbie. You were so funny, no wonder he likes you so much, you are such a good player. Now bend over, let me warm your arse for you before the others start moaning. And don't worry, I will take it nice and slow for you."

"Thanks, Nats! That has put my mind to rest." Before I bend over I look over to Lloyd; he nods his head to me and I smile nervously.

I bend over, take some deep breaths and wiggle my arse as a sign that the game is on.

Swipe.

Not so bad.

Wiggle, swipe.

OK, just eighteen more like this will be fine. I close my eyes and take a deep breath.

Swipe, and then a little rub with the paddle.

"Hi up there!"

"Lloyd, what are you doing here?" He is lying on the floor looking at me.

"Just checking my assets and making sure they are OK."

"Well, if I am your asset, yes, I am fine, thank you."

"Good, you enjoying yourself?"

"You never told me I was being auctioned in that way and you didn't bid once!"

Swipe.

"Why would I want to pay money for something I can have anytime I want for free?"

"Lloyd, that isn't the point, that nasty fat Dom might

have got me and then your assets might not have been any longer."

Swipe, rub.

"Oh, Charlotte, you're not going to sulk with me, are you, because if you are I am sure everyone will enjoy a demonstration of how to spank a stroppy sub."

Swipe, rub.

"Now, Lloyd, you have made me lose count – go away."

"It's OK, Nats won't have done." He kisses me on the lips; then he is gone.

Swipe, swipe, swipe.

I bite my bottom lip.

"Lloyd, I know that is you," I snap.

"Yes, the colour didn't please my eye, Charlotte. It's a nice glowing red, now enjoy," he says, laughing as I see him sit back down. I'll give you a nice glowing red.

"You OK there, Charlotte?" Nats bends down to ask.

"Yes, fine, Nats, thank you."

"All ready and warmed up. You OK with this?"

"Yes, fine. I can see Lloyd and I can see the door to my side and in front. Steve will be there all night so I am more than fine."

"You know they are really gonna swipe at your arse, and probably a lot harder than Lloyd has ever swiped at it?"

"Yes, I know and I wouldn't like to bet that it will be a lot harder than Lloyd – he is mean when he wants to be."

"I don't doubt it at all, Charlotte. Well, enjoy yourself – you know they are betting on you, don't you?"

"No, who? Oh, let me guess, Lloyd and Anthony."

"Got it in one, it's to see who is the closest to the first 'ouch'."

"Might have known. Do you know what they think, then?"

"No, I don't. I shouldn't have told you about the bet but I thought it was fair."

"OK, Nats, thanks."

"Well, enjoy. Here comes first paddler to swipe at your arse." And she laughs, walking away out the door.

I feel the paddle touch my arse as whoever has got it squares it up to my arse. I take a deep breath in and slowly out.

Swipe.

Geez, what the sub just hit me? My eyes have bounced right out of their sockets. I bite my tongue. I am not going to say 'ouch' on the first hit. Lloyd turns his hands up, asking me if I am OK – well, if he was in earshot he would have got the long answer, which he most certainly wouldn't have liked, so he got my right hand on and off my ankle which means yes; if I move my left hand it means maybe OK, so he will give Steve a nod so he can give me a small break; if I take both hands off my ankles it means I need time out.

Swipe.

Another swipe from hell. Again I bite my tongue. God, where have they got these guys from? Deep breath in and relax. I see Lloyd get up off the sofa and move to the door. George is talking with Anthony, and then Lloyd joins in on the conversation. I watch as they talk, and someone else takes a swipe at my arse…which doesn't seem so hard, or it could be because I am more interested in what is being spoken about. Then Lloyd returns to the sofa. Anthony keeps looking over at Lloyd, but George has disappeared. Something is going on, I know it. Lloyd looks around the room. Then back at me.

Swipe.

"Ah, ah, ah, nope, not going to say ouch just yet," I mutter through gritted teeth.

Lloyd gets up again. I can see there is a little bit of a debate going on. Then Lloyd leaves the room altogether, followed by Anthony. Oh no, they have both gone – where have they gone? This isn't supposed to happen.

Swipe.

Concentrate. I have to keep focused.

Swipe.

Aww, help, that was a little quick.

"You OK, Charlotte?" Steve bends down.

"Yes, smarting a little but OK. Where has Lloyd gone?"

"I'm not sure, but I am sure he will not be long. Are you staying down there?"

"I might as well."

"OK, do some breathing exercises. I will tap my right foot when someone is going to swipe again, OK?"

"Yes, fine."

"And don't worry, you are doing fine."

"Thanks."

I take some deep breaths, close my eyes and relax, mentally visualising someone, namely Lloyd, rubbing the smarting away from my arse. This is harder than I thought it was going to be.

I open my eyes and fix a stare on Steve's foot, waiting for him to tap it.

"OK, Lloyd?" Steve says. I look round and Lloyd is coming back into the room. Lloyd puts up his hand as if to say yes; then swoops down, taking my hand and dragging me off. I barely have a chance to stand up straight, and stumble as we go.

I look back at Steve, who just shrugs. There is no Anthony and no George in sight; I can't even see Nats. We go to the front door, he opens it and we go outside.

"Where are we going?" I ask, but there is no answer.

We fly down the steps to a car; he opens the back door and flings me in, closing the door behind me. He gets into the driver's seat, starts the car and we set off.

I lean forward. "Where are we going?"

He holds up his hand as if to say 'shut up', so I sit back in the seat and buckle my belt.

"OK, if you are not going to say than I will enjoy the ride, Lloyd. I know you said mystery but I wasn't expecting a mystery tour, though I will play along with the game, if that's what you want."

Chapter Twenty-Five

The car finally stops and he gets out, opens my door, grabs me by the wrist and drags me out of the car.

"Ouch, Lloyd, OK, you have an ouch. What's the matter, are you cross because I didn't say ouch and you lost your bet with Anthony?"

He still doesn't say anything. I look around where the car has stopped.

"Oh no, is this some kind of sick joke, Lloyd, I am not going in there." We are outside the warehouse where Lloyd got my outfit made.

"Come on, Lloyd, very funny, now let's go." I try to pull away, but his grip gets tighter. He pushes the door open, drags me inside and swings me in front of him so he can close the door. He un-Velcros the back of his mask and rips it off.

"What the hell? Where is Lloyd? Is he here?" I ask, as Lloyd said he would be the only one wearing this mask.

"No, he is not." The man grabs my wrist then drags me towards the door of the changing room.

I struggle with the man trying to get free.

"Let me go. Why are you doing this? I want to leave right now."

"Now you be a good girl and I am sure all will become

clear soon." He swings me around into the dark and dingy room.

"No, no, wait, where is Lloyd? He is the only person with that mask, he had it made by the woman that owns this place."

"Yes, I know, she is my sister, I got her to make me one exactly the same so that once we got Lloyd, Anthony and George away from you I could just walk in and take you without anyone batting an eyelid – good, huh?"

"Lloyd will work it out, you know, he will know that it's you, and he will have you locked away in the loony house with your other little friend you brought to the club."

"That's where you are wrong, Charlotte. He escaped with a little help – that is, a few days ago – so you see, Lloyd and your friends are all looking for him and not me. I have him hidden away quite nicely until the time is right, and they will never think of you being here, that's for sure, and I have my sister on a permanent holiday, if you get my drift. Now I have some things to sort out, so try and behave yourself."

I move towards him.

"Please don't do this let me go"

He slams the door shut.

BANG!

To be continued...

χ χ

Acknowledgements

I owe thanks to all those, professional and non-professional, who have encouraged and supported me with my books. I feel privileged and honoured to have such wonderful people in my life.

A special thanks to JM whose support has been beyond measure.

I would also like to thank my readers for their honest reviews, which have given me the confidence to carry on.